A horror from  east appeared b... and head were h... handsome: swarthy, hooknosed, and proud, beard falling in curling ringlets over broad chest. But its arms were the snapping chelae of a monster scorpion. A scorpion's jointed tail grew from the base of its spine, sting gleaming at the tip. With a bellow that should have come from the throat of a bull, the demon Luhuzantiyas sprang at Gerin and Van.

It was a nightmare fight. Quicker on its feet than any human, the demon used its tail like a living spear. The sting flashed past Gerin's face, so close that he caught the acrid reek of its poison. It scored a glittering line across Van's corselet. Those terrible claws chewed the outlander's shield to bits. Only a backward leap saved his arm.

He and Gerin landed blow after blow, but the demon would not go down, though dark ichor pumped from a score of wounds and one claw was sheared away. Not until Van, with a strength born of loathing, smashed its skull and face to bloody pulp with frenzied strokes of his mace did it fall. Even then it writhed and thrashed in the mire, still seeking its foes.

Gerin drew in a long, shuddering breath. "Now, wizard," he grated, "join your devil in the fiery pit that spawned it."

Baen Books by Harry Turtledove

The Case of the Toxic Spell Dump
Agent of Byzantium
Werenight
Prince of the North (*forthcoming*)

HARRY TURTLEDOVE

WERENIGHT

Copyright © 1994 by Harry Turtledove

The parts of this novel have been published separately, in substantially different form, as *Werenight* (1979) and *Wereblood* (1979). This edition is the first publication of this novel in a single volume.

A Baen Books Original

Baen Publishing Enterprises
P.O. Box 1403
Riverdale, N.Y. 10471

ISBN: 0-671-72209-3

Cover art by Larry Elmore

First printing, February 1994

Distributed by
SIMON & SCHUSTER
1230 Avenue of the Americas
New York, N.Y. 10020

Printed in the United States of America

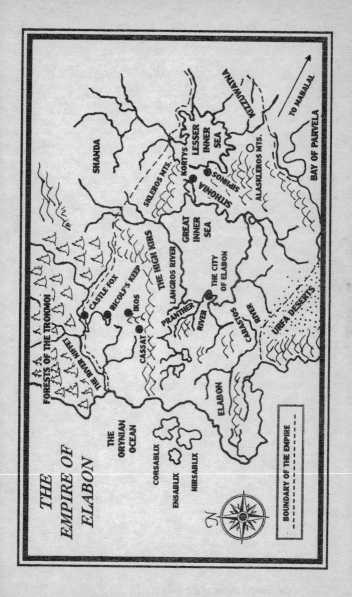

I

"Duin, you're a damned fool if you think you can fight from horseback," Drago the Bear said, tossing a gnawed bone to his trencher.

Duin the Bold slammed his tankard down on the long table. Ale slopped over the rim. "Fool, is it?" he shouted, his fair face reddening. "You're the fool, you thickskulled muckbrain!"

Drago stormed up with an oath, murder in his eyes. His thick arms groped toward Duin. The slimmer man skipped back. His hand flashed to his swordhilt. Cries of anger and alarm rang through Castle Fox's great hall.

Gerin the Fox, baron of Fox Keep, sprang to his feet. "Stop it!" he shouted. The shout froze both angry men for a moment, giving their benchmates a chance to crowd between them. Drago sent one man flying with a shrug of his massive shoulders, but was brought up short by a grip not even his massive thews could break. Van of the Strong Arm grinned down at him. Almost a foot taller than the squat Bear, the outlander was every bit as powerfully made.

Gerin glowered at his fractious vassals, disgust plain in every line of his lean body. The men grew shame-faced under his glare. Nothing would have pleased him more than breaking both their stupid heads. He lashed them with his voice instead, snapping, "I called you here to fight the Trokmoi, not each other. The woodsrunners will be a tough enough nut to crack without us squabbling among ourselves."

"Then let us fight them!" Duin said, but his blade was back in its scabbard. "This Dyaus-damned rain has cooped us up here for ten days now. No wonder we're quarreling like so many snapping turtles in a pot. Turn us loose, lord Gerin!" To that even Drago rumbled agreement. He was not alone.

The Fox shook his head. "If we try to cross the River Niffet in this weather, either current or storm will surely swamp us. When the sky clears, we move. Not before."

Privately, Gerin was more worried than his liege-men, but he did not want them to see that. Since spring he'd been sure the northern barbarians were planning to swarm south over the Niffet and ravage his holding. He'd decided to strike first.

But this downpour—worse than any he could remember in all his thirty years on the northern marches of the Empire of Elabon—balked his plans. For ten days he'd had no glimpse of sun, moons, or stars. Even the Niffet, a scant half mile away, was hard to spy.

Rumor also said the Trokmoi had a new wizard of great power. More than once, the baron had seen fell lights dancing deep within the northern forests. His ever-suspicious mind found it all too easy to blame the Trokmê mage for the rude weather.

Duin started to protest further. Then he saw the scar over Gerin's right eye go pale: a sure danger signal. The words stayed bottled in his throat. He made sheepish apologies to Drago, who frowned but, under Gerin's implacable gaze, nodded and clasped his hand.

As calm descended, the baron took a long pull at his own ale. It was late. He was tired, but he was not eager for bed. His chamber was on the second floor, and the roof leaked.

Siglorel Shelofas' son, when sober the best Elabonian wizard north of the High Kirs, had set a five-year calking spell on it only the summer before, but the old sot must have had a bad day. Water trickled through the roofing and collected in cold puddles on the upper story's floor. Spread rushes did little to soak it up.

Gerin plucked at his neat black beard. He wished for carpets like those he had known in his younger days south of the mountains. Study was all he'd lived for then, and the barony the furthest thing from his mind. He remembered the fiasco that had resulted when exasperation drove him to try the book of spells he'd brought north from the capital.

History and natural lore had always interested him more than magecraft. His studies at the Sorcerers' Collegium began late and, worse, were cut short after fewer than a hundred days: a Trokmê ambush took both his father and elder brother, leaving him the unexpected master of Fox Keep.

In the eight years since, he'd had little cause to try wizardry. His skill was not large. Nor did age improve it: his incantation raised nothing but a cloud of stinking black smoke and his vassals' hackles. On the whole, he counted himself lucky. Amateur wizards who played with forces stronger than they could control often met unpleasant ends.

A snatch of drunken song made him look up. Duin and Drago sat with their arms round each other's shoulders, boasting of the havoc they would wreak among the Trokmoi when the cursed weather finally cleared. The baron was relieved. They were two of his stoutest fighting men.

He drained his mug and rose to receive the salutes of his vassals. Head buzzing slightly, he climbed the soot-grimed oak stairway to his bedchamber. His last waking thought was a prayer to Dyaus for fair weather so he could add another chapter to the vengeance he was taking on the barbarians. . . .

A horn cried danger from the watchtower, tumbling him from his bed with the least ceremony imaginable. He cursed the bronzen clangor as he stumbled to a window. "If that overeager lackwit up there is tootling for his amusement, I'll have his ears," he muttered to himself. But the scar over his eyes throbbed and his fingers were nervous in his beard. If the Trokmoi had found a way to cross the Niffet in the rain, no telling how much damage they might do.

The window was only a north-facing slit, intended more for shooting arrows than sight. The little Gerin saw was enough. Jabbing forks of lightning revealed hand after hand of Trokmoi, all searching for something to carry off or, failing that, to burn. The wind blew snatches of their lilting speech to his ears.

"May the gods fry you, Aingus, you tricky bastard, and your pet wizard too," Gerin growled. He wondered how the Trokmê chieftain had got so many men across the river so fast. Then he raised his eyes further and saw the bridge bulking impossibly huge over the Niffet.

It had to be sorcerous: a silvery band of light leading from the northern woods into Gerin's holding. It had not been there when the baron went to his rest.

As he watched, Trokmê nobles poured over it in their chariots, retainers loping beside them. Once long ago, Gerin thought, he had read something of such spans. He could not recall where or when, but the half-memory sent a pang of fear icing up his spine.

No time for such worries now. He hurled himself into trousers and hobnailed sandals, buckled on his sword, and rushed down dim-lit passageway and creaking stair to the great hall, where his vassals had hung their corselets when they arrived. That hall was a swearing jumble of men donning bronze-faced leather cuirasses and kilts, strapping on greaves, jamming pot-shaped helms onto their heads, and fouling each other as they waved spears in the air. Like Gerin, most had skin that took the sun well and dark hair and eyes, but a few freckled faces and light beards told of northern blood—Duin, for one, was fair as any Trokmê.

"Ho, captain!" Van of the Strong Arm boomed. "Thought you'd never get here!"

Even in the rowdy crew Gerin led, Van stood out. Taller than the Fox's six feet by as many inches, he was broad enough not to look his height. A sword-cut creased his nose and disappeared into the sun-colored mat of beard covering most of his face. Little hellish lights flickered in his blue eyes.

His gear was as remarkable as his person, for his back-and-breast was cast of two solid pieces of bronze. Not even the Emperor had a finer one. Unlike the businesslike helms his comrades wore, Van's was a fantastic affair with a scarlet horsehair plume nodding above his head and leather cheekpieces to protect his face. Looking more war-god than man, he shook a spear like a young tree.

If his tale was true, he'd been trying to cross the Trokmê forests from north to south, and had all but done it till he fell foul of Aingus' clan. But he'd escaped them too, and had enough left in his giant frame to swim the Niffet, towing his precious armor behind him on a makeshift raft.

His strength, bluff good humor, and wide-ranging stories (told in the forest tongue until he learned Elabonian) had won him a home at Fox Keep for as long as he wanted to stay. But when Gerin asked him his homeland, he politely declined to answer. The Fox did not ask twice; if Van did not want to talk, it was his affair. That had been only two years ago, Gerin thought with a twinge of surprise. He had trouble remembering what life had been like without his burly friend at his side.

The Fox's own armor was of the plainest, leather much patched, plates battered and nicked. The leather was firm and supple, though, and every plate sound. To Gerin's way of thinking, the figure he cut was less important than staying alive himself and putting a quick end to his foes.

The warriors wallowed through thick mud to the stables. It squelched underfoot, trying to suck their sandals and boots into its cold, slimy mouth. The chaos was worse inside the stables, as boys tried to hitch unwilling horses to their masters' chariots.

Gerin strung his bow and stowed in on the right side of his car next to his quiver; on the left went an axe. Like many of the Fox's vassals, Van affected to despise the bow as an unmanly weapon. He bore sword, dagger, and a wickedly spiked mace on his belt.

His shield and the Fox's, yard-wide discs of bronze-faced wood and leather, topped the car's low sidewalls when put in their brackets. Gerin's was deliberately dull, Van's burnished bright. Despite their contrasting styles, the two formed one of the most feared teams on the border.

Gerin's driver, a gangling youth named Raffo,

leaped into the chariot. A six-foot shield of heavy leather was slung on a baldric over his left shoulder. It gave Gerin cover from which to shoot. Taking up the reins, Raffo skillfully picked his way through the confusion.

After what seemed far too much time to the Fox, his men gathered in loose formation just behind the gatehouse. Shrieks from beyond the keep told plain as need be that the Trokmoi were plundering his serfs. Archers on the palisade kept up a sputtering duel with the barbarians, targets limited to those the lightning showed.

At Gerin's shouted command, the gatehouse crew flung wide the strong-hinged gates and let the drawbridge thump down. The chariots lumbered into action, trailing mucky wakes. Van's bellowed oaths cut off in midword when he saw the bridge. "By my beard," he grunted, "where did it come from?"

"Magicked up, without a doubt." Gerin wished he were as calm as he sounded. No Trokmê hedge-wizard could have called that spell into being—nor could the elegant and talented mages of the Sorcerer's Guild down in the capital.

An arrow whizzing past his ear shattered his brief reverie. Trokmoi swarmed out of the peasant village to meet his men. They had no mind to let their looting be stopped. "Aingus!" they shouted, and "Bala-mung!"—a name the Fox did not know. The Elaboni-ans roared back: "Gerin the Fox!" The two bands met in bloody collision.

A northerner appeared at the left side of the Fox's chariot, sword in hand. The rain plastered his long red hair and flowing mustaches against his head; he wore no helm. The reek of ale was thick about him.

Reading his mind was easy. Van would have to twist his body to use his spear, Raffo had his hands full, and Gerin, who had just shot, could never get off another arrow before the Trokmê's blade pierced him. Feeling like a gambler playing with loaded dice, the Fox snatched up his axe with his left hand. He drove it into the barbarian's skull. The Trokmê toppled, a look of outraged surprise still on his face.

Van exploded into laughter. "What a rare sneaky thing it must be to be left-handed," he said.

More barbarians were hustling stolen cattle, pigs, sheep, and serfs across the gleaming bridge to their homeland. The villeins had no chance against the northern wolves. Huddled in their huts against the storm and the wandering ghosts of the night, they were easy meat. A few had tried to fight. Their crumpled bodies lay beside their homes. Sickle, flail, and scythe were no match for the sword, spear, bow, and armor of the Trokmê nobles, though their retainers were often little better armed than the peasants.

Gerin almost felt pity as he drove an arrow into one of those retainers and watched him thrash his life away. He knew the northerner would have had no second thoughts about gutting him.

A few Trokmoi had managed to light torches despite the downpour. They smoked and sputtered in the woodsrunners' hands. The rain, though, made the thatched roofs and wattle walls of the cottages all but impossible to light.

With a wave and a shout, Gerin sent half his chariots after the pillagers. His own car was in the middle of the village when he shouted, "Pull up!"

Raffo obediently slowed. Gerin slung his quiver over his shoulder. He and Van slid their shields onto their arms and leaped into the mire. Raffo wheeled the horses and made for the safety of Fox Keep's walls. The chariot-riders not chasing looters followed the Fox to the ground. Panting footsoldiers rushed up to stiffen their line.

A Trokmê sprang on the baron's back before he

could find his footing in the mud. His bow flew from his hand. The two struggling men fell together. The barbarian's dagger sought Gerin's heart, but was foiled by his cuirass. He jabbed an elbow into the Trokmê's unarmored middle. The fellow grunted and loosened his grasp.

Both men scrambled to their feet. Gerin was quicker. His foot lashed out in a roundhouse kick. The spiked sole of his sandal ripped away half the Trokmê's face. With a dreadful wail, the marauder sprawled in the ooze, his features a gory mask.

Duin the Bold thundered by on a horse. Though his legs were clenched round its barrel, he still wobbled on the beast's bare back. Since a rider did not have both hands free to use a bow and could not deliver any sort of spearthrust without going over his horse's tail, Gerin thought fighting from horseback a foolish notion.

But his fierce little vassal clung to the idea with the tenacity of a bear-baiting dog. Duin cut down one startled Trokmê with his sword. When he slashed at another, the northerner ducked under his stroke and gave him a hefty push. He fell in the mud with a splash. The horse fled. The Trokmê was bending over his prostrate victim when an Elabonian with a mace stove in his skull from behind.

Van was in his element. Never happier than when on the field, he howled a battle song in a language Gerin did not know. His spear drank the blood of one mustachioed barbarian. Panther-quick, he brought its bronze-shod butt back to smash the teeth of another raider who thought to take him from behind.

A third Trokmê rushed at him with an axe. The barbarian's wild swipe went wide, as did Van's answering thrust. The impulse of the blows left them breast to breast. Van dropped his spear and seized the barbarian's neck with his huge fist. He shook him once, as a dog does a rat. Bones snapped. The Trokmê went limp. Van flung him aside.

Gerin did not share his comrade's red joy in slaughter. The main satisfaction he took from killing was the knowledge that the shuddering corpse at his feet was one enemy who would never trouble him again. As far as he could, he stood aloof from his fellow barons' internecine quarrels. He fought only when provoked, and was fell enough to be provoked but seldom.

Toward the Trokmoi, though, he bore a cold, bitter hatred. At first, it had been fueled by the slaying of his father and brother, but now revenge was only a small part of it. The woodsrunners lived only to destroy. All too often, his border holding tasted of that destruction as it shielded the softer, more civilized southlands from the sudden bite of arrows and the baying of barbarians in the night.

Almost without thinking, he ducked under a flung stone. Another glanced from his helmet and filled his head with a brief shower of stars. A spear grazed his thigh; an arrow pierced his shield but was turned by his corselet.

His archers shot back, filling the air with death. Spouting bodies disappeared in the mud, to be trampled by friend and foe alike. The Trokmoi swarmed round Gerin's armored troopers like snarling wolves round bears, but little by little they were driven back from the village toward their bridge. Their chieftains fought back, making fierce charges across the Fox's fertile wheatfields, crushing his men beneath the flailing hooves of their woods ponies, sending yard-long arrows through cuirasses into soft flesh, and lopping off arms and heads with their great slashing swords.

At their fore was Aingus. He had led his clan for nearly as long as Gerin had been alive, but his splendid red mustachioes were unfrosted. Almost as tall as Van, if less wide through the shoulders, he was proud in gilded armor and wheel-crested bronze helm. Golden fylfots and the ears of men he had slain adorned his chariot. His right hand held a dripping sword, his left the head of an Elabonian who had tried to stand against him.

His long, knobby-cheekboned face split in a grin when he spied Gerin. "It's himself himself," he roared, "come to be corbies' meat like his father. Thinking to be a man before your ape of a friend, are you, laddie?" His Elabonian was fluent enough, though flavored by his own tongue.

Van shouted back at him; Gerin, silent, set himself for the charge. Aingus swung up his sword. His driver, a gaunt, black-robed man the Fox did not know, whipped his beasts forward.

On came the chariot, its horses' hooves pounding like doom. Gerin was lifting his shield to beat back Aingus' first mighty stroke when Van's spear flashed over his shoulder and took one of the onrushing ponies full in the chest.

With the awful scream only wounded horses make, the shaggy pony reared and then fell. It dragged its harness-mate down with it. The chariot overturned and shattered, sending one wheel flying and spilling both riders into the muck.

Gerin ran forward to finish Aingus. The Trokmê lit rolling and rushed to meet him. "A fine thing will your skull be over my gate," he shouted. Then their blades joined with a clash of sparks and there was no more time for words.

Slashing and chopping, Aingus surged forward, trying to overwhelm his smaller foe at the first onset. Gerin parried desperately. Had any of the Trokmê's cuts landed, he would have been cut in two. When Aingus' blade bit so deep into the edge of his shield that it stuck for a moment, the Fox seized the chance for a thrust of his own. Aingus knocked the questing point aside with a dagger in his left hand; he had lost his bloody trophy when the chariot foundered.

The barbarian would not tire. Gerin's sword was heavy in his hands, his battered shield a lump of lead on his arm, but Aingus only grew stronger. He was bleeding from a cut under his chin and another on his arm, but his attack never slowed.

Crash! Crash! An overhand blow smashed the Fox's shield to kindling. The next ripped through his armor and drew a track of fire down his ribs. He groaned and sank to one knee.

Thinking him finished, the Trokmê loomed over him, eager to take his head. But Gerin was not yet done. His sword shot up and out with all the force of his body behind it. The point tore out Aingus' throat. Dark in the gloom, his lifeblood fountained forth as he fell, both hands clutching futilely at his neck.

The baron dragged himself to his feet. Van came up beside him. There was a fresh cut on his forearm, but his mace dripped blood and brains and his face was wreathed in smiles. He brandished the gory weapon and shouted, "Come on, captain! We've broken them!"

"Is it to go through me you're thinking?"

Gerin's head jerked up. The Tromê's voice seemed to have come from beside him, but the only northerner within fifty yards was Aingus' scrawny driver. He wore no armor under his sodden robes and carried no weapon, but he strode forward with the confidence of a demigod.

"Stand aside, fool," Gerin said. "I have no stomach for killing an unarmed man."

"Then have not a care in the world, southron darling, for I'll be the death of you and not the other way round at all." Lightning cracked, giving Gerin a glimpse of the northerner's pale skin stretched drumhead tight over skull and jaw. Like a cat's, the fellow's eyes gave back the light in a green flash.

He raised his arms and began to chant. An invocation poured forth, sonorous and guttural. Gerin's blood froze in his veins as he recognized the magic-steeped speech of the dreaming river valleys of ancient Kizzuwatna. He knew that tongue, and knew it did not belong in the mouth of a swaggering woodsrunner.

The Trokmê dropped his hands, screaming, *"Ethrog, O Luhuzantiyas!"*

A horror from the hells of the haunted east appeared before him. Its legs, torso, and head were human, the face even grimly handsome: swarthy, hooknosed, and proud, beard falling in curling ringlets over broad chest. But its arms were the snapping chelae of a monster scorpion. A scorpion's jointed tail grew from the base of its spine, sting gleaming at the tip. With a bellow that should have come from the throat of a bull, the demon Luhuzantiyas sprang at Gerin and Van.

It was a nightmare fight. Quicker on its feet than any human, the demon used its tail like a living spear. The sting flashed past Gerin's face, so close that he caught the acrid reek of its poison. It scored a glittering line across Van's corselet. Those terrible claws chewed the outlander's shield to bits. Only a backward leap saved his arm.

He and Gerin landed blow after blow, but the demon would not go down, though dark ichor pumped from a score of wounds and one claw was sheared away. Not until Van, with a strength born of loathing, smashed its skull and face to bloody pulp with frenzied strokes of his mace did it fall. Even then it writhed and thrashed in the mire, still seeking its foes.

Gerin drew in a long, shuddering breath. "Now,

wizard," he grated, "join your devil in the fiery pit that spawned it."

The Tromê had put twenty or so paces between himself and the Fox. His laugh—an unclean chuckle that scraped across Gerin's nerves—made plain his lack of fear. "It's a strong man you are, lord Gerin the Fox"—the contempt he packed into that stung— "and this day is yours. But we'll meet again; aye, indeed we will. My name, lord Gerin, is Balamung. Mark it well, for you've heard it twice the now, and hear it again you will."

"Twice?" Gerin only whispered it, but Balamung heard.

"Not even remembering, are you? Well, 'twas three years gone by I came south, having it in mind to take up sorcery. You made me sleep in the stables, with the reeking horses and all, for some fatgut from the south and his party of pimps filled the keep all to bursting, you said. When the next time comes for me to sleep at Fox Keep—and 'twill be soon—I shan't bed in the stables.

"So south I fared, stinking of horsedung, and in Elabon the town only their hinder parts did the Sorcerers' Collegium show me. They called me savage, and that to my face, mind! After you, it's them to pay their price.

"For, you see, quit I didna. I wandered through desert and mountain, and learned from warlocks and grizzled hermits and squinting scribes who cared nought about a 'rentice's accent, so long as he did their bidding. And in a cave lost in the snows of the High Kirs, far above one of the passes the Empire blocked, I found what I had learned to seek: the Book of Shabeth-Shiri the sorcerer-king of Kizzuwatna long ago.

"Himself had died there. When I took the Book from his dead fingers, he turned to a puff of smoke and blew away. And today the Book is mine, and tomorrow the northlands—and after that, the world is none too big!"

"You lie," Gerin said. "All you will own is a nameless grave, with no one to comfort your shade."

Balamung laughed again. Now his eyes flamed red, with a fire of their own. "Wrong you are, for the stars tell me no grave will ever hold me. They tell me more, too, for they show me the gates of your precious keep all beat to flinders, and that inside two turns of the bloody second moon."

"You lie," Gerin growled again. He ran forward, ignoring the pain that lanced up from his wound. Balamung stood watching him, hands on hips. The Fox lifted his blade. Balamung was unmoving, even when it came hissing down to cleave him from crown to breastbone.

The stroke met empty air—like the light of a candle suddenly snuffed, the wizard was gone. Gerin staggered and almost fell. Balamung's derisive laugh rang in his ears for a long moment, then it too faded. "Father Dyaus above!" the shaken Fox said again.

Van muttered an oath in an unknown tongue. "Well, captain," he said, "there's your warlock."

Gerin did not argue.

The Trokmoi seemed to lose their nerve when the sorcerer disappeared. Faster and faster they streamed over Balamung's bridge, their feet silent on its misty surface. Only a snarling rearguard held Gerin's men at bay. Those warriors slipped away to safety one by one. With deep-throated roars of triumph, the Elabonians swarmed after them.

Like a phantasm compounded of coils of smoke, the bridge vanished. Soldiers screamed as they plunged into the foaming Niffet, the bronze they wore for safety dragging them to a watery doom. On the shore, men doffed armor with frantic haste and splashed into the water to save their comrades. Jeering Trokmoi on the northern bank shot at victims and rescuers alike.

It took two men to save Duin. Impetuous as always, he had been farthest along the bridge when it evaporated, and he could not swim. Somehow he managed to stay afloat until the first rescuer reached him, but his grip was so desperate that he and his would-be savior both would have drowned had another swimmer not been nearby. A few others were also hauled out, but Balamung's trap took more than a dozen.

A plashing downstream made Gerin whirl. Matter-of-fact as a river godlet, Drago the Bear came out of the water, wringing his long beard like a peasant wench with her man's breeches. Incredibly, armor still gleamed on his breast.

If anyone could survive such a dip, thought Gerin, it would be Drago. He was strong as an ox and lacked the imagination to let anything frighten him. "Nasty," he rumbled in a voice like falling trees. He might have been talking about the weather.

"Aye," an abstracted Gerin muttered. At the instant the bridge had melted away, the rain stopped. Pale, dim Nothos, nearing full, gleamed in a suddenly star-flecked sky, while ruddy Elleb, now waning toward third quarter, was just beginning to wester. The other two moons, golden Math and quick-moving Tiwaz, were both near new and hence invisible.

Hustling along a doubled handful of disheveled prisoners, most of them wounded, the weary army trudged back to the keep. Gerin's serfs met them at the village. They shouted thanks for having their crops, or most of them, saved. Their dialect was so rustic that even Gerin, who had heard it since birth, found it hard to follow.

Gerin ordered ten oxen slaughtered, laying the fat-wrapped thighbones on the altars of Dyaus and the

war-god Deinos which stood in his great hall. The rest
of the meat vanished into his men. To wash it down,
barrel after barrel of smooth, foaming ale and sweet
mead was broached and emptied. Men who found
combat raising a different urge pursued peasant
wenches and servant wenches, many of whom preferred being chased to chaste.

At first the baron did not join the merrymaking.
He applied an ointment of honey, lard, and astringent
herbs to his wound (luckily not deep), and winced at
its bite. Then he had the brightest-looking captive, a
tall mournful blond barbarian who kept his left hand
clutched to a torn right shoulder, bandaged and
brought into a storeroom. While two troopers stood
by with drawn swords, Gerin cleaned his nails with a
dagger from his belt. He said nothing.

The silence bothered the Trokmê, who fidgeted.
"What is it you want of me?" he burst out at last.
"It's Cliath son of Ailech I am, of a house noble for
more generations than I have toes and fingers, and
no right at all do you have to treat me like some low
footpad."

"What right have you," Gerin asked mildly, "to rob
and burn my land and kill my men? I could flay the
hide off your carcass in inch-wide strips and give it
to my dogs to eat while what was left of you watched,
and no one could say I did not have the right. Thank
your gods Wolfar did not catch you; he would do it.
But tell me what I need to know, and I will set you
free. Otherwise"—his eyes flicked to the two hard
men by him—"I'll walk out this door, and ask no
questions after."

One of Cliath's eyes was swollen shut. The other
peered at the Fox. "What would keep you from doing
that anyway, once I've talked?"

Gerin shrugged. "I've held this keep almost eight
years. Men on both side of the Niffet know what

my word is worth. And on this you have that word: you'll get no second chance."

Cliath studied him. The Trokmê made as if to rub his chin, but grimaced in pain and stopped. He sighed. "What would you know of me, then?"

"Tell me this: what do you know of the black-robed warlock who calls himself Balamung?"

"Och, that kern? Till this raid it's little I've had to do with him, and wanted less. It's bad cess for any man to have truck with a wizard, say I, for all he brings loot. No glory in beating ensorceled foes is there, no more than in cutting the throat of a pig, and it tied, too. But those who go with Balamung grow fat, and the few as stand against in him die, and in ways less pretty than having the skins of them flayed off. I mind me of one fellow—puir wight!—who no slower than a sneeze was naught but a pile of twisty, slimy worms—and the stench of him!

"Nigh on a year and a half it is since the wizard omadhaun came to us, and for all we're friends now with Bricriu's clan and thieving Meriasek's, still I long for the days when a man could take a head without asking the leave of a dried-up little turd like Balamung. Him and his dog-futtering talisman!" The Trokmê spat on the hard-packed dirt floor.

"Talisman?" Gerin prompted.

"Aye. With my own eyes I've seen it. 'Tis squarish, perhaps as long as my forearm, and as wide, but not near so thick, you understand, and opening out to double that. And when he'd fain bewitch someone or magic up something, why, the talisman lights up almost like a torch. With my own eyes I've seen it," Cliath repeated.

"Can you read?" the baron asked.

"No, nor write, no more than I can fly. Why in the name of the gods would you care to know that?"

"Never mind," Gerin said. "I know enough now."

More than I want, he added to himself: Bricriu's clan and Meriasek's had been at feud since the days of their grandfathers.

The Fox tossed his little knife to the barbarian, who tucked it into the top of one of his high rawhide boots. Gerin led him through the main hall, ignoring his vassals' stares. He told his startled gatekeepers to let Cliath out, and said to him, "How you cross the river is your affair, but with that blade perhaps you won't be waylaid by my serfs."

Good eye shining, Cliath held out his left hand. "A puir clasp, but I'm proud to make it. Och, what a clansmate you'd have been.

Gerin took the offered hand but shook his head. "No, I'd sooner live on my own land than take away my neighbor's. Now go, before I think about the trouble I'm giving myself by turning you loose."

As the northerner trotted down the low hill, Gerin was already on his way back to the rollicking great hall, a frown on his face. Truly Deinos was coursing his terrible warhounds through the northern forests, and the baron was the game they sought.

After he had downed five or six tankards, though, things looked rosier. He staggered up the stairs to his room, arm round the waist of one of his serving wenches. But even as he cupped her soft breasts later, part of his mind saw Castle Fox a smoking ruin, and fire and death all along the border.

II

He woke some time past noon. By the racket coming from below, the roistering had never ceased. Probably no one was on the walls, either, he thought disgustedly; could Balamung have roused his men to a second attack, he would have had Fox Keep in the palm of his hand.

The girl was already gone. Gerin dressed and went down to the great hall, looking for half a dozen of his leading liegemen. He found Van and Rollan the Boar-Slayer still rehashing the battle, drawing lines on the table in sticky mead. Fandor the Fat had a beaker of mead, too, but he was drinking from it. That was his usual sport; his red nose and awesome capacity testified to it. Drago was asleep on the floor, his body swathed in furs. Beside him snored Simrin Widin's son. Duin was nowhere to be found.

The Fox woke Simrin and Drago and bullied his lieutenants up the stairs to the library. Grumbling, they found seats round the central table. They stared suspiciously at the shelves full of neatly pigeonholed scrolls and codices bound in leather and gold leaf. Most of them were as illiterate as Cliath and held reading an affectation, but Gerin was a good enough man of his hands to let them overlook his eccentricity. Still, the books and the quiet overawed them a bit. The baron would need that today.

He scratched his bearded chin and remembered how horrified everyone had been when, after his father was killed, he'd come back from the southlands clean-shaven. Duin's father, dour old Borbeto the Grim, had managed the barony till his return. When he saw Gerin, he'd roared, "Is Duren's son a fancy-boy?" Gerin had only grinned and answered, "Ask your daughter"; shouts of laughter won his vassals to him.

Duin wandered in, still fumbling at his breeches. Bawdy chuckles greeted him. Fandor called, "Easier to stay on a lass than a horse, is it?"

"It is, and more fun besides," Duin grinned, plainly none the worse for his dunking. He turned to Gerin, sketched a salute. "What's on your mind, lord?"

"Among other things," Gerin said drily, "the bridge that was almost your end."

"Downright uncanny, I call it," Rollan murmured. He spoke thickly, for his slashed lip had three stitches holding it shut. Tall, solid, and dark, he ran his fief with some skill, fought bravely, and never let a new thought trouble his mind.

"Me, I have no truck with wizards," Drago said righteously. He sneezed. "Damn! I've taken cold." He went on, "There's no way to trust a body like that. Noses always in a scroll, think they're better than simple folk."

"Remember where you are, fool," Simrin Widin's son hissed.

"No offense meant, of course, lord," Drago said hastily.

"Of course." Gerin sighed. "Now let me tell you what I learned last night." The faces of his men grew grave as the tale unfolded, and there was a silence when he was through.

Duin broke it. Along with his auburn hair, his fiery temper told of Trokmê blood. Now he thumped a fist down on the table and shouted, "A pox on wizardry! There's but one thing to do about it. We have to hit the whoreson before he can hit us again, this time with all the northmen, not just Aingus' clan."

A mutter of agreement ran down the table. Gerin shook his head. This was what he had to head off at all costs. "There's nothing I'd like better," he lied, "but it won't do. On his home ground, their mage would squash us like so many bugs. But from what the braggart said, we have some time. What I'd fain do is go south to the capital and hire a warlock from the Sorcerers' Collegium there so we can fight magic with magic. I don't relish leaving Fox Keep under the axe, but the task is mine, for I still have connections in the southlands. We can settle Balamung properly once I'm back."

"It strikes me as a fool's errand, lord," Duin said, plain-spoken as always. "What we need is a good, hard stroke now—"

"Duin, if you want to beard that wizard without one at your back, then you're the fool. If you had to take a keep with a stone-thrower over its gate, you'd find a stone-thrower of your own, wouldn't you?"

"I suppose so," Duin said. His tone was surly, but there were nods round the table. Gerin was relieved. He was coming to the tricky part. With a little luck, he could slip it by them before they noticed.

"Stout fellow!" he said, and went on easily, "Van will need your help here while I'm gone. With him in charge, nothing can go too badly wrong."

It didn't work. Even Fandor and Simrin, both of whom had kept those noses buried in their drinking jacks till now, jerked up their heads. Diffidently, Rollan began, "Begging your pardon, my lord—" and Gerin braced for insubordination. It came fast enough: "The gods know Van of the Strong Arm has proven himself a man, time and again, and a loyal and true vassal as well. But for all that, he is an outlander and owns no land hereabouts, guesting with you as he does. It'd be downright unseemly for us, whose families have held our fiefs for generations, to take orders from him."

Gerin gathered himself for an explosion. Before he loosed it, he saw all the barons nodding their agreement. He caught Van's eyes; the outlander shrugged. Tasting gall, the Fox yielded with as much grace as he could. "If that's how you would have it, so be it. Van, would it please you to ride with me, then?"

"It would that, captain," Van said, coming as close as he ever did to Gerin's proper feudal title. "I've never been south of the Kirs, and I've heard enough about Elabon's capital to make me want to see it."

"Fine," Gerin said. "Duin, you have the highest standing of any here. Do you think you can keep things afloat while I'm away?"

"Aye, or die trying."

Gerin feared the latter, but merely said, "Good!" and whispered a prayer under his breath. Duin was more than doughty enough and not stupid, but he lacked common sense.

Drago and Rollan decided to stay at Fox Keep themselves and leave the defense of their own castles to the vassal contingents they would send home; Gerin dared hope they might restrain Duin. After his other liegemen had gone, he spent a couple of hours giving Duin instructions on matters probable, matters possible, and as many matters impossible as his fertile mind could envision. He finished, "For Dyaus' sake, send word along the West March Road and the Emperor's Highway. The border barons must know of this, so they can ready themselves for the storm."

"Even Wolfar?"

"As his holding borders mine, news has to go through him anyway. But the slug happens to be out a-courting, and his man Schild, though he has no love for me, won't kill a messenger for the sport of it. Also, you could do worse than to get Siglorel here; he has the most power of any Elabonian wizard north of the Kirs, even if he is overfond of ale. Last I heard, he was in the keep of Hovan son of Hagop east of here, trying to cure Hovan's piles."

Duin nodded, hopefully in wisdom. He surprised Gerin by offering a suggestion of his own: "If you're bound to go through with this wizard scheme, lord, why not go to Ikos and ask the Sibyl for her advice?"

"You know, that's not a bad thought," Gerin mused. "I've been that way once before, and it will only cost me an extra day or so."

Next day he decided—not for the first time—that mixing ale and mead was a poor idea. The cool, crisp early morning air settled in his lungs like sludge. His side was stiff and sore. His head eached. The creaks and groans of the light wagon and steady pound of hooves on stone roadbed, sounds he usually failed to notice, rang loud in his ears. The sun seemed to have singled him out for all its rays.

Worst of all, Van was awake and in full song. Holding his throbbing head, Gerin asked, "Don't you know any quiet tunes?"

"Aye, several of 'em," Van answered, and returned to his interrupted ditty.

Gerin contemplated death and other delights. At last the song came to an end. "I thank you," he said.

"Nothing at all, captain." Van frowned, then went on, "I think yesterday I was too hellishly worn out to pay as much attention to what you were saying as I should. Why is it such a fell thing for Balamung to have got his claws on Shabeth-Shiri's book?"

The Fox was glad to talk, if only to dull the edge of his own worry. "Shabeth-Shiri was the greatest sorcerer of Kizzuwatna long ago: the land where all wizardry began, and where it flourishes to this day. They say he was the first to uncover the laws behind their magic, and set them down in writing to teach his pupils."

"Now, that can't be the book Balamung was boasting of, can it?"

"No. I have a copy of that one myself, as a matter of fact. So does everyone who's ever dabbled in magic. It's not a book of spells, but of the principles by which they're cast. But, using those principles, Shabeth-Shiri worked more powerful warlockery than any this poor shuddering world has seen since. He made himself king as well as mage, and he fought so many wars he ran short of men, or so the story goes. So he kept his rule alive by raising demons to fight for him, and by many other such cantrips. Think how embarrassed an army that thought itself safe behind a stream would be to have it flood and drown their camp, or turn to blood—or to see Shabeth-Shiri's men charging over a bridge like the one Balamung used against us."

"Embarrassed is scarcely the word, captain."

"I suppose not. Shabeth-Shiri wrote down all his most frightful spells, too, but in a book he showed to no one. He meant it for his son, they say, but for all his wizardry he was beaten at last: all the other mages and marshals of Kizzuwatna combined against him, lest he rule the whole world. His son was killed in the sack of his last citadel, Shaushka—"

"Shaushka the Damned? That was his? I've seen it with my own eyes. It lies in the far north of Kizzuwatna, at the edge of the plains of Shanda, and the plainsmen showed it to me from far away: stark, dark, and dead. Nothing grows there to this day, even after—how many years?"

Gerin shuddered. "Two thousand, if a day. But the winners never found Shabeth-Shiri's body, or his book either, and sorcerers have searched for it from that day to this. The legends say some of its pages are of human skin. It glows with a light of its own when its master uses it." The baron shook his head. "Cliath saw it, sure as sure."

"A nice fellow, this Shabeth-Shiri, and I think he'd be proud of the one who has his Book now. It seems all Kizzuwatnans have a taste for blood, though," Van said. "Once when I was traveling with the nomads—" Gerin never found out about the Kizzuwatnan Van had fallen foul of, for at that moment two hurtling bodies burst from the oaks that grew almost to within bowshot of the road.

One was a stag, proud head now low as it fled. But it had not taken more than three bounds when a tawny avalanche struck it from behind and smashed it to the grass. Great stabbing fangs tore into its throat, once, twice. Blood spurted and slowed; the stag's hooves drummed and were still.

Crouched over its kill, the longtooth snarled a warning at the travelers. It settled its short hind legs under its belly and began to feed. Its stumpy tail quivered in absurd delight as it tore hunks of flesh from the stag's carcass. When the men stopped to watch, it growled deep in its throat and dragged its prey into the cover of the woods.

Van was all for flushing it out again, but Gerin

demurred; like rogue aurochs, longtooths were best hunted by parties larger than two. Rather grumpily, Van put away his spear. "Sometimes, Gerin," he said, "you take all the fun out of life."

The Fox did not answer. His gloomy mood slowly cleared as the sun rose higher in the sky. He looked about with more than a little pride, for the lands he ruled were rich ones. And, he thought, the wealth they made stayed on them.

The lands between the Kirs and the Niffet had drawn the Empire of Elabon for their copper and tin and as a buffer between its heartland and the northern savages. Once seized, though, they were left largely to their own devices.

Not a measure of grain nor a pound of tin did Elabon take from Gerin's land, or from any other borderer lord's. The Marchwarden of the North, Carus Beo's son, kept his toy garrison in Cassat under the shadow of the Kirs. So long as the borderers held the Trokmoi at bay, the Empire let them have their freedom.

Traffic on the great road was light so near the Niffet. The only traveler Gerin and Van met the first day was a wandering merchant. A thin, doleful man, he nodded gravely as he headed north. A calico cat with mismatched eyes and only one ear sat on his shoulder. It glared at Gerin as they passed.

When night began to near, the baron brought a brace of fowls from a farmer who dwelt by the road. Van shook his head as he watched his friend haggle with the peasant. "Why not just take what you need, like any lord?" he asked. "The kern is your subject, after all."

"True, but he's not my slave. A baron who treats his serfs like beasts of burden will see his castle come down round his ears the first time his crops fail. Serve him right, too, the fool."

After they stopped for the evening, Gerin wrung a hen's neck and drained its blood into a trough he dug in the rich black soil. "That should satisfy any roving spirits," he said, plucking and gutting the bird and skewering it to roast over the campfire.

"Any that wouldn't sooner drink *our* blood instead," Van said. "Captain, out on the plains of Shanda the ghosts have real fangs, and they aren't shy of watchfires. Only the charms the nomads' shamans magic up can keep them at bay—and sometimes not those, either, if most of the moons are dark. A bad place."

Gerin believed him. Any land that made his hard-bitten comrade leery sounded like a good place to avoid.

They drew straws for the first watch. Within seconds, Van was curled in his bedroll and snoring like a thunderstorm. Gerin watched Tiwaz and Math, both thin crescents almost lost in the skirts of twilight, follow the sun down to the horizon. As they sank, full Nothos rose. Under his weak grayish light, field and forest alike were half-seen mysteries. Small night-creatures chirped and hummed. Gerin let the fire die into embers, and the ghosts came.

As always, the eye refused to grasp their shapes, sliding away before they could be recognized. They swarmed round the pool of blood like great carrion flies. Their buzzing filled Gerin's mind. Some shouted in tongues so ancient their very names were lost. Others he almost understood, but no true words could be heard, only clamor and loss and wailing.

The Fox knew that if he tried to grasp one of the flittering shapes it would slip through his fingers like so much mist, for the dead kept but a pallid semblance of life. Grateful for the boon of blood, they tried to give him such redes as they thought good, but only a noise like the rushing wind filled his head. Had he not granted them that gift, or had the fire not been there, they likely would have driven him mad.

He kept watch until midnight, staring at stars and full Nothos and the half-seen shapes of spirits until Elleb, a copper disc almost half chewed away, was well clear of the dark woods on the horizon. No man disturbed him: few travelers were so bold as to risk moving in the dark of the sun.

When Gerin roused Van, he woke with the instant awareness of a seasoned warrior. "The ghosts are bad tonight," the baron mumbled, and then he was asleep.

Van announced the dawn with a whoop that jerked the Fox awake. Trying to pry his eyes open, he said, "I feel as if my head were filled with sand. 'Early in the morning' says the same thing twice."

"An hour this side of midday is counted as morning, is it not?"

"Aye, it is, and too bloody early in the bargain. Oh for the days when I was in the capital and not one of the wise men I listened to thought of opening his mouth before noon."

Gerin gnawed leathery journeybread, dried fruit, and smoked sausage, washing them down with bitter beer. He had to choke the bread down. The stuff had the virtue of keeping nearly forever, and he understood why: the bugs liked it no better than he.

He sighed, stretched, and climbed into his armor, wincing as his helm slipped down over one ear bent permanently outward by a northerner's club in a long-ago skirmish. "The birds are shining, the sun is chirping, and who am I to complain?" he said.

Van gave him a curious glance. "You feeling all right, captain?" he asked, a note of real concern in his voice.

"Yes and no," Gerin said thoughtfully. "But for the first time since I came back from the southlands, it doesn't matter at all. Things are out of my hands, and they will be for a while now. If someone pisses in the soup-pot, why, Duin will just have to try and take care of it without me. It's a funny feeling, you know. I'm half glad to be free and half afraid things will fall apart without me. It's like running a long way and then stopping short: I've got used to the strain, and feel wrong without it."

They moved south steadily, but not in silence. Van extracted a clay flute from his kit and made the morning hideous with it. Gerin politely asked if he'd been taking music lessons from the ghosts, but he shrugged a massive shrug and kept on tweedling.

A pair of guardhouses flanked the road where it crossed from Gerin's lands to those of Palin the Eagle. Two sets of troopers sprawled in the roadway, dicing the day away. At the creak of the wagon, they abandoned the game and reached for their weapons.

Gerin looked down his long nose at the wary archers. "Hail!" he said. "Would that you'd been so watchful last summer, when you let Wacho and his brigands sneak south without so much as a challenge."

The guard captain shuffled his feet. "Lord, how was I to know he'd forged his safe-conduct?"

"By the hand of it, and the spelling. The lout could barely write. Too late now, but if it happens again you'll find a new lord, probably in the underworld. Do we pass your inspection?"

"You do that, lord." The guard waved the wagon on. Gerin drew sword as he passed the ancient boundary stone separating his holding from Palin's. Palin's guardsmen returned his salute. For long generations the two houses had been at peace. The stone, its time-worn runes covered by gray-green moss, had sunk almost half its height into the soft earth.

Once past the guards, Van turned and said to Gerin, "You know, Fox, when I first came to your land I thought Palin the Eagle had to be some fine

warrior, to judge by what his folk called him. How
was I to know they were talking of his nose?"

"He's no Carlun come again, I will say." Gerin
chuckled. "But he and his vassals keep order well
enough that I don't fear a night or so in the open in
his lands, or perhaps with one of his lordlets."

"You don't want himself to guest you?"

"No indeed. He has an unmarried sister who must
be rising forty by now and desperate, poor lass.
Worse, she cooks for him too, and badly. The last
time I ate with Palin, I thought the belly-sickness had
me, not just a sour stomach."

When the travelers did stop for the night, it was at
the ramshackle keep of one of Palin's vassals, Raff the
Ready. A blocky boulder of a man, he was very much of
the old school, wearing a forked beard that almost
reached his waist. His unflappable solidity reminded the
Fox of Drago; so, less hearteningly, did his disdain
for cleanliness.

Withal, he set a good table. He had killed a cow
that day, and along with the beef there was a stew of
frogs and mussels from a nearby pond, fresh-baked
bread, blueberries and blueberry tarts, and a fine, nut-
like ale with which to wash them down.

Gerin sighed in contentment, loosened his belt,
belched, and then, reluctantly, gave Raff his news.
His host looked uneasy. He promised to spread the
word. "You think your men won't be able to hold
them at the Niffet, then?" he asked.

"I'm very much afraid they won't."

"Well, I'll tell my neighbors, not that it'll do much
good. All of us are looking south, not north, waiting
for the trouble in Bevon's barony to spill over into
ours."

"There's fighting there?" Van asked hopefully.

"Aye, there is that. All four of Bevon's sons are
brawling over the succession, and him not even dead

yet. One of them ran twenty sheep off Palin's land, too, the son of a whore."

With that warning, they left early, almost before dawn. They carried a torch to keep the ghosts at bay. Even so, Gerin's skin crawled with dread until the spirits fled the rays of the sun.

He spent a nervous morning hurrying south through Bevon's strife-torn barony. Every one of Bevon's vassals kept his castle shut tight. The men on the walls gave Gerin and Van hard stares, but no one tried to stop them.

Around noon, they heard fighting down an approaching side road. Van looked interested, but Gerin cared far more about reaching the capital than getting drawn into an imbroglio not his own.

The choice did not stay in his hands. Two spearmen and an archer, plainly fleeing, burst onto the highway. The archer took one quck glance at Gerin and Van, shouted "More traitors!" and let fly. His shaft sailed between them, perhaps because he could not pick either one as target.

He got no second shot. Gerin had been sitting with bow ready to hand, and no confusion spoiled his aim. But even as the archer fell, his comrades charged the wagon. Gerin and Van sprang down to meet them.

The fight was short but savage. The footsoldiers seemed to have already despaired of their lives, and thought only of killing before they fell. Cool as usual in a fight, the Fox ducked under his foe's guard and slid the point of his blade between the luckless fellow's ribs. The man coughed blood and died.

The baron wheeled to help Van, but his friend needed no aid. A stroke of his axe had shattered his man's spearshaft, another clove through helm and skull alike. Only a tiny cut above his knee showed he had fought at all. He rubbed at it, grumbling, "Bastard pinked me. I must be getting old."

The triumph left the taste of ashes in Gerin's mouth. What fools the men of Elabon were, to be fighting among themselves while a storm to sweep them all away was rising in the northern forests! And now he was as guilty as any. Warriors who might have been bold against the Trokmoi were stiffening corpses in the roadway—because of him.

"Where you're going makes you more important than them," Van said when he voiced that worry aloud.

"I hope so." But in his heart, Gerin wondered if the southern wizards could withstand Balamung and the Book of Shabeth-Shiri.

He sighed with relief when at last he spied the guardhouse of Bevon's southern neighbor, Ricolf the Red. He was not surprised to see it had a double complement of men.

The baron returned the greetings Ricolf's guardsmen gave him. He knew a few of them, for he had spent several pleasant weeks at Ricolf's keep on his last journey to the southlands. "It's been too long, lord Gerin," one of the guards said. "Ricolf will be glad to see you."

"And I him. He was like a second father to me."

"Peace be with you, wayfarers," Ricolf's man called as they drove past.

"And to you also peace." Van made the proper response, for he held the reins. He had been quick to pick up the customs of Gerin's land.

The sun was dying in the west and Gerin felt the first low keenings of long-dead wraiths when Ricolf's castle came into view, crowned by a scarlet banner. Somewhere high overhead, an eagle screamed. Van's sharp eyes searched the sky till he found the moving speck. "On our right," he said. "There's a good omen, if you care for one."

"I mislike taking omens from birds," Gerin said.

"They're too public. Who's to say a foretelling is meant for him and not some lout in the next holding who has to squint to see it?"

A boy's clear voice floated from Ricolf's watch-tower: "Who comes to the holding of Ricolf the Red?"

"I am Gerin, called the Fox, guest-friend to your master Ricolf, and with me is my friend and companion, Van of the Strong Arm. By Dyaus and Rilyn, god of friendship, we claim shelter for the night."

"Bide a moment." After a pause, Gerin heard Ricolf's deep voice exclaim, "What? Let them in, fool, let them in!" The drawbridge swung down. The lad cried, "In the names of Dyaus and Rilyn, welcome, guest-friend Gerin! Be you welcome also, Van of the Strong Arm."

Ricolf's keep, more sophisticated than Gerin's frontier fortress, had stone outwalls instead of a log palisade. Its moat was broad and deep; limp-looking plants splashed the slick surface of the water. A vile stench rose from the moat. Sinuous ripples made Gerin suspect water plants were not the only things to call it home.

Ricolf greeted his guests at the gatehouse. He was stout, perhaps fifty, with a square, ruddy face and blue eyes. His tunic and trousers were brightly checked and modish in cut, but the sword swinging at his belt was a plain, well-battered weapon that had seen much use. He had more gray in his red hair and beard than Gerin remembered, and lines of worry the Fox had not seen before bracketed his eyes and mouth.

When Gerin scrambled down from the wagon, Ricolf enfolded him in a bearhug, pumping his hand and thumping his back. "Great Dyaus above, lad, is it ten years? They've made a man of you! Ten years indeed, and us not living five days' ride from each other. This must never happen again!"

Untangling himself, Gerin said, "True enough, but I doubt if either one of us had a five-day stretch free and clear in all those years." He explained why he was traveling south. Ricolf nodded in grim comprehension. Gerin went on, "If what traders say is true, you've had your own troubles."

"I did, until I sent my unloving cousin Sarus to the afterworld this past winter," Ricolf agreed. He focused on Van. "Is this your new lieutenant? I thought what news I heard of him so much nonsense, but I see it was just the truth."

"My comrade, rather," Gerin said, and made the introduction. Van acknowledged it with grave respect. His broad hand, back thick-thatched with golden hair, swallowed Ricolf's in its clasp.

"I greet you as well, Van of the Strong Arm. Use my home as you own for as long as you would. Speaking of which" —Ricolf turned back to Gerin— "would you like to scrub off the dust of the road in my bathhouse before we eat? You have the time, I think."

"Bath-house?" Geirn stared. "I thought I'd have to shiver in the streams or reek like a dungheap till I got south of the mountains."

Ricolf looked pleased. "So far as I know, I have the first up here. I had it put in last summer, when I sent messages to the unmarried barons of the north-country—and to some south of the Kirs, too—that any who thought himself worthy of my daughter Elise's hand should come here, to let me decide which man I thought most suited to her. My wife Yrse gave me no sons who lived, you know, nor have I hopes for any legitimate ones now, as I've no real intention of marrying again. I had three bastard boys, and one a lad of promise, too, but the chest-fever carried them off two winters back, poor lads, so when I die the holding passes to Elise and whomever she weds. Gerin, you must have got my invitation to join us; I know you're still wifeless."

"Yes, I did, but I had an arrow through my shoulder. It was a nasty one, and I was afraid the wound would rot if I traveled too soon. I sent my regrets."

"That's right, so you did. I remember now. I was truly sorry; you've done yourself a fine job since Duren and Dagref, er, died."

"It wasn't the trade I was trained for," Gerin shrugged. "My father always counted on Dagref; besides being older than me, he was a fighter born. Who would have thought the Trokmoi could get them both at once? I know my father never did. As for me, I'm still alive, so I suppose I haven't disgraced myself."

He changed the subject; remembering his father still hurt. "Now you'd better show me where that bath-house of yours is, before your dogs decide I'm part of the midden." He scratched the ears of a shaggy, reddish hound sniffing his ankles. Its tail switched back and forth as it grinned up at him, tongue lolling out. A half-memory flickered, but he could not make it light.

"Go away, Ruffian!" Ricolf snapped. The dog ignored him. "Beast thinks the place belongs to him," Ricolf grumbled. He took Gerin's arm and pointed. "Right over there, and I'll see to it your horses are tended."

Ricolf's tubs were carved limestone. The delicate frieze of river godlets and nymphs carved round them told Gerin they'd been hauled up from the south, for local gravers were less skilled. Soaking in steaming water, the Fox said, "Ricolf gives the suitors nothing but the finest. I never thought I'd feel clean again."

Van's bulk almost oozed out of the tub, but he grunted contented agreement. He asked, "What is this daughter of Ricolf's like?"

Gerin paused to rinse suds from his beard. "Your guess is as good as mine. Ten years back, she was small and skinny and rather wished she were a boy."

They dried off. Van spent a few minutes polishing imaginary dull places on his cuirass and combing the scarlet crest of his helm. Gerin did not re-don his own armor, choosing instead a sky-blue tunic and black breeches.

"With your gear, you could go anywhere," he said, "but I'd look a mere private soldier in mine. Even this is none too good; the southerners will doubtless have their hair all curled and oiled and wear those toga things they affect." He waved a limp-wristed hand. "And they talk so pretty, too."

"Don't have much use for them, eh, captain?"

Gerin smiled wryly. "That's the funniest part of it. I spent the happiest part of my life south of the Kirs. I'm a southerner at heart some ways, I suppose, but I can't let it show at Fox Keep."

Ricolf led them into his long hall. At the west end, a great pile of fat-wrapped bones smoked before Dyaus' altar. "You feed the god well," Gerin said.

"He has earned it." Ricolf turned to the men already at the tables. "Let me present the baron Gerin, called the Fox, and his companion Van of the Strong Arm. Gentlemen, we have here Rihwin the Fox—"

Gerin stared at the man who shared his sobriquet. Rihwin stared back, his clean-shaven face a mask. His smooth cheeks alone would have said he was from the south, but he also wore a flowing green toga and a golden hoop in his left ear. Gerin liked most southern ways, but he had always thought earrings excessive.

Ricolf was still talking. "Also Rumold of the Long Bow, Laidrad the Besieger, Wolfar of the Axe—"

Gerin muttered a polite unpleasantry. Wolfar, a

dark-sinned lump of a man with bushy eyebrows, coarse black hair, and an unkempt thicket of beard that almost reached his swordbelt, was the Fox's western neighbor. They'd fought a bloody skirmish over nothing in particular two winters ago, before Wolfar went to seek Ricolf's daughter.

While Ricolf droned on, introducing more suitors and men of his household, Gerin got hungrier and hungrier. Finally Ricolf said, "And last but surely not least, my daughter Elise."

The baron was dimly aware of Van's sweeping off his helmet and somehow bowing from the waist in full armor. What Elise's long golden gown contained reminded him acutely of how much little girls could grow in ten years. He vaguely regretted she did not follow the bare-bodiced southern style, but the gown showed plenty as it was. Long brown hair flowed over her creamy shoulders.

Her laughing green eyes held him. "I remember you well, lord Gerin," she said. "When last you were here, you bounced me on your knee. Times change, though."

"So they do, my lady," he agreed mournfully.

He took a seat without much attention to his benchmates, and found himself between Rihwin and Wolfar. "Bounced her on your knee, forsooth?" Rihwin said, soft voice turning words in elaborate southern patterns. "I should be less than a truthteller were I to say some such idea had not crossed my mind at one time or another, and I daresay the minds of others here as well. And now we meet a man who has accomplished the fondest dreams of a double hand of nobles and more: in good truth, a fellow manifestly to be watched with the greatest of care."

He raised a mug in mocking salute, but Gerin thought the smile on his handsome face real. The baron drained his own tankard in return. Rihwin seemed to wince as he downed his ale; no doubt he preferred wine. Most southerners did, but grapes grew poorly north of the Kirs.

An elbow nudged Gerin's ribs. Wolfar grinned at him, displaying snaggled teeth. Gerin suspected he had were-blood in him. His hairiness varied marvelously as the moons whirled through the sky. Three years before, when Nothos and Math were full at the same time, a tale went round that he'd gone all alone into the forests of the Trokmoi and slain men with his teeth.

At the moment, he seemed civil—and civilized—enough. "How fare you, Fox?" he asked.

"Well enough, until now," Gerin answered smoothly. From the corner of his eye, he saw Rihwin cock an eyebrow in an expression he was more used to feeling on his own face than seeing on another. He felt he had passed an obscure test.

His belly was growling when the repast appeared. Rihwin's cooks did not have the spices and condiments the Fox had known south of the mountains, but the food was good and they did no violence to it. There was beef both roasted and boiled, fowls fried crisp and brown, mutton, ribs of pork cooked in a tangy sauce, creamy cheese with a firm, tasty skin, thick soup from the stockpot, and mountains of fresh-baked bread. Ricolf's good beer was an added delight. Serving wenches ran here and there, food-laden bronze platters in their hands, trying to keep ahead of the gobbling suitors.

Rihwin and one or two others discreetly patted the girls as they went by. Gerin understood their caution; it would not have done for a noble intent on marrying Ricolf's daughter to get one of his wenches with child. Van had no such worries. When a well-made lass came by, he kissed her and gave her a squeeze. She squealed and almost dropped her tray. Her face was red as she pulled away, but she smiled back at him.

The feasters tossed gnawed bones onto the hall's dirt floor, where Ricolf's dogs snarled and fought over them. Whenever the battles grew too noisy, a couple of cleaned-up serfs in stout boots toed the hounds apart. Even so, the din was overpowering.

So were the smells. The odors of dog and man vied with the smell of cooking meat. Smoke from the torches and the great hearth next to Dyaus' altar hung in a choking cloud.

Gerin ate until he could barely move, then settled back, replete and happy. Everyone rose as Elise made her exit, flanked by two maids. When she was gone, the serious drinking and gambling began.

Wolfar, Gerin knew, was a fanatic for dicing, but tonight, for some reason, he declined to enter the game. "I never bet in my life," he declared loftily, pretending not to hear the Fox's snort.

"I wish I could say that," a loser mourned as his bet was scooped up.

"Why can't you? Wolfar just did," Rihwin said. Gerin grinned at him with genuine liking. In the southlands the smooth insult was a fine art, one the baron had enjoyed but one too subtle for Castle Fox. Rihwin nodded back; maybe he had aimed the remark for Gerin's ears. It always warmed the Fox when a southerner born and bred took him for an equal. They were a snobbish lot on the other side of the Kirs. That Rihwin's target was Wolfar only made things more delightful.

Rihwin had a capacity for ale that belied his soft looks. Gerin valiantly tried to keep up, emptying his mug again and again until the room spun as he rose. His last clear memory was of Van howling out a nomad battlesong and accompanying himself with the flat of his blade on the tabletop.

* * *

To his surprise, the baron woke up the next morning in a bed. He had scant notion of how or when he'd reached it. Little wails of delight and Van's hoarse chuckle from the next room told him the outlander had not wasted his night sleeping.

The Fox found a bucket of cold water outside his door. He poured half of it over his head. Spluttering, he walked down the passageway and into the yard. He found Ricolf there, halfheartedly practicing with the bow. Though the older man had not tried to pace his guests, he looked wan.

"Does this sort of thing happen every night?" Gerin asked.

"The gods forbid! Were it so, I'd have been long dead. No, I plan to announce my choice tonight, and it would be less than natural if tension didn't build. For near a year I've seen these men—all but Sigiber the South, poor wight, who got a spear through his middle—in battle, heard them talk, watched them. Aye, my mind's made up at last."

"Who?"

"Can you keep it quiet? No, that's a foolish question; you could before, pup though you were, and it's not the sort of thing to change in a man. For all his affected ways—I know some call him 'Fop' and not 'Fox'—Rihwin is easily the best of them. After him, perhaps, would be Wolfar, but a long way back."

"Wolfar?" Gerin was amazed. "You can't mean it?"

"Aye, I do. I know of your trouble with him, but you can't deny he's a doughty warrior. He's not as slow of wit as his looks would make you think, either."

"He's a mean one, though. Once in hand-to-hand he almost bit my ear off." Something else occurred to the Fox. "What of your daughter? If the choice were hers, whom would she pick?"

It was Ricolf's turn for surprise. "What does that

matter? She'll do as I bid her." He turned back to his archery.

Gerin was tempted to leave, but knew his old friend would think him rude to vanish on the eve of the betrothal. He spent the day relaxing, glancing at the couple of books Ricolf owned, and making light talk with some of the suitors.

Van emerged in the early afternoon, a smile on his face. The outlander was rubbing a callus on his right forefinger when he found Gerin. The baron remembered the heavy silver ring he'd worn there. Van explained, "It's only right to give the lassie something to remember me by."

"You, I don't think she's likely to forget."

"I suppose not," Van said happily.

A bit before sunset, a wandering minstrel appeared outside Ricolf's gate and prayed shelter for the night. The baron granted it, on condition that he sing after Elise's betrothal was announced. The minstrel, whose name was Tassilo, agreed at once. "How not?" he said. "After all, 'tis the purpose of a singer to sing."

The evening meal was like the one the night before. Tonight, though, Ricolf opened jugs of wine brought up from the south along with griffin-headed ivory rhytons and eared cups of finest Sithonian ware—beautiful scenes of hunting, drinking, and the deeds of the gods were painted under their glaze. Gerin's thrifty soul quailed when he thought of what Ricolf must have spent.

Rihwin, who seemed to expect his coming triumph and hadn't tasted the wine he loved in a year, began pouring it down almost faster than he could be served. He held it well at first, regaling his comrades with bits of gossip from the Emperor's court. Though this was a year old, most of it was new to Gerin.

The feasters finished. An expectant hush fell on the hall.

Just as Ricolf began to rise, Rihwin suddenly clambered onto the table. The boards creaked. Voice wine-blurred, Rihwin called out, "Ha, bard, play me a tune, and make it a lively one!"

Tassilo, who had looked at the bottom of his cup more than once himself, struck fiery music from his mandolin. Rihwin went into a northern dance. Gerin stared at him. He was sure Ricolf would not like this. But Rihwin found the jig too sedate. He shifted in mid-step to a wild, stamping nomad dance.

Ricolf, watching the unmanly performance, looked like a man bathing in hellfire. He had all but beggared himself to provide the best for these men and make his holding as much like the elegant southland as he could. Was this his reward?

Then, with a howl, Rihwin stood on his hands and kicked his legs in the air in time to the music. His toga fell limply around his ears. He wore nothing under it.

At that spectacle, the maids hustled Elise from the hall. Gerin did not quite catch her expression, but thought amusement a large part of it.

In agony, Ricolf cried, "Rihwin, you have danced your wife away!"

"I could hardly care less," Rihwin said cheerfully. "Play on, minstrel!"

III

After that, there was little Ricolf could do. He tried to make the best of the fiasco by proclaiming to everyone that Wolfar of the Axe was his true choice as Elise's groom. Wolfar acknowledged his honor with a gracious grunt, which only disconcerted Ricolf more. There were scattered cheers, including a sardonic one from Rihwin.

Gerin muttered insincere congratulations to Wolfar. Then he left the feast, claiming he wanted to make an early start in the morning. That held just enough truth to make mannerly his escape from his enemy's triumph. Van had already disappeared with another wench and a jug of wine. Ignoring the raucous celebration in the great hall, Gerin blew out the little flame flickering from the middle fingertip of the hand-shaped clay lamp by his bed and fell asleep.

He woke to the sound of someone fumbling at the barred door. Elleb's crescent, just now topping the walls of Ricolf's keep, peeped through the east-facing slit window and sent a pale pink stripe of light across the bed to the door. Sunrise was still two or three hours away.

Head aching, Gerin groped for his clothes. He slid into trousers, but wrapped his tunic round his right arm for a shield. The fumbling went on. Knife in hand, he padded to the door and flung it open.

Whatever outcry he had intended clogged in his throat. "Great Dyaus, Elise, what are you doing here?" he gurgled. He almost had not known her. No longer was she gowned and bedecked. She wore stout boots, breeches, and a sheepskin jacket so baggy it all but hid her curves. A knife swung at her belt. Her long hair was tucked up under a shapeless leather traveler's hat.

For a long moment, she stared at the blade in his left hand. Its nicked edge glittered in the fading light of the hallway torches. Then she brushed past the stunned Fox and shut the door behind them. Voice low and fast, she said, "I need help, lord Gerin, and of all the men here, I think I can only ask it of you. I was willing to try my father's idiot scheme as long as I thought I had some chance of getting a husband I could endure, but Wolfar of the Axe—"

Gerin wished he had not drunk so much. His head still buzzed and his wits were slow. "All the northland knows I have no love for Wolfar, but what do you want of me?" he asked, already afraid he knew the answer.

She looked up at him, eyes enormous in the gloom. "I know you are going to the capital—take me with you! My mother was of a southern house, and I have kin there. I'd be no burden to you. I've been daughter and son both to my father, and I can live from the land like any warrior—"

"Don't you see I can't?" Gerin broke in. "It's impossible.

What would my life be worth if someone were to find you here even now?" Alarmed at that, he added, "By the gods, where are your maids?"

"As soon as I knew my father had chosen Wolfar, I put a sleeping powder in their cups. The ninnies were still clucking over poor besotted Rihwin. He wasn't a bad fellow, for all his silly ways."

The baron felt a twinge of annoyance at her mentioning the drunken fool with kindness, but stifled it. He said, "That's one for you, then. But why won't Ricolf think I ran off with you against your will?"

"Nothing simpler: I let a note in my room saying just what I was doing, and why. There are things in it only he and I know; he'd not think it forced from me."

Gerin stared. Women who read and wrote were not of the ordinary sort. *Well*, he thought, *I've already found that out*. But he shook his head, saying, "You have all the answers, it seems. But answer me this: would you have me break the sacred oath of guest-friendship I hold with your father? No luck comes to the oath-breaker; gods and men alike turn from him."

She inspected him. Her eyes filled with tears. He felt himself flinch under her gaze. "You've forgotten the oath you gave me all those years ago, then?" she asked bitterly. "How old was I? Eight? Ten? I don't know, but I've remembered from then till now that you treated me like a real person, not just a brat underfoot. You swore if ever I needed you, there you would be. Is an oath less an oath because given to a child? Am I less a person because I have no beard? You called on Dyaus; by Dyaus, lord Gerin, could you see yourself wed to Wolfar, were you a woman?" The tears slid down her cheeks.

"No," he sighed, understanding what the truth meant but unable to lie to her.

"No more could I. I would sooner die."

"There's no need of that," he said, awkwardly patting her shoulder. He shrugged on the rolled-up tunic and climbed into his cuirass. "What sort of gear do you have?"

"No need to worry about that. I've already stowed it in your wagon."

He threw his hands in the air. "I might have known. You know, Van will call me nine different kinds of fool, and every one of them true, but you'll be useful to have around. You could talk a longtooth into eating parsnips.

"Wait here," he added, and stepped into the hall. He tried Van's door. It was barred. He swore under his breath. He was about to tap when the door flew open. Van loomed over him, naked as the day he was born. His mace checked its downward arc inches from the Fox's head.

"Captain, what in the five hells are you up to?" he hissed. Behind him, a woman made drowsy complaint. In the half-light, the curve of her hip and thigh made an inviting shadow on the bed. "It's all right, love," the outlander reassured her. She sighed and went back to sleep. Van turned to Gerin: "Don't come scratching round my door. It isn't healthy."

"So I see. Now will you put that fornicating thing down and listen to me?"

When the baron finished, there was nothing but astonishment on Van's face. He whistled softly. "I will be damned. Spend two years thinking a man stodgy and then he does this to you." His shoulders shook with suppressed mirth. "What are you standing here gawking for? Go on, get the horses hitched up; I'll be with you in a few minutes." Softly but firmly, he shut the door in Gerin's face.

Blinking, the baron retrieved Elise and hurried down the hallway. The only sounds were faint cracklings from the guttering torches and snoring from behind almost every door. Gerin thanked the gods for the flooring of rammed earth. On planking, the nails in his sandals would have clicked like the wooden snappers some Sithonian dancers wore on their fingers.

"How can I thank you?" Elise whispered. "I—" Gerin clamped a hand over her mouth: someone else was in the hall.

Wolfar, stumbling to his bed, had rarely felt better in his life. He had spent most of the night thinking of Gerin chopped into dogmeat after he took over Ricolf's lands as well as his own; Elise was a tasty baggage, too. Every other feaster had long since either lurched off to bed or slid under the table, but Wolfar, buoyed by visions of glory and mayhem, was still mostly himself after drinking them all down.

He gaped when Gerin appeared before him. "Ah, the Fox," he said jovially. "I was just thinking of you." His piggy eyes went wide when he saw the baron's companion.

Gerin saw Wolfar fill his lungs to shout. He snatched a dead torch from its dragon-headed bronze sconce and broke it over his rival's bald spot. Wolfar sank without a sound, mouth still open. Gerin and Elise darted for the stables, not knowing how long he would stay stunned.

They slowed once they got outside the castle. Attracting the gate crew's attention was the last thing they wanted.

The horses looked resentful as Gerin harnessed them. His fingers leaped over the leather straps. Each had to go in its proper place, lest the whole harness come apart. He expected an alarm at any moment. But the horses were hitched and Elise hidden under blankets in the back of the wagon, and all stayed quiet. Van, however, did not come. Gerin waited and worried.

A footfall in the doorway made him whirl. His hand leaped for his swordhilt, but that gigantic silhouette could only belong to one man. "What kept you?" the baron barked.

"Some things, a gentleman never hurries," Van said with dignity. "You laid Wolfar out cold as a cod; he'll have himself a ten-day headache. Now let's be off, shall we? Ah, you've already got a torch lit. Good. Here, start another. The light may keep the worst of the ghosts away. Or, of course, it may not. I know few men who've gone night-faring, and fewer still who came back again, but now it's a needful thing, I think."

He climbed aboard, took the reins, and set the horses moving. Harness jingling, they rode up to the gate. A couple of Ricolf's hounds sniffed about the wagon's wheels. Van flicked them away with his whip.

The gate guards made no move to let down the drawbridge. They looked curiously at Van and Gerin. One asked, "Lords, why are you on your way so early?"

Van stopped breathing. It was a question for which he had no good answer. But Gerin only grinned a lopsided grin. He laughed at the guards and said, "I'm running away with Ricolf's daughter; she's much too good for anyone here."

The soldier shook his head. "Ask a question like that and you deserve whatever answer you get, I suppose. Come on, Vukov," he said to the other watchman, "let down the bridge. If they want to take their chances with the ghosts, it's their affair and none of mine."

Smothering a yawn, Vukov helped his comrade with the winch. The bridge slowly lowered, then dropped the last few feet with a thump. To Gerin, the clop of the horses' hooves on it seemed the loudest thing in the world.

Trying not to bellow laughter, Van wheezed and choked. Between splutters, he said, "Captain, that was the most outrageous thing I've ever seen! You've got to promise me you'll never, ever let me gamble with you. I have better things to do than throwing my money away."

"It's ill-done to lie in the house of a guest-friend. If his men choose not to believe, why, that's their affair and none of mine." Gerin shrugged, mimicking the guardsman.

As soon as they left the shelter of Ricolf's keep, the ghosts were on them, keening loss and shrieking resentment of any who still kept warm blood in their veins. Without the boon of blood to placate them, they sent an icy blast of terror down on the travelers.

The horses rolled their eyes, shying at things only they saw. Gerin stopped his ears with his fingers in a vain effort to shut out the ghosts' wails. He saw Van work his massive jaw, but no word of complaint passed the outlander's lips. Elise, shivering, came up to sit with them under the scant protection the torches gave.

Ricolf's lands shot by in a gray blur, as if Van thought to outrun the ghosts by fleeing south. The horses did not falter; rather they seemed glad to run. False dawn was touching the east with yellow light when the wagon sped past the little guardpost Ricolf kept on his southern border. Gerin was not much surprised to see the guards curled up asleep inside; fire and blood warded them from the night spirits. They did not stir as the wagon clattered past.

The Fox had been looking back over his shoulder as long as he was in Ricolf's lands. When he saw how Van slowed their pace once past the border, he knew he had not been the only one to worry. He cocked an eyebrow at his friend. "For all his willingness to help carry off the lady," he said to no one in particular, "I seem to notice a certain burly accomplice of mine lacking a perfect faith in the power of her notes to soothe ruffled tempers."

"If all that noise means me," Van rumbled, "then you've hit in the center of the target. It would have been downright awkward to have to explain to a horde of warriors just what I was doing with their lord's daughter."

Elise made a face at him. She, at least, seemed confident there would be no followers. Gerin wondered what it took to put trust in someone unknown for a double handful of years. His mind stalked round the idea like a cat with ruffled fur. He was still astonished any pleading of hers could have convinced him to bring her along.

At last the sun touched the eastern horizon, spilling out ruddy light like a huge hand pouring wine from a jug. The ghosts gave a last frightened moan and returned to whatever gloomy haunts they inhabited during the day.

The morning wore on with no sign of anyone on Gerin's trail, but he still felt uneasy for no reason he could name. It could not have been the land. Save for the High Kirs, now a deep blue shadow on the southern skyline, nothing was much different from what he knew in his own barony.

Meadow and forest alternated, and if there were a few more elms and oaks and a few less pines and maples, that mattered little. The woods did grow closer to the road than the Fox would have liked: south of Ricolf's holding, the highway marked the boundaries of two barons said to be rivals, and to Gerin's way of thinking they should have kept the undergrowth well trimmed so no one could use it for cover.

Once a little stream wound close by the roadway. When Van pulled off to water the horses and let them rest for a few minutes, frogs and turtles leaped from mossy rocks and churned away in senseless terror, just as they would have near Fox Keep. No, the Fox thought as he stared back at a suspicious turtle, the land was not what troubled him.

The peasants seemed much the same, too. They lived in little villages of wattle and daub, the community oxen housed about as well as the people. Scrawny chickens picked around cottages and squawked warnings at dogs, who snarled back. Little naked herdboys guided flocks of sheep and cattle with sticks, helped by the shortlegged brown and white dogs native to the north country. Men and women in colorless homespun worked in the fields, as hard as the draft animals laboring with them.

Not until Gerin lifted his eyes to the keeps could he finger what troubled him. Castles crowned many hills, but here and there the banks of their moats were beginning to crumble into the water. Some lesser barons let stands of trees big enough to shelter scores of warriors grow almost within bowshot of their walls.

Gerin had no desire to claim shelter from any of these nobles. The few he saw on the road distressed him. Their chariots were decorated with inlays of gold and bright stones, but plainly had never seen combat. More than one man wore cloth instead of mail. What cuirasses were to be seen were covered with studs and curlicues of bronze: beautiful to look at, but sure to catch and hold a spearpoint.

The footsoldiers were not much better. They were well armed, but soft jaws and thick middles said they were unblooded troops. Behind the shield of the border, where the Trokmoi were always ready to pounce on the weak, Elabon's northern province was starting to rot.

Van saw it too. "This land is ripe for the taking," he said. Gerin could only nod.

The sun rose high and hot. Gerin felt the sweat trickle down his back and chest. He wished he could scratch through his armor.

With fairer skin, Van suffered more, tanned though he was. He finally took off his proud helm and carefully stowed it in the back of the wagon, then poured over his head a bucket of cool water from the brook where they had stopped. He puffed and snorted as the water poured down his face and dripped through his beard. "Ahhh!" he said. "That's better, even if I do sound like a whale coming up for air."

"A whale?" Elise said. She had shed her jacket. In tunic and trousers, she was more comfortable than either of the men. Her hat she kept on, for her fairness was not like that of Van, who grew golden under the sun: she would burn and freckle and peel and never really tan at all. She went on, "I've heard the word. Some kind of fish, is it not? I've never seen one."

"Nor I," Gerin said. "The farthest I've traveled is to the capital, and there are no whales in the Inner Seas."

"Well, captain, I'll tell you—and you, my lady—I've seen whales right enough, and closer than I wanted, too. Do you know the land called Mabalal?"

Elise shook her head. Gerin said, "I've heard the name. It's far to the south and east, I think."

"That's the one, captain. And sultry—why, this is nothing beside what it's like there. I thought I'd melt like a lump of wax in a fire. The people are little and dark, and they seem to like it well enough. For all their swarthy hides, the women are not uncomely, and what they do—" Van abruptly broke off. Gerin was amused to see his huge friend could blush.

"But I was talking about whales," Van went on. "They come in all sizes, and the sailors like the little ones, and wouldn't think of harming them. But the big ones hate men, and sink whatever boats they can. Now, one of them had lived outside the harbor at Jalor—that's the capital thereabouts—for years, and he'd sunk maybe twenty ships. He had a reddish skin they knew him by, and they called him 'Old Crimson,' since crimson is the color their kings wear. Five times they'd tried to kill him, and neither of the two harpooners who lived was whole.

"It got so bad the captains wouldn't ship out of Jalor, and if they did they couldn't find a soul to man the oars. Didn't that put a pretty squeeze on the merchants! So they decided to have another go at him, and when one of their big traders, a fellow named Kariri, saw me in some dive, he thought I would make a good oarsman, having more in the way of muscle than his countrymen. I was game; things had been dull since I'd had to leave Shanda, and the price he promised was good. It had to be, to get rowers for that boat! Most of us were foreigners of one kind or another: the folk of Jalor knew better.

"So off we sailed, the only ship in the water, though the docks and beach were black with people watching. Now, in those part the way they lure whales is this: they catch a lot of fat tunny and pickle them with salt in big jars, and when they're nice and ripe, they soak rags in the fish-grease and dump 'em in the water where they think the whales are. The first thing any of us knew of Old Crimson being round was a sort of a loud hiss and a cloud of evil-smelling steam. Whales aren't like other fish. They have to come to the surface every so often to get a breath of air and blow out the old. That's what he'd done, not fifty yards to starboard.

"I tell you, I missed a stroke, and I wasn't the only one. Then he came all the way out of the water, and I never want to see such a sight again. That ruddy hide of his was all scarred and torn from the ships he'd sunk, and I saw three spearpoints stuck in just back of his head, but not deep enough to do more than drive him mad with pain over the years. I don't lie when I say I'd've sooner been elsewhere right then. He was bigger than our boat, and not by a little, either.

"But the harpooning crew knew what to do if they—and we—were going to come home alive. They tossed ten or twelve pounds of that pickled tunny toward the monster, and he snapped it up. It's a funny thing, but the stuff makes whales drunk, and Old Crimson lay still in the water. If he were a kitten, he would have purred.

"Once that happened, the harpooners slipped out of their clothes (not that they wore much, just rags round their middles) and swam over to him, quiet as they could. One trailed his barbed harpoon, the second a little stand for it, and the third, who had more brawn than most men of Mabalal, took a big mallet with him. They climbed up on Old Crimson's head, and he never stirred. We lay dead quiet in the water, for fear of rousing him.

"They set up the harpoon just aft of his head, right behind the others that hadn't gone deep enough to kill. Then the fellow with the mallet swung it up over his head and hit the butt end of the harpoon with everything he had. I swear by all the gods there are that the whale leaped clean out of the water, with the harpooners still clinging to him. They might have screamed, but we never would have heard them. We were backing water for all we were worth, but still I saw that great tail like a fist over the bow.

"When it came down, the ship just went all to splinters. I'm hazy about what happened next, because something hit me right between the eyes. I must have grabbed an oar; the next thing I remember is being fished out of the water by one of the little boats that came out as soon as the people on shore saw Old Crimson was really dead. Thirty-four people were on our boat when we set out, and six of us lived: only one of the harpooners, the fellow with the little stand.

"Anyway, the fishermen who rescued me took me to shore, and the Jalorians took the whale's carcass ashore too, for they valued the meat and oil of it. The head of the merchants' guild kissed all of us who had lived, and gave each of us a tooth worried out of the whale's head: I don't lie when I say it was more than half a foot long.

"But do you know what? I didn't make a copper more from it, for that fat merchant sitting on his arse on the shore just called me a filthy foreigner and wouldn't pay. For all that, though, I drank my way through the grogshops for ten days straight without touching a coin of my own, and to this day no one in Jalor knows how old Kariri's warehouses burned down."

"You know," Gerin said thoughtfully, "if they were to put a line on the end of their harpoons with floats—sealed empty casks, maybe—every hundred paces or so, they could spear their whales without having to climb onto them, and if the wound didn't kill on the spot, the whales couldn't escape by diving, either."

Van stared at him. "I do believe it'd work," he said at last. "Why weren't you there then to think of it? The gods know I never would have." He looked to Elise. "Gerin, I do believe our guest thinks my yarn would be good for making flowers grow, but not much else, though since she's kind as she is fair she's too polite to say so. Hold the reins a bit for me, will you?"

Elise started to protest, but Van was not listening to her. He stepped into the back of the wagon. Gerin heard him rummaging in the battered leather sack where he kept his treasures. After a minute or two, he grunted in satisfaction and emerged, handing Elise what he held.

Gerin craned his neck to look too. It was an ivory tusk unlike any he had ever seen: though no longer than the fang of the longtooth he knew, this was twice as thick, and pure white, not yellowish. Someone had carved a whale and the prow of an unfamiliar ship on the tooth; the whale was tinted a delicate pink.

Seeing the baron's admiration, Van said, "A friend of mine made it while I was out roistering. You'll notice it isn't done, but I got out of Jalor in a hurry, and he didn't have time to finish."

Elise was silent.

Gerin kept the reins. Van had been yawning all morning, and now he tried to snatch some sleep in the cramped rear of the wagon. The Fox was looking for one particular dirt track of the many joining the Elabon Way. Each path had a stone post set beside it, carved with the marks of the petty barons to whose keeps the roadlets ran. It was past noon before Gerin saw the winged eye he sought. He almost passed it by, for the carving was so ancient that parts of it had weathered away; startling red lichens covered much of what remained.

"Where are we going?" Elise asked when he turned down the track. She coughed as the horses kicked up dust.

"I thought you knew all my plans," Gerin said. "I'd like to hear what the Sibyl at Ikos tells me. I stopped there once before, when I went south for the first time, and she warned me I'd never be a scholar. I laughed at her, but two years later the Trokmoi killed my father and my brother, and I had to quit the southlands."

"That I had heard," Elise said softly. "I'm sorry." Gerin could feel the truth in her words. He was touched, and at the same time annoyed with himself for letting her sympathy reach him. He felt relieved when she returned to her original thought: "Where we go matters little to me; I simply didn't know. Any place away from Wolfar is good enough, though I've heard evil things of the country round Ikos."

"I've heard them too," he admitted, "but I've never seen much to make me think them true. This road goes over the hills and through some of the deepest forest this side of the Niffet before it reaches the Sibyl's shrine. It's said strange beasts dwell in the forest. I never saw any, though I did see tracks on the roadway that belong to no animals the outer world knows."

The more prosperous petty barons and their lands clung leechlike to the Elabon Way. A few hours' travel from it, things were poorer. Freeholders held their own plots, men not under the dominion of any local lordling. They were of an ancient race, the folk who had been on the land between the Niffet and the High Kirs even before the coming of the Trokmoi whom the Empire had expelled. Slim and dark, they spoke the tongue of Elabon fluently enough, but among themselves used their own soft, sibilant language.

The road narrowed, becoming little more than a winding rutted lane under frowning trees. The sinking sun's light could barely reach through the green arcade overhead. Gerin jumped when a scarlet finch shot across the roadway, taken aback by the flash of color in the gloom. As the sun set, he pulled off the road and behind a thick clump of trees.

He routed Van from his jouncing bed. Together they unharnessed the horses and let them crop what little grass grew in the shade of the tall beeches.

They had but a scanty offering for the ghosts: dried beef mixed with water. It was not really enough, but Gerin hoped it would serve. Elise wanted to take one watch. The Fox and Van said no in the same breath.

"Please yourselves," she shrugged, "but I could do it well enough." A knife appeared in her hand and then, almost before the eye could see it, was quivering in a treetrunk twenty feet away.

Gerin was thoughtful as he plucked the dagger free, but still refused. Elise looked to Van. He shook his head and laughed: "My lady, I haven't been guarded by women since I was old enough to keep my mother from learning what I was up to. I don't plan to start over now."

She looked hurt, but said only, "Very well, then. Guard me well this night, heroes." He half-sketched a salute as she slipped into her bedroll.

Van, who was rested, offered to take the first watch. Gerin got under a blanket, twisted until he found a position where the fewest pebbles dug into him, and knew no more until Van prodded him awake. "Math is down, and—what do you call the fast moon? I've forgotten."

"Tiwaz."

"That's it. As well as I can see through the trees, it'll set in an hour or so. That makes it midnight, and time for me to sleep." Van was under his own blanket—the gold-and-black striped hide of some great hunting beast—and asleep with the speed of the experienced wanderer. Gerin stretched, yawned, and heard the ghosts buzz in his mind like gnats.

In the dim red light of the embers, the wagon was

a lump on the edge of visibility, the horses a pair of dark shadows. Gerin listened to their unhurried breathing and the chirp and rustle of tiny crawling things. An owl overhead loosed its hollow, eerie call. Somewhere not far away, a small stream chuckled to itself. A longtooth roared in the distance, and for a moment everything else was quiet.

The baron turned at a sound close by. He saw Elise half-sitting, watching him. Her expression was unreadable. "Regrets?" he asked, voice the barest thread of sound.

Her answer was softer still. "Of course. To leave all I've ever known ... it's no easy road, but one I have to travel."

"You could still go back."

"With Wolfar's arms waiting? There's no returning." She started to say more, stopped, began again. "Do you know why I came with you? You helped me once, long ago." Her eyes were looking into the past, not at Gerin. "The first time I saw you was the most woeful day of my life. I had a dog I'd raised from a pup; he had a floppy ear and one of his eyes was half blue, and because of his red fur I called him Elleb. He used to like to go out and hunt rabbits, and when he caught one he'd bring it home to me. One day he went out as he always did, but he didn't come back.

"I was frantic. I looked for two days before I could find him, and when I did, I wished I hadn't. He'd run down a little gully and caught his hind leg in a trap."

"I remember," Gerin said, realizing why the dog Ruffian had seemed familiar. "I heard you crying and went to see what the trouble was. I was heading south to study."

"Was I crying? I suppose I was. I don't remember. All I could think of was poor Elleb's leg shredded in the jaw of the trap, and blood dried black, and the flies. The trap was chained to a stake, and I couldn't pry it loose from him.

"Hurt as he was, I remember him growling when you came up, still trying to keep me safe. You knelt down beside me and patted him and poured some water from your canteen on the ground for him to drink, and then you took out your knife and did what needed to be done.

"Not many would tried to make friends with him first, and not many would have sat with me afterwards and made me understand why an end to his pain was the last gift he could get from someone who loved him. By the time you took me home, I really did understand it. You were kind to me, and I've never forgotten."

"And because of so small a thing you put your trust in me?"

"I did, and I have no regrets." Her last words were sleep-softened.

Gerin watched Nothos and the stars peep through holes in the leafy canopy and thought about the obligations with which he had saddled himself. After a while, he decided he too had no regets. He fed bits of wood to the tiny fire, slapped at the buzzing biters lured by its light, and waited for the sun to put the ghosts to rout.

At dawn he woke Van. His comrade knuckled his eyes and spoke mostly in sleepy grunts as they harnessed the horses. Elise doused and covered the fire before Gerin could tend to it. They breakfasted on hard bread and smoked meat. To his disgust, Gerin missed a shot at a fat grouse foolish enough to roost on a branch not a hundred feet away. It flapped off, wings whirring.

The track wound through the forest. Trailing shoots

and damp hanging mosses hung from branches overhead, eager to snatch at anything daring to brave the
wood's cool dim calm. The horses were balky. More
than once Van had to touch them with the whip
before they would go on.

Few birds trilled to ease the quiet. Almost the only
sounds were the creaking of branches and the rustling
of leaves in a breeze too soft to reach down to the
road.

Once a sound almost softer than silence paced the
wagon for a time. It might have been the pad of great
supple feet, or perhaps nothing at all. Gerin saw—or
thought he saw—a pair of eyes, greener than the
leaves, measuring him. He blinked or they blinked
and when he looked again they were gone. The rattle
of the wagon's wheels was swallowed as if it had never
been.

"Place gives me the bloody shivers!" Van said. To
Gerin, his friend's voice sounded louder than needful.

The baron thought the day passing faster than it
was, so thick was the gloom. He bit back an exclamation of surprise when they burst from shadow into the
brightness of the late afternoon sun. He had not realized how much the thought of camping again in the
forest chilled him until he saw he would not have to.

The hills cupped the valley in which Ikos lay. Travelers could look down on their goal before they
reached it. The main road came from the southwest.
Gerin could see little dots of moving men, carriages,
and wagons, all come to consult the Sibyl. His own
road was less used. The border lords usually put more
faith in edged bronze than prophecy.

A tiny grove surrounded the temple. Probably in
days long past the forest had lapped down from the
hilltops into the valley, but the sacred grove was all
that was left of it there. The shrine's glistening marble
roof stood out vividly against the green of the trees.

Around the temple proper were the houses of the priests, the attendants, and the little people who, while not really connected with the Sibyl, made their livings from those who came to see her: sellers of images and sacrificial animals, freelance soothsayers and oracle-interpreters, innkeepers and whores, and the motley crew who sold amulets, charms—and doubtless curses too.

Around the townlet were cleared fields, each small plot owned by a freeholder. Gerin knew the temple clung to the old ways. He did not grudge it its customs, but still thought freeholding subversive. A peasant could not produce enough wealth to equip himself with all the gear a proper warrior needed. Without the nobles, the border and all the land behind would have been a red tangle of warfare, with the barbarians howling down to loot and burn and kill.

"Should we go down before the light fails?" Van asked.

Gerin thought of Ikos' dingy hostels. He shook his head. "We'd get nothing done at this hour. From what I recall of the inns, we'll find fewer bugs here."

The evening meal was spare, taken from the same rations as breakfast. Gerin knew those had been packed with the idea of feeding two people, not three. He reminded himself to lay in more. *Pretty sorry scholar you are*, he jeered at himself—*worrying over smoked sausages and journeybread*.

He must have said that aloud, for Van laughed and said, "Well, someone has to, after all."

The baron took the first watch. In Ikos below, the lights faded until all was dark save for a central watchfire. The hills to the southwest were dotted with tiny sparks of light Gerin knew to be camps like his own. In its grove, the temple was strange, for the light streaming out from it glowed blue instead of the comfortable red-gold of honest flame.

Magic, Gerin decided sleepily, or else the god walking about inside. When Math's golden half-circle set, he roused Van, then dove headfirst into sleep.

He woke to the scent of cooking; luckier than he had been the morning before, Van had bagged a squirrel and two rabbits and was stewing them. Elise contributed mushrooms and a handful of herbs. Feeling better about the world with his belly full, Gerin hitched up the horses. The wagon rolled down the path toward the Sibyl.

IV

Gerin soon discovered his memory had buried a lot about Ikos. First of all, the place stank. It lay under a cloud of incense so cloying that he wished he could stow his nose in the wagon. Mixed with the sweet reek were the scents of charring fat from the sacrifices and the usual town odors of stale cookery, garbage, ordure, and long-unwashed animals and humanity.

The noise was as bad. Gerin's ears had not faced such an assault since he returned to the north country. It seemed as if every peddler in Ikos rolled down on the wagon, each crying his wares at the top of his lungs: swordblades, rare and potent drugs, sanctified water, oats, pretty boys, savory cooked geese, collected books of prophetic verse, and countless other things. A fat bald man in greasy tunic and shiny leather apron, an innkeeper from the look of him, pushed his way through the pressed and bowed low before the bemused Fox, who had never seen

65

him before. "Count Stoffer, I believe?" he said, back still bent.

Patience exhausted, Gerin sanpped, "Well, if you believe that, you'll believe anything, won't you?" and left the poor fellow to the jeers of his fellow townsmen.

"Is this what the capital is like?" Elise asked faintly.

"It is," Gerin said, "but only if you will allow that a map is like the country it pictures."

She used a word he had not suspected she knew.

Van chuckled and said, "It's the same problem both places, I think: too many people all pushed together. Captain, you're the only one of us with pockets. Have a care they aren't slit."

Gerin thumped himself to make sure he was still secure. "If any of these fine bucks tries it, he'll be slit himself, and not in the pocket." He suddenly grinned. "Or else not, depending on how lucky I am."

They pushed their slow way through Ikos and into the clearing round the sacred grove. The sun was already high when they reached it. They bought cheese and little bowls of barley porridge from the legion of vendors. Men from every nation Gerin knew cursed and jostled one another, each trying to be the first to the god's voice on earth.

One lightly built chariot held two nomads from the eastern plains. They were little and lithe, flat of face and dark of skin, with scraggly caricatures of beards dangling from their chins. They dressed in wolfskin jackets and leather trousers, and bore double-curved bows reinforced with sinew. They carried small leather shields on their left arms; one was bossed with a golden panther, the other with a leaping stag. When Van noticed them, he shouted something in a language that sounded like hissing snakes. Their slanted eyes lit as they gave eager answer.

There were Kizzuwatnans in heavy carts hauled by straining donkeys: squat, heavy-boned men with swarthy skins; broad, hook-nosed faces; and liquid, mournful eyes. Their hair and beards curled in ringlets. They wore long linen tunics that reached to their knees.

There were a few Sithonians, though most of them preferred the oracle at Pronni in their own country. Slimmer and fairer than the Kizzuwatnans, they wore woolen mantles with brightly dyed edgings. They scornfully peered about from under broad-brimmed straw hats: though they had been subjects of the Empire for five centuries, they still saw themselves as something of an elite, and looked down on their Elabonian overlords as muscular dullards.

Even an Urfa from the deserts of the far south had come to Ikos. He must have ridden all the way around Elabon's Greater Inner Sea, for he was still perched atop his camel. Gerin looked at its reins and saddle with interest, thinking how fascinated Duin would have been. The desert-dweller peered down at the wains and chariots around him. He growled guttural warning when they came too close. That was seldom; horses shied from his evil-looking mount.

The Urfa was wrapped in a robe of grimy wool. Eyes and teeth flashed in a face darkened by dirt and long years of sun. Save for a nose even larger than the Kizzuwatnans', his features were delicate, almost feminine. He wore a thin fringe of beard and, for all his filth, seemed to think himself the lord of creation.

Gerin had a hard time naming some of the other outlanders. Van claimed one black-haired, fair-skinned giant belonged to the Gradi, who lived north of the Trokmoi. The man was afoot, and sweating in his furs. He carried a stout mace and a short-handled throwing axe. Gerin knew almost nothing of the Gradi, but Van spoke of them with casual familiarity.

"Do you know their tongue?" Elise asked.

"Aye, a bit," Van said.

"Just how many languages do you know?" Gerin asked.

"Well, if you mean to say hello in, and maybe swear a bit, gods, I've lost track long since. Tongues I know fairly well, though, perhaps ten or a dozen. Something like that."

"Which is your own?" Elise asked.

"My lady," Van said, with something as close to embarrassment as his deep voice could produce, "I've been on the road a lot of years now. After so long, where I started matters little."

Gerin grinned wryly; he'd got much the same answer when he asked that question. Elise looked to want to pursue it further, but held her tongue.

One group of foreigners the Fox knew only too well: the Trokmoi. Three chieftains had come to consult the Sibyl. Their chariots stayed together in the disorder.

They were from deep in the northern woods: Gerin, who knew the clans on the far side of the border as well as he knew the barons warding it, recognized none of them, nor were the clan patterns of bright checks on their drivers' tunics familiar to him. Chiefs and drivers alike were tall thin men; four had red hair and two were blond. All wore their hair long and had huge drooping mustachioes, though they shaved their cheeks and chins. Two clutched jugs of ale to themselves; another wore a necklace of human ears.

Priests circulated through the crowd. Gerin looked with scant liking at the one approaching the wagon. A robe of gold brocade was stretched across his overample belly, and his beardless cheeks shone pink. Everything about him was round and soft, from his limpid blue eyes to the toes peeking sausage-like from his sandals. He was a eunuch, for the god accepted no whole man as his servitor.

The tip of his tongue played redly across his lips

as he asked, "What would your business be, gentles,
with the Sibyl of my lord Biton?" His voice was soft
and sticky, like the caress of a hand dripping with
honey.

"I'd sooner not speak of it in public," Gerin said.

"Quite, quite. Your servant Falfarun most definitely
agrees. You have, though, a suitably appropriate offering for the god, I hope?"

"I think so." Gerin swung a purse into Falfarun's
pudgy fist.

The priest's face was blank. "Doubtless all will be
well when your question is heard."

"I do hope, my dear Falfarun, it will be heard
soon," Gerin said in his suavest voice. He handed the
priest another, larger purse, which vanished into a
fold of Falfarun's robe.

"Indeed. Yes, indeed. Come this way, if you
please." Falfarun neared briskness as he elbowed
aside less forethoughtful seekers of divine wisdom.
Clucking to the horses, Van steered after him. Falfarun led the wagon into the sacred grove around the
temple precinct. Seeing the Fox's success, the Trokmoi pulled off rings, armlets, and a heavy golden pec-
toral and waved them in the face of another plump
priest.

"You gauged the size of your second sack about
right," Van whispered.

"Praise Dyaus for that! The last time I was here, I
spent three days cooling my heels before I got to go
before the Sibyl. I was still too young to know the
world runs on gold."

"Was the wench worth looking at, once you finally
saw her?"

"Scarcely. She was a wrinkled old crone. I wonder
if she still lives."

"Why have hags to give prophesies? It seems to me
they'd hardly be fitting mates for whatever god runs

the shrine here. Give me a young, juicy lass every time," Van said, drawing a sniff from Elise.

"Biton has spoken through her since she was chosen for him when she was still a child," Gerin explained. "Whenever a Sibyl dies, the priests search among families of the old race; this valley has always been their stronghold. When they find a girl-child with a certain mark—what it is they keep secret, but it's been Biton's sign for ages—she becomes the new Sibyl for as long as she remains a maiden: and her chastity is guarded, I assure you."

The tumult behind them faded under the trees. Images of all-seeing Biton were everywhere in the grove, half of them turned to show the two eyes in the back of his head. Another priest led the Trokmoi along a different path. Far from being struck by the holiness of the wood, they argued loudly in their own language.

High walls of gleaming white marble warded the outer courtyard of Biton's temple. The gates were flung wide, but spear-carrying temple guards stood ready to slam them shut should trouble threaten. Here and there the shining stone was chipped and discolored, a mute reminder of the great invasion of the Trokmoi two hundred sixty years before, when Biton himself, the priests maintained, made an appearance to drive the barbarians from his shrine.

Before they could go in, Falfarun summoned a green-robed underpriest. The fat priest said, "It is not permitted to enter the courtyard save on foot; Arcarola here will take your wagon to its proper place. Fear not, for there is no theft on the grounds of the temple. A loathsome plague unfailingly smites any miscreant daring to attempt such rapine."

"How many are thus stricken?" Gerin asked skeptically.

"The body of the latest is one of the curiosities

within the outer walls. Poor wretch; may he edify others."

Sobered, Gerin descended from the wagon, followed by Elise and Van. When Arcarola climbed up, the horses rolled their eyes and tried to rear, feeling the unfamiliar touch at the reins. Van put a heavy hand on each one's muzzle and growled, "Don't you be stupid, now," following that with an oath in the harsh tongue Gerin guessed was his own. The beasts subsided and let themselves be led away.

The Trokmoi came up about then. More green-robes took their chariots. The priest who was leading them drew Falfarun aside and spoke softly with him. The Trokmoi were talking too, and not softly: the argument they'd begun under the trees of the sacred grove was still in full swing. Gerin was about to greet them in their own tongue until he heard what they were quarreling about.

One of the northerners looked suspiciously at the Fox and his comrades. "Not so loud should you make it, Catuvolcus," he said. He sounded worried, and his scarred hands made hushing motions.

Catuvolcus was not going to be hushed. Gerin guessed he was a bit drunk. His eyes were shot with red, his speech slurred. He toyed with his gruesome necklace. "Divico," he said, "you can take a flying futter at fast Fomor." He used the northern name for the quickest moon. "What's the chance we would find someone this far south who speaks the real language?"

"There's no need to take a chance for no purpose."

"But I'm saying it's no chance at all. And if you will remember, now, 'twas your scheme to come here. And what was the why of it? Just to have the privacy we could scarce be getting from our own oracles."

"A proper notion it was, too. I'd liefer not have that Balamung omadhaun know it's less than full faith I have in him. Who is the spalpeen, anyhow, and why should we fight for him? If I go hunting with a bear, why, I want to be sure he'll not save me for the main course."

Listening as hard as he could without seeming to, Gerin barely noticed Falfarun return. He was trailed by the other priest, who was even fatter than he. Falfarun coughed and said, "Good sir, my colleague Saspir" —he indicated his companion, whose smooth eunuch's face belied the years shown by his graying hair and sagging jowls— "and I have decided that these northern gentlemen should precede you to the Sibyl, as their journey has been longer than yours and they have urgent business in their own land which requires them to make haste."

"You are trying to tell me they paid you more," Gerin said without much rancor.

Falfarun's chins quivered. His voice was hurt as he answered, "I would not put it so crassly—"

"—But it's still true," Gerin finished for him. "Be it so, then, if we can follow them directly."

"But of course," Falfarun said, relieved to find him so agreeable. Saspir gave the Trokmoi the good news and took them into the temple courtyard. Falfarun followed, his reedy voice loud in the ears of Gerin, who would much rather have listened to the barbarians. Another golden-robed hierarch conducted a toga-clad noble out from the holy precinct; the man's thin, pale face bore a troubled expression. The nomads from the plains of Shanda came up just as Gerin entered the courtyard. He heard a priest override their loud objections to being separated from their chariot.

Even the Trokmoi had fallen silent in the temple forecourt. They were gawking, necks craning every which way, trying to see everything at once. Gerin thought they looked like so many hungry hounds licking their chops in front of a butcher's shop. He did not much blame them, for the sight of so much treasure affected him the same way. The would-be thief's corpse, covered with hideous raw-edged lesions and bloated and stinking after some days in the open, did little to dampen his enthusiasm. Beside him Van whistled, soft and low.

Only the choicest gauds were on display. Most of the riches Biton's shrine had accumulated over the centuries were stored away in strong-walled vaults behind the temple or in caves below it. What was visible was plenty to rouse a plunderer's lusts.

Chief among the marvels were twin ten-foot statues of gold and ivory, one of the Emperor Oren II, who had built the temple in the ancient grove, the other of his father, Ros the Fierce, who drove the Trokmoi north of the River Niffet and won the land between the Kirs and the Niffet for Elabon. Oren wore the toga and held in his upraised right hand the orb of empire; Ros, mailed, had a javelin ready to cast and leaned upon a narrow-waisted shield of antique design.

Ros' stern craggy face, with its thrusting nose and lines carved deep on weathered cheeks, still brought awe after four hundred years. Gerin shivered when he looked up into those cold eyes of jet.

A huge golden mixing bowl celebrated Biton's triumph over the Trokmoi. Wider even than Van's outstretched arms, it was set upon a claw-footed tripod of bronze, and held the images of barbarians fleeing the god's just wratch—and the prostrate bodies of those his arrows had struck down.

On a pedestal of purple marble next to it was a splendid statue of a dying Trokmê. The naked warrior was on his right side, propping himself up with his right arm. That hand still clung to swordhilt. The other clutched a gaping gash in his right side; the red-painted blood streamed down his flank to form a puddle at his hip. His face was turned up to stare at his unportrayed conqueror. Its grimace showed agony and defiance, but not a hint of fear. The statue's features were blunter than those usual among the long-faced, thin-nosed Trokmoi. Probably the sculptor, himself a Sithonian, had used a countryman as model, adding only long hair and mustaches to make clear the statue's race.

There was much else to see: the silver-and-gold longtooth, its leap onto an aurochs frozen by a master artisan of long ago; the chalices and urns of precious metals, alabaster, cinnabar, and multicolored jades; the stacks of ingots and bars of gold and silver, each with a plaque telling which accurate prophesy it commemorated . . . but Falfarun was leading Gerin up to the steps of the temple, and that was a sight in itself.

Oren's architect had tried to harmonize the sparely elegant columned shrines the Sithonians loved with the native brickwork fanes of Elabon, and his effort was a noble one. The sides of Biton's shrine were marble blocks; spacious glazed windows helped illuminate the interior. The front wall was pure Sithonian, with its triangular entablature supported by delicately fluted columns of whitest stone.

Between architrave and overhanging eaves the frieze, carved by a team of workmen from drawing by the creator of the dying Trokmê, showed Biton, hand outstretched, guiding an imperial column against a horde of Trokmoi. Ros, his harsh features easy to recognize, stood in the lead chariot. His men had a tough uniformity in striking contrast to the disorderly foe they battled—and to the barons who had come after them.

Up the seven marble steps they went, Falfarun chattering all the while. When Elise heard statue and frieze sprang from the same man's mind, she asked his name. Falfarun looked shocked and shook his head. "I have no idea," he said. "The work is far too holy to be polluted by such mundanities."

Gerin's eyes needed a moment to adjust to the inside of Biton's shrine, accustomed as they were to bright sunshine. They went wide as he saw the splendor within, for it had faded in his memory.

Limiting himself to simple white stone for the outside of the building, its designer had let color run riot within. Twin rows of crimson granite columns, polished mirror-bright, led the eye to the altar. That was of sandalwood overlain with gold and encrusted with all kinds of precious stone. It threw back in coruscating sheets the light cast on it by dozens of fat candles in three arabesqued chandeliers overhead.

The temple's inner walls were faced with rare green marbled shot with gold. That stone came from only one quarry, near Siphnos in Sithonia. The Fox could but marvel at the sweat and gold needed to haul it here, a journey of several hundred miles over the Greater Inner Sea and the royal roads of Elabon. Like the columns, it was buffed till it gleamed; it tinged niche-set gold and silver statues with its own color.

Chanting acolytes paced here and there, intent on Biton's rituals. Their slippers swished over the floor mosaics, their swinging censers filled the air with the fragrances of aloes, myrrh, and other costly incenses. Folk who wanted Biton's aid but needed no sight of the future knelt and prayed in pews flanking the granite columns. Some kept their heads lowered; others raised them to the ceiling frescoes, as if seeking inspiration from the scenes of the god's begetting by Dyaus on a princess and of his subsequent adventures, most of them caused by the jealousy of the heavenly queen Darza.

Only in two respects was Biton's shrine unlike many even more superb temples in the lands south of the mountains. One was the image of the god behind the altar. Here he was no graceful youth. A square column of rough black stone stood there, drinking in the light and giving back none. Immeasurably old, it could have been a natural pillar, save for the faint images of eyes round its top and a jutting phallus stabbing forward from its middle.

Biton's priests had only smiled when Oren proclaimed their deity a son of Dyaus. In their hearts they knew whose god was the elder. Seeing that image, Gerin was not inclined to doubt them. Biton's power was rooted in the earth, and in the square of bare earth to the left of the altar was a rift leading down below the roots of the sacred grove to the Sibyl's cave, a rift whose like was unknown in the tamer south.

The Trokmoi made obeisance before Biton's altar, the three chieftains on their knees and the drivers flat on their bellies. They rose, dusted themselves off, and followed their guide into the yawning mouth of the cave. One driver, a freckled youth with face tight-set against fear, flexed the fingers of one hand in a sign to avert evil. The other was tight on the hilt of his blade.

Falfarun brought up his charges to take the barbarians' place. All bent the knee before Biton, Falfarun panting as he eased his bulk to the floor. Gerin looked up at the ancient idol. For an instant, he thought he saw eyes brown as his own looking back at him, but when he looked again they were only scratches on stone.

Rising, Falfarun asked, "Would it please you to take more comfortable seats while waiting to meet the Sibyl?"

Gerin sat in the foremost pew. He ignored the puffing Falfarun, who dabbed at his forehead with a square of blue silk. His thoughts were on the Trokmoi: if these barbarians, men from so deep in the forests he knew nothing of them, had allied their clans with Balamung, how many more had done the same? Fox Keep, it seemed, was in the way of an onsalught more terrible than the attack whose scars still showed on the temple forecourt's walls.

He grew more and more jittery until the Trokmoi emerged from the cavemouth. All were grim-faced: they had no liking for what they'd heard. The young driver who had made the wardsign was white as an exterior column, the freckles on his nose and cheeks standing out like spatters of dried blood.

The two chiefs who had been quarreling outside the temple forecourt were still at it. Divico, even more worried than before, waved a hand in front of Catuvolcus' face. "Are you not glad now we came?" he said. "Plain as day the witch-woman told us there'd be naught but a fox gnawing our middles if we joined Balamung, plain as day."

"Ox ordure," Catuvolcus said. "The old gammer has no more wits than teeth, the count of which is none. On all the border there's but one southron called the Fox, and were you not listening when himself told us the kern'd be ravens' meat in no more than days? It must be done by now, so where's your worry?"

Gerin stood and gave the Trokmoi his politest bow. "Begging your pardon," he said, using their tongue with a borderer's ease, "but a wizard's word a coin I'd bite or ever I pocketed it. But if you're after the Fox, I am he, and I tell you this: the raven who'll pick my bones is not yet hatched, no, nor his grandsire either."

He had hoped his sudden appearance would show the barbarians the folly of their way. Instead he saw the rashness of his, for Catuvolcus bellowed an oath, rasped sword from scabbard, and rushed. His five comrades followed.

Leaping to his feet, Van lifted Falfarun over his head as easily as if the fat eunuch had been stuffed with down. He pitched him into the Trokmoi, bowling over two of them and giving himself and Gerin time to free their blades. At the same instant Elise hurled a dagger, then skipped back to safety. The freckled driver fell, throat pumping a torrent of blood round the hilt suddenly flowering there and sword slipping from nerveless fingers.

Catuvolcus ducked under the hurtling priest. He swung up his sword two-handed, brought it down in a cut to cleave Gerin from crown to chin. Sparks flew as the Fox blocked the stroke. His arms felt numb to the elbow. He ducked under another wild slash, edged bronze whizzing bare inches above his head.

His own sword bit into the Trokmê's belly. He ripped it free to parry the lunge of one of the drivers. The northerner seemed confused at facing a lefthanded swordsman. Gerin beat down another tentative thrust, feinted at his enemy's throat, and guided his sword into the barbarian's heart. More surprise than pain on his face, the Trokmê swayed and fell. He gasped for air he could not breathe, tried to speak. Only blood gushed from between his lips.

The Fox looked round for more fight, but there was none. Van leaned on his blade and puffed; he watched the shrilling, scrambling eunuchs with distaste. Half the proud crest of his helm was sheared away. His armor was drenched with gore, but none was his. Red hair matted by redder blood, the head of one barbarian stared glassily at its body. The ghastly corpse lay across another, whose entrails and pouring blood befouled the gentle meadow of the mosaic floor.

Horror on her face, Elise came up to survey the carnage. With a flourish, Van plucked her dagger from its victim's throat and handed her the dripping weapon. "As fine a throw as I've ever seen, and as timely, too," he said. She held it a moment, then threw it to the floor as hard as she could and gagged, reeling back against the pews.

Gerin put a hand on her shoulder to comfort her. She clung to him and sobbed. He murmured wordless reassurance. He was nearly as much an accidental warrior as was she, and recalled only too well puking up his guts in a clump of bushes after his first kill. Now he was just glad he was still among the living, and tried not to think of the ruined humanity at his feet.

He offered his canteen to Elise so she could rinse her mouth. She took it with a muffled word of thanks.

A squad of temple guardsmen rushed down the main aisle, brushing aside the plainsmen (who had watched the fight with interest) and their guide. The guard captain, his corselet gilded to show his rank, shook his head when he heard Gerin's story, though Saspir confirmed it. Tugging his beard, the officer, whose name was Etchebar, said, "To slay a priest of the god, even to save your own lives, is foully done. Surprised am I Biton did not smite you dead."

"Slay?" Van shouted. "Who in the five hells said anything about slaying a priest, you jouncebrained lump of dung?" Etchebar's spearmen bristled at that, but restrained themselves at his gesture. "The great tun is no more slain than you, as you'd find out if you flipped water in his fat face. And if we'd waited for *your* aid, it'd be the Trokmoi you were jabbering with here!" He spat into the pool of red. "Look!"

As smoothly as before, he lifted Falfarun. The priest had still been on top of the inert Divico. Van set him on his feet as blood dribbled from the hem of his robe. The outlander slapped him gently, once or twice. He groaned and clutched his head. He did not seem much hurt, however shaken he was.

Gerin turned all his powers of persuasion on the guard captain and the priest, one of whose eyes was already beginning to blacken. He broke off in midsentence when he saw Van stooping over Divico, plainly intending to finish off the unconscious man. The baron made a quick grab for his friend's arm.

"Captain, are you daft?" Van said.

"I hope not." Gerin took Van's place over the fallen Trokmê and shook him.

Divico came to himself with a thunderstorm in his head. He moaned and opened his eyes. That accursed Fox was bending over him, the scar above his eye white against his tan, his square face hard. The Trokmê gathered himself for a spring until he felt the cold kiss of a blade at his throat. He rolled his eyes down until he saw its upper edge, still smeared with blood.

Impotent rage flashed across his face. "I willna beg for my life, if it's that you're after," he said. "Slit my weasand and have done."

"A warrior's answer," Gerin nodded, still speaking the forest tongue with a fluency Divico found damnable. "Can it be you're wise as well?"

He sheathed his sword and helped the bewildered Trokmê sit. The chieftain hissed when he saw his slaughtered comrades.

Gerin waved at them and went on, "You and your friends heard the Sibyl's words, but did they heed them? Not a bit, and see what's become of them now. Sure as sure the same'll befall you and your clansmen if you go following Balamung's war-trumpets. If I give you your life, would you go and tell them that, aye, and others you meet on the way?"

Divico's red brows came together as he thought. At last he said, "I would that. For Catuvolcus and Arviragus I cared not a fart. Poor Togail is another matter, though. Black shame 'twill be to me to tell my brother Kell his son had his lovely throat torn out while I return revengeless. Still, I will do it, to keep the same from befalling all my kin. Fox, I like you not, but I will. By Taranis, Teutates, and Esus I swear it."

That was the strongest oath the Trokmoi knew, Gerin thought; if it would not bind Divico to his word, nothing would. "Good man!" he said, clasping his hand and helping him to his feet. He almost told the Trokmê he thought like an Elabonian, but judged the proud chieftain would think it an insult.

"A moment," Etchebar said drily. "You have not the only claim on this man. Because of him, blood was shed in the holy precinct, which is abhorrent to our lord Biton." He touched his eyes and the back of his head in reverence. Falfarun nodded vigorous agreement. The guardsmen level their spars at Divico, who shrugged and relaxed but kept his hand near his sword.

"I am sure we can come to an understanding," Gerin said, propelling guard captain and priest into a quiet corner. There they argued for some minutes. The Fox reminded them that Divico had opposed Catuvolcus, who started the unholy combat. Furthermore, he pointed out, Biton was able to deal with those who offended him, as he had proved on the body of the luckless thief who was displayed in the forecourt.

Etchebar growled a curt order and Divico was set free. The Trokmê bowed to Gerin and left, one hand still clutched to his aching skull.

Another discreet offering of gold "for the temple" salved Falfarun's bruises. Etchebar was a harder case, for Van's chaffing had wounded his pride. He wanted satisfaction, not gold. Making sure the outlander was not in earshot, Gerin apologized profusely.

Black-robed temple servitors dragged away the dead Trokmoi and began to mop up their spilled gore, which had already attracted a few flies. Eyes still unhappy under bushy eyebrows, Etchebar gathered up his men and led them back to the forecourt. "And now, gentles, to the Sibyl at last," Falfarun said, with quite as much solemn aplomb as he had had before he was tossed about and his gleaming robe befouled.

The mouth to the Sibyl's cave was a black, grinning slit. Elise, still wan, took Gerin's hand. Looking down into the inky unknown, he was glad of the touch. Van fumed blasphemously as he tried to scrub sticky drying blood from his cuirass.

Falfarun vanished down the cavemouth. "You need have no fear for your footing," he called. "Since the unhappy day a century ago when the cousin of the Emperor Forenz (the second of that name, I believe) tumbled and broke an ankle, it was thought wise to construct regular steps and flooring to replace rocks and dirt. Such is life." He sighed, a bit unhappy at tradition flouted.

The subterranean corridor to the Sibyl's caved went down and down, twisting until Gerin lost all idea of which way he was going. A few dim candles set in brackets of immemorial antiquity gave pale and fitful light, making the flapping shadow of Falfarun's robe a monstrous thing. Cross-branches of the caverns were holes of deeper blackness in the gloom. Elise's grip on Gerin's hand tightened.

Most of the cave wall was left in its natural state. Now and again a bit of rock crystal would gleam for a moment in the candlelight and then fade. A few stretches were walled off by brickwork of a most antique mode which had its origins in the timeworn river land of Kizzuwatna, where men first lived in cities: not truly square like most bricks, these had convex tops and looked like buns of baked earth.

When Gerin asked the reason for the brickwork, Falfarun answered with a shiver, "Behind the bricks are charms of great fellness, for not all branches of these caves are safe for men. As you have seen, some we use for armories, others to store grain or treasure. But in some branches dread things dwell, and men who tried to explore them never returned. Those ways were stopped, as you see, to prevent such tragedies. More than that I cannot tell you, for it was done ages ago."

Imagining the pallid monsters that could inhabit such dismal gloom, Gerin shivered himself. He tried not to think of the tons of rock and earth over his head. Van muttered something that might have been prayer or curse and hitched the swordbelt higher on his hip.

An ancient statue of Biton smiled its secret smile at them as they neared the Sibyl. The candles gave way to brighter torches. The corridor widened to form a small chamber. A gust of cool, damp wind blew past Gerin's face. He heard the deep mutter of a great subterranean river far below.

When Falfarun touched his elbow, he started. "Your gifts entitle you to privacy with the Sibyl, if such is your desire," the priest said.

Gerin thought, then nodded.

Surprisingly, Falfarun's bruised face crinkled into a half-smile. "Good," he said. "Did the answer you received please you not, belike your brawny friend would undertake to pitch me through a wall." Van sputtered in embarrassment. Falfarun went on, "Good fortune attend you, gentles, and I leave you with the Sibyl." He waved at the throne set against the rear wall of the chamber and was gone.

"By my sword," Van said softly, "if I didn't know better, I'd say it was carved from one black pearl." Taller than a man, the high seat glimmered nacreously in the torchlight; crowns of silver shone on its two back posts.

The throne's splendor made the bundle of rags sitting on it altogether incongruous. Though the Trokmoi had called the Sibyl a crone, Gerin hadn't been able to believe the withered body through which the god had spoken ten years before still held life. But it was she, one eye dim, the other whitened by cataract. Her face was a badlands of wrinkles; her scalp shone through thinning strands of yellowish hair.

The mind behind that ruined countenance was still sharp, though. She raised on withered claw in a gesture of command. "Step forward, lass, lads," she said, voice a dry rustle. Gerin knew she would have called his father "lad" had he been before her, and she would have been as right.

"What would you know of my master Biton?" she asked.

For some days Gerin had mulled the question he would put. Still, in that place his tongue stumbled as he asked, "How best may I save myself and my lands and destroy the wizard who threatens them?"

She did not reply at once. Thinking she had not heard, the baron opened his mouth to ask the question again. But with no warning, her eyes rolled back, showing only vein-tracked whites. Her scrawny fists clenched; her body shook and trembled, throwing her robe off one dry shoulder to reveal an empty dug. Her face twisted. When she spoke, it was not in her own voice, but that of a powerful man in the first flush of strength. Hearing the god, Gerin and his companions went to their knees as his words washed over them:

"Buildings fall in flame and fire:
Against you even gods conspire.
Bow before the mage of the north
When all his power is put forth
To crush you down, to lay you low:
For his grave no man will know."

The god's voice and power gone, the Sibyl slumped forward in a faint.

V

Evening came. Gray clouds scudded across the sky. The wet-dust smell of rain was in the air. Grim and silent, Gerin began to help Van make camp. Elise, worry in her voice and on her face, said, "Not three words have you spoken since we left the temple."

All the rage and helplessness the baron had contained since he stalked frozen-faced past Falfarun to reclaim the wagon came out in a torrent of bile. He slammed his helmet to the ground. It spun into the undergrowth. "What difference does it make?" he said bitterly. "I might as well cut my own throat and save that perambulating corpse the work. The Sibyl told me the same thing he did, only from him I hadn't believed it. I was a fool to go to her; I wanted advice, not a death sentence. A plague take all oracles!"

At that, Van looked up. While Gerin stormed, he had quietly gone on setting up camp. He'd started a fire and drained the blood of a purchased fowl into a trench to propitiate the ghosts. "I knew a man who said something like that once, captain," he said.

"Is there a story to go with the knowing?" Elise asked, seemingly searching for any way to draw Gerin out of his inner darkness.

"Aye, that there is," Van agreed. He understood well enough what she was after, and pitched his words to the Fox. Elise settled herself by the fire to listen. "Captain, you know—or you've heard me say—the world is round, no matter what any priest may blabber. I know. I should; I've been round it.

"Maybe ten years ago, when I was at the far eastern edge of this continent, I hired on as a man-at-arms under a merchant named Zairin. He was moving a shipment of jade, silk, and spices from a place called Ban Yarang to Selat, a couple of hundred miiles southeastward. The folk are funny round those parts, little yellow-skins with slanting eyes like the Shanda nomads'. It looks better on the women, I must say. Still, that's no part of the yarn.

"Zairin was one of those people who have no truck with the gods. Now, in those parts it's customary to check the omens by watching the way the sacred peacocks peck at grain. If they eat well, the journey will be a good one. If not, it's thought wiser to try again some other time.

"There we were, all ready to set out, and Zairin's right-hand man—a fat little fellow named Tzem—brought us a bird from the shrine. He poured out the grain, but the peacock, who probably hadn't much liked traveling slung under his arm for more than a mile, just looked at it. He wouldn't touch it for anything, not that bird.

"Zairin sat watching this, getting madder and madder. Finally the old bandit had himself a gutful. He got up on his feet and roared out, 'If he won't eat, let him drink!' May my beard fall out if I lie, he picked up that peacock, chucked it into the Kemlong river (which runs through Ban Yarang) and started off regardless."

Gerin was caught up in spite of himself. "Dyaus! It's not a chance I'd like to take," he said.

"And you the fellow who curses oracles? You can imagine what we were thinking. Most of the way, though, things went well enough. The road was only a little track through the thickest jungle I've ever seen, so we lost a couple of porters to venomous snakes the poor barefoot fools stepped on, and one more to a blood-sucking demon that left him no more than a withered husk when we found him the next morning. But on a trip like that, you learn to expect such things. Zairin was mightily pleased with himself. He kept laughing and telling anyone who'd listen what a lot of twaddle it was to pay any attention to a fool bird.

"Well, a day and a half before we would have made Selat and proved the old croaker right, everything came unraveled at once. A dam broke upstream from where we were fording; five men and half our donkeys drowned. The customs man Zairin knew at the border had been transferred, and I shudder to think of the silver his replacement gouged out of us. Half the men got a bloody flux. It bothered me for two years. And just to top everything off, old Zairin came down with the crabs. From then on, captain, he was a believer, I can tell you!"

"Go howl!" Gerin said. "I was hoping you'd cheer me with a yarn where a prophesy turned out wrong. I know enough of the other sort myself. For that you can stand first watch."

"Can I, now? Well, *you* can—" The outlander scorched Gerin in more tongues than the Fox knew. Finally he said, "Captain, fair is fair: I'll wrestle you for it."

"Aren't you the bloodthirsty one? I thought you'd had enough fighting for one day."

Gerin got up and pulled off his tunic. He helped Van undo the leather laces of his back-and-breast. His friend sighed as the weight came off. In kilt and sandals, Van seemed more a war-god than ever. His muscles ripped as he stretched. The forest of golden hair on his chest and belly flashed in the firelight. Only his scars told of his humanity—and his turbulent past. One terrible gash ran from right armpit to navel; every time Gerin saw it, he wondered how the outlander had lived.

Not that he was unmarked himself: sword, spear, knife, and arrow had left their signatures on his skin, and the cut Aingus had given him was only half healed. Seeing Elise's eyes travel from Van's enormous frame to him, he knew he seemed a stripling beside his companion, though he was a well-made man of good size.

But he had a name as a wrestler on both sides of the Niffet. He had learned more tricks from masters south of the Kirs than his neighbors ever imagined, and threw men much bigger than himself. For all that, though, Van's raw strength was enough to flatten him as often as he could finesse his way to victory. When word went out that they would tussle, even Trokmoi came to watch and bet.

Embarrassed that her look had been seen and understood, Elise dropped her eyes. Gerin grinned at her. "He won't chuck me through a tree, girl."

"Who says I won't?" Van bellowed. He charged like an avalanche. Gerin sprang to meet him. Ducking under the thick arms that would quickly have squeezed breath from him, he hooked his own left arm behind Van's right knee and rammed a shoulder into his friend's hard-muscled middle.

Van grunted and went down, but a meaty paw

dragged Gerin after him. They rolled, thrashed, and grappled in the dirt. Gerin ended up riding his friend's broad back. His hands had slid under the outlander's shoulders; his hands were clasped behind Van's neck. Van slapped the ground. Gerin let him up. He shook his head and rubbed his eye to rout out some dust.

"You'll have to show me that one again, Gerin," he said. "Another fall?"

The baron shrugged. "All right, but the last one was for the watch." Van nodded. In mid-nod, he leaped. Gerin had no chance to use any of his feints or traps. He was seized, lifted, and slammed to earth with rib-jarring force. Van sprang on him like a starving lion onto a fat sheep.

Thoroughly pinned, Gerin grumbled, "Get off me, you pile of suet!" Van snorted and pulled him to his feet. They both swore as they swabbed each other's scratches with beer-soaked rags. The stuff stung foully.

After supper, Gerin began to regret not having the first watch. He was sure he was too full of troubles to sleep, despite the day's exertions. He tossed, wriggled until a small stone no longed gouged his back, wished the crickets were not so loud. . . .

Van watched his friend's face relax as slumber overtook him. He was not too worried about the baron's dejection; he had seen him downhearted before, and knew he recovered quickly. But the Fox deeply felt his responsibilities. If anything, a menace to his lands hit him harder than a threat against himself.

More and more clouds blew in from the west, pale against the dark blue dome of the sky. Math, a day past first quarter, and mottled Tiwaz, now nearly full, jumped in and out of sight. A couple of hours before midnight, dim Nothos' waning gibbous disk joined them. The wind carried a faint salt tang from the

Orynian Ocean far away. Van scrubbed dried blood from his armor and helm, waiting till it was time to wake Gerin.

Rain threatened all through the Fox's watch. It was still dark when the first spatters came. Elise jerked as a drop splashed her cheek; she woke up all at once, like a soldier. Smiling at Gerin, she said, " 'The gods in the heaven send dripping-tressed rain/ To nourish sweet hope in a desert of pain'—or so the poet says, anyway."

He stared at her. The passage of a night had eased much of his gloom; now surprise banished the rest. "Where did you learn to quote Lekapenos? And whose rendering as that? Whoever did it knows his Sithonian well."

"As for the rendering—" She shrugged. "It's mine. That passage always appealed to me. And where else would I learn my letters than from the epics?"

That held much truth. The baron still recalled the godlike feeling he'd had when the curious marks on parchment began to correspond with the verses he'd learned by ear. Thoughtfully, he started getting ready to travel again.

Gerin was glad to exchange the dirt road that led to Ikos for the main southbound highway before the former became a bottomless river of mud. Moments later, he was wondering at the wisdom of his choice. From behind him came a drumming of hooves, the deadly clangor of bronze on bronze, and wheels rumbling on a stone roadbed—a squadron of chariotry, moving fast.

Van unshipped his spear and Gerin began to string his bow. Then a deep voice sounded above the rising clatter: "Way! Way for the men of Aragis the Archer!"

The baron pulled off the road with almost unseemly haste. Ignoring the rain, Aragis' troopers pounded past, brave in surcoats of scarlet and silver. A handful of draggled bandits were their reluctant companions.

Proud hawk face never smiling, Aragis' captain—or maybe it was Aragis himself—raised one arm in salute as his men thundered by. Some of them had leers for Elise, stares for Van's fine cuirass. The bandits looked stolidly ahead. Gerin guessed they could already see the headsman's axe looming large across their futures, and precious little else.

"Whew!" Van said as the chariots disappeared into the rain ahead. "This trip will make a fine yarn, but it's not something I'd like to do more than once."

"Which is true of most things that make good stories," Gerin said. Van laughed and nodded.

From Ikos to Cassat was a journey of two days. To the baron, they were a time of revelation. For years his mind had not reached further than the harvest, the balance of a blade, or the best place to set an ambush. But Elise had read many of the works that were his own favorites and, better yet, thought on what she read. They passed hour after hour quoting passages they liked and arguing meanings.

Gerin had almost forgotten talk like this existed. Over the years, all without his knowing it, his mind had grown stuffy and stale. Now he relished the fresh new breeze playing through it.

Van chimed in too, from time to time. He lacked the background Gerin and Elise shared, but he had seen more of the varied ways of man than either, and his wit was keen.

The purple bulk of the High Kirs, a great rampart looming tall on the southern horizon, came to dominate the landscape. Eternal snow clung to many peaks, scoffing at high summer below. Eight passes traversed the mountains; seven the Empire had painstakingly blocked over the years, to keep out the northern barbarians. In the foothills before the eighth squatted the town of Cassat, a monument to what might have been.

Oren II had planned it as a splendid capital for the new province his father had won. Its great central square was filled with temples, triumphal arches, law courts, and a theater. But fate had not been kind. Birds nested under the eaves of the noble buildings; grass pushed up between marble paving-blocks. The only reality to Cassat was its barracks, squat, unlovely structures of wood and grimy plaster where a few hundred imperial soldiers pretended to rule the northlands. A few streets of horsetraders, sword-smiths, joyhouses, and taverns met their needs. The dusty wind blew mournful through the rest of the town.

The Empire's dragon flag, black on gold, flew only over the barracks. There did Carus Beo's son, the Marchwarden of the North, perform his office; mice alone disputed in the courthouse Oren had built.

Once, Carus had been a favorite at court. He had earned his present post some years back, when the Urfa massacred a column he led. Because of what he saw as exile to the cheerless north, he despised and resented the border barons.

Gerin called on him nonetheless. Few as they were, Carus' men would help hold the border against the Trokmoi, could he be persuaded to send them north. Elise accompanied the baron. Van took the wagon to a leading trader of horseflesh, seeking fresh animals to replace Gerin's weary beasts.

The Marchwarden of the North sat at a well-scuffed desk piled high with parchments of all sizes. He was sixty or a bit over; his yellowish-white hair had retreated to a ruff round his ears and the back of his neck, leaving his pink scalp bare but for a meager forelock. His eyes had dark pockets under them. His jowls quivered when he lifted his head from whatever bureaucratic inconsequentiality Gerin's arrival had interrupted.

"My man tells me you seek the assistance of the Empire against the Trokmoi. Surely the boldness of the brave holders of Elabon's frontier cannot have declined to such an abysmal level?" he said, looking at Gerin with no liking at all.

Then his narrow eyes swiveled to Elise, and a murky gleam lit them. The Fox saw a liking there, sure enough, but only of the sort that made him want to kick Carus' stained teeth down his throat. Elise studied a point on the wall directly behind the Marchwarden's forehead.

"Surely not," Gerin said. Ignoring the fact that he had not been offered a seat, he handed Elise into a chair and took another for himself. Carus' sallow cheeks reddened. As if nothing had happened, the Fox resumed, "At the present time, however, circumstances are of unusual difficulty." He told the Marchwarden of Balamung and his threatened invasion.

Carus was drumming his nails on top of his desk by the time the Fox finished. "Let me see if I understand you correctly," he said. "You expect the troops of the Empire to get you out of trouble with this wizard, into which you have gotten yourself. Now to justify this request for service, you may point to—what?"

"Among other things, that we border barons have kept the Trokmoi out of the Empire for two hundred years and more."

"A trivium." Carus waved his hand in a languid southern gesture which might have seemed courtly from Rihwin but was only grotesque in a man of the Marchwarden's years and girth. "If I had my way, we would merely send a few thousand tons of stone down behind the Great Gate. That would quite nicely seal off the barbarians for all time."

"Horseballs," Gerin muttered. Elise heard him and grinned. Carus heard him too. The baron had not intended that.

"Horseballs?" Carus' mouth moved in what might have been a smile, but his eyes stayed cold. "Ah, the vivid turn of phrase of the frontier. But do let me return to what I was saying: indeed, I think the Empire would be as well off without you. What do we gain from you, after all? No metals, no grain—only trouble. Half the rebels of the past two hundred years have had northern ties. You corrupt the calm, orderly way of life we crave. No, my good lord Gerin, if the barbarians can eat you up, they are welcome to you."

The Fox had not really expected help from the Marchwarden, but he had not expected outright hatred, either. He drew in a long, angry breath. Elise pressed his hand in warning, but he was too furious to pay heed. He spoke in the same polished phrases Carus had used, and the same venom rode them: "You complain the Empire receives nothing from us? Up on the border, we wonder what we get from you. Where are the men and chariots of the Empire, to help us drive away the northern raiders? Where are they when we fight among ourselves? Do you care? Not a bit, for if we are kept distracted, we cannot think of rebellion. You judge, and rightly, our flesh and blood a better shield than any you might make of stone or wood, and so we die, for nothing."

Bowing to Carus, Gerin stood to go. "And you, my fine Marchwarden, you have gained most of all from our thankless toil. While we sweat and bleed to keep the border safe, here you have stayed for the past twenty-five years, shuffling parchments from one pile to the next and sitting on your fat fornicating fundament!" The last was a roar of surprising volume.

Carus leaped to his feet, fumbling for his sword but finding only an empty scabbard. Gerin laughed mockingly. "Guards!" the Marchwarden bleated. When the men appeared, he gabbled, "Clap this insolent lout in chains and cast him in the dungeon until he learns politeness." His eyes lingered on Elise. He reached out a flabby hand to take her arm. "I will undertake to instruct the wench personally."

The befuddlement on the guards' faces was ludicrous; they had not seen their master so active in years. Gerin made no move for his own blade. He said mildly, "Do you know what will happen if you seize us? As soon as the barons learn of it, they will come down in a body and leave your precious barracks so much kindling. Not long after that, the Trokmoi will be here to light it. I'm almost sorry you won't live to watch."

"What? What nonsense are you spewing now? I'll— *gark!*" Carus' voice abruptly disappeared. Elise was tickling the soft skin under his chin with the tip of her dagger. She smiled sweetly at him. The blood drained from his face, leaving it the color of the parchment on his desk. Moving very carefully, he let go of her arm. "Go," he said, in ragged parody of the tone he had used a moment before. "Get out. Guards, take them away."

"To the dungeons, sir?" asked one, scorn in his voice.

"No, no, just go." Carus sank back into his chair, hands shaking and sweat gleaming on his bald head. With as much ceremony as if it were a daily occurrence, his men conducted Gerin and Elise from the Marchwarden's presence.

The sun was still high in the soutwest; the audience had made up in heat what it lacked in length. Gerin turned to Elise and said, "I knew having you along would be a nuisance. Once he caught a glimpse of you, the old lecher couldn't find a way to get me out of there fast enough."

"Don't be ridiculous. I'm a mess." Of itself, her hand moved to brush at her hair.

The baron surveyed her. There was dust in her hair and a smudge of grime on her forehead, but her green eyes sparkled, the mild doses of sun she allowed herself had brought out a spray of freckles on her nose and cheeks, her lips were soft and red, and even in tunic and trousers she was plainly no boy. . . .

Easy there, Gerin told himself: *do you want to make Ricolf your irreconcilable enemy too, along with the Trokmoi and Wolfar?* He gave his beard a judicious tug. "You'll do," he said. "You'll definitely do."

She snorted and poked him in the ribs. He yelped and mimed a grab at her; she made as if to stab him. They were still smiling half an hour later, when Van pulled up in the wagon. He smelled of horses and beer, and had two new beasts in the traces. A grin split his face when he saw how happy Gerin looked. "Himself gave you the men, did he?"

"What? Oh. No, I'm afraid not." The Fox explained the fiasco; Van laughed loud and long. Gerin went on, "I expected nothing much, and got just that. You seem to have been busy, though—what sort of horse do you have there, anyway?" He jerked a thumb at one of Van's newly acquired animals.

Unlike its companion, a handsome gray gelding, this rough-coated little beast was even less sightly than the shaggy woods-ponies of the Trokmoi. But Van looked scandalized. He leaped down and rubbed the horse's muzzle.

A quick snap made him jerk his hand away. Even so, he said, "Captain, don't tell me you don't know a Shanda horse when you see one? The fool trader who had him didn't. He thought he was putting one over on me. Well, let him laugh. A Shanda horse will go all day and all night; you can't wear one down if you try. I like the bargain, and you will too."

"All right, show me." Gerin helped Elise up, then climbed on himself. Van followed. The wagon clattered out of Cassat toward the Great Gate, the sole remaining link the Empire allowed itself with its northern provinces.

It was a long pull through the Gate. Toward the end, the gray horse was lathered and blowing, but the pony from the plains showed no more sign of strain than if it had spent the day grazing. Gerin was impressed.

Though Elabon had not blocked this last way through the Kirs, her marshals had done their best to make sure no enemy could use it. Fortresses of brick and stone flanked the roadway. Watchmen tramped smartly along their battlements, alert against any mischance. The towers' bronze-sheathed wooden gates were closed now, but could open to vomit forth chariots and footsoldiers against any invader.

Wizards, too, aided in defending the Empire. They had their own dwellings, twin needle-like spires of what seemed to be multicolored glass, off which the late afternoon sun shimmered and sparkled. Should the fortresses' armed might fail to blunt an attack, the warlocks would set in motion the thousands of boulders heaped on either side of the pass, and thus block it forever.

The arrangement left Gerin uneasy: what wizardry had made, it could unmake. He cheered slightly when he discovered the warriors in the fastnesses could also start the avalanche by purely natural means: paths led up to the tops of the piles of scree, and triggering rocks there had levers under them. The Fox did not envy the men who would work those levers.

The succession of powerful strongholds awed even Van. "Folk who huddle behind forts are dead inside," he said, "but with forts like these it will be a while yet before anyone notices the reek of the corpse."

A brown and buff lizard chased a grasshopper into the road. It danced madly under hooves and wagon wheels, then vanished into a crevice in the rocks on the far side. Gerin never knew whether it had caught its bug.

Traffic through the Great Gates was heavy. Traders headed north. Their donkeys brayed loud disgust at the weight of the packs they bore. Traders came south. Their donkeys brayed loud disgust over nothing at all. Mercenaries, wandering wise men, wizards, and a good many travelers who fell into no neat scheme—all used the imperial highway.

Nearly two hours went by before the wagon reached the end of the pass. Golden under the light of the setting sun, the southern land spread out ahead like a picture from a landscape master's brush. Field and forest, town and orchard, all were plain to see, with brooks and rivers like lines of molten copper.

"It's a rare pretty country," Van said. "What are the people like?"

"People," Gerin shrugged.

"I'd best keep an eye on my wallet, then."

"Go howl! You'd bit a coin free-given."

"Likely I would, if I planned to spend it."

"Scoffer!"

Just then a warm, dry breeze wafted up from the south. It was sweet and spicy, with the faintest tang of salt from the distant Inner Sea, and carried scents the baron had forgotten.

Like a swift stream breaching the dam that restrained it, long-buried memories flooded up in Gerin. He thought of the two years free from care he had spent in the capital, then of the sterile, worry-filled time since—and was appalled.

"Why did I ever leave you?" he cried to the waiting

land ahead. "Father Dyaus, you know I would sooner have been a starving schoolmaster in the capital than king of all the northlands!"

"If that's how you feel, why not stay in the south?" Elise asked. Her voice was gentle, for the fair land ahead had enchanted her as much as the Fox.

"Why not indeed?" Gerin said surpised. He realized the notion had never crossed his mind, and wondered why. At last he sighed and shook his head. "Were the danger behind me less great, I'd leap at the chance like a starving longtooth. But for better or worse, my life is on the cooler side of the mountains. Much depends on me there. If I stay, I betray more than my own men, I think. The land will fall to Balamung, and I doubt it will slake his evil thirst. That may happen yet; the gods have given the northland little enough hope. It's partly my fault Balamung is what he is; if I can make amends, I will."

"I think you will do well," Elise said slowly. "Often, it seems, the most glory is won by those who seek it least."

"Glory? If I can stay alive and free without it, I don't give a moldy loaf of journeybread for glory. I leave all that to Van."

"Ha!" Van said. "Do you want to know the real reason he's bound to go back, my lady?"

"Tell *me*," Gerin said, curious to see what slander his friend would come up with.

"Captain, you'd need more than a wizard to drive you away from your books, and you know it as well as I do." There was enough truth in that to make Gerin throw a lazy punch at Van, who ducked. A good part of the barony's silver flowed south to the copyists and bookdealers in Elabon's capital.

They wound their way down from the pass, hoping to reach a town before the sun disappeared. Gerin was less worried about the ghosts than he would have been on the other side of the mountains; peace had reigned here for many years, and the spirits were relatively mild. For his part, Van grew eloquent about the advantages of fresh food, a mug of ale (or even wine!), a comfortable bed, and perhaps (though he did not say so) a wench to warm it.

The road was flanked by a grove of fruit trees of a kind unknown north of the Kirs. Not very tall, they had gray-brown bark, shiny light-green leaves, and egg-shaped yellow fruit. Both leaves and fruit were fragrant, but Gerin remembered how astonishingly sour the fruit was to the tongue. It was called . . . he snapped his fingers in annoyance. He had forgotten the very name.

As the trees began to thin, another smell made its presence known through their perfume: a faint carrion reek. The baron's lips drew back in a mirthless grimace. "I think we've found our town," he said.

The road turned, the screen of trees disappeared, and sure enough the town was there. It was not big enough to have a wall. The Fox was sure folk living ten miles from it had never heard its name. Nonetheless, it aspired to cityhood in a way open to the meanest of hamlets: by the road stood a row of crucifixes, each with its slow-rotting burden. Under them children played, now and then shying a stone upward. Dogs slunk there too, dogs with poor masters or none, waiting for easy meals.

Some of the spiked and roped criminals were not yet dead. Through sun-baked and blistered lips they begged for water or death, each according to the strength left in him. One, newly elevated or unnaturally strong, still howled defiance at gods and men.

His roars annoyed the carrion birds nearby. Strong black bills filled with noisome food, they flapped lazily into the sky, staring down with fine impartiality on town, travelers, and field. They knew all would come to them in good time.

Van's face might have been carved from stone as he surveyed the wretches. Elise was pale. Her eyes went wide with horror. Her lips shaped the word "Why?" but no sound emerged. Gerin tried not to remember his own thoughts when he'd first encountered the malignant notions of justice the southerners had borrowed from Sithonia.

"Maybe," he said grimly, "I had my reasons for going home, after all."

VI

The town (Gerin learned its name was Fibis) did little to restore the luster of the southlands in the baron's eyes. The houses lining the north-south road were little finer than the huts of his peasants. Only muddy alleys ankle-deep in slops led away from that road.

The sole hostel Fibis boasted was of a piece with the rest. It was low-roofed, dingy, and small. The sign outside had faded past legibility. Within, the smell of old grease fought with but could not overcome the odor of stale urine from the dyeworks next door and the never-absent stench of the crosses.

And the townsfolk! City ways that had been sophisticated to the youth who traveled this road ten years before now seemed either foppish or surly. Gerin tried to strike up a conversation with the innkeeper, a dour, weathered old codger named Grizzard, but got only grunts in return. He gave up and went back

103

to the rickety table where his friends awaited supper. "If I didn't know better," he said, "I'd take oath the fellow was afraid of me."

"Then he thinks you've already tasted his wine," said Van, who was on his third mug. "What swill!" He swigged, pursed his lips to spit, but swallowed instead.

The rest of the meal was not much better than the wine. Plainly, lack of competition was all that kept Grizzard in business. Disgusted with the long, fruitless day he had put in, Gerin was about to head for bed when a cheery voice said, "Hello, you're new here! What's old Grizzard given you to drink?"

Without so much as a by-your-leave, the fellow pulled up a chair and joined them. He sniffed the wine, grimaced, and flipped a spinning silver disk to the innkeeper, who made it disappear. "You can do better than this, you thief," he said. To the Fox's surprise, Grizzard could.

The baron studied his new acquaintance curiously, for the man seemed made of pieces which did not belong together. Despite his heartiness, his voice soon dropped so low Grizzard could not hear what he said. While his mouth was full of slang from the capital, his homespun tunic and trousers were both rustic. Yet his chin sported a gray imperial and his shoes turned up at the toes: both Sithonian styles. The name he gave—just Tevis, without patronymic or sobriquet— was one of the three or four commonest south of the mountains.

Whoever he was, he had a rare skill with words. Softly, easily, he enticed from Gerin (usually as close-mouthed as any man alive) the story of his travels, and all without revealing a bit of his own purpose. It was almost as if he cast a spell. He paused a while in silent consideration, his clear dark eyes studying the

Fox. "You have not been well-used by the Empire," he said at last.

Gerin only shrugged. His caution had returned. He was wary of this smooth-talking man of mystery. Tevis nodded, as if he had expected nothing more. "Tell me," he said, "do you know of Moribar the Magnificent, his imperial majesty's governor at Kortys?"

Van, who had drunk deep, stared at Tevis in owlish incomprehension. Elise was nearly asleep, her head warm on Gerin's shoulder. Her hair tickled his cheek. The scent of it filled his nose. But in his mind the stench of the rood was stronger still. Here was the very thing Carus Beo's son had feared most: a potential rebel in the capital of Sithonia, seeking northern help.

At any other time, the baron would have shed no tears to see the Empire go up in civil war, but now he needed whatever strength he could find at his back. He chose his words with care: "Tevis, I don't know you and I didn't ask to know you. If you say one word more to me, you will have spoken treason, and I will not hear it. True, I've had my quarrels with some of his majesty's servants, but if he does not plot against me in my land, I have no right to plot against him in his. I would not have drunk with you had I known what was in your mind. Here, take this and go." He set a coin on the table to pay for the jug of wine.

Tevis smiled faintly. "Keep it," he said, "and this as well." He took something from the pouch on his belt, tossed it next to the coin, and was gone into the night while Gerin still gaped at what he had thrown: a tiny bronze hand, fingers beginning to curl into a fist.

"Oh, great Dyaus above!" he said. "An Imperial Hand!" He propped his chin on his palm and stared at the little token before him. He could have been no more startled had it sprung up and slapped him in the face.

Bristles rasped under Van's fingers as he scratched his jaw. "And what in the five hells is that?" he asked with ponderous patience.

"A secret agent, spy, informer . . . call him what you will. That doesn't matter. But if I'd shown any interest in setting Moribar on the throne, by this time tomorrow we'd be on crosses side by side, waiting for the vultures to pick out our eyes."

"Ha! I'd bite off their heads!" Van seemed more concerned with the vultures than the crucifixion that would invite them.

"That's one way of dealing with them, I suppose," Gerin agreed mildly. He woke Elise. She yawned and walked sleepily to the one room Grizzard grudged female travelers. Van and Gerin headed for their own pallets, hoping they would not be bug-ridden. Almost as an afterthought, the Fox scooped up the diminutive but deadly emblem Tevis had left behind.

Though weary, he slept poorly. The quarrel with Carus, his jarring reintroduction to the dark side of the southlands, and above all the brush with doom in the form of Tevis kept him tossing all night. The bed was hard and lumpy, too. When he awoke, half a dozen red, itchy spots on his arms and chest proved he had not slept alone.

Van was unusually quiet at breakfast. "Head hurt?" Gerin asked as they walked to the stables.

"What. Oh. No, it's not that, captain." Van hesitated. Finally he said, "I'll tell you right out, Gerin, last night I almost decided to buy myself a gig and get the blazes out of this crazy country."

Gerin had imagined disaster piled on disaster, but never in his worst nightmares had he imagined his friend leaving. Ever since Van came to Fox Keep the two of the had been inseparable, fighting back to back and then carousing and yarning far into the night. Each owed the other his life several times. With a shock, the baron realized Van was a larger, gustier version of his dead brother Dagref. Losing him would be more than parting with a comrade; part of the baron's soul would go with him.

Before he could put what he felt into words, Elise spoke first: "Why would you want to leave now? Are you afraid? The danger is in the north, not here." She seemed unwilling to believe her ears."

At any other time, the outlander's wrath would have kindled if his courage was questioned. Now he only sighed and kicked at a pebble. Genuine distress was in his voice as he answered, "My lady, look about you." His wave encompassed not just the grubby little hamlet of Fibis and the crosses outside it, but all the land where the writ of the Empire was law. "You've seen enough of me to know what I am and what my pleasures are: fighting, talking, drinking, aye, and wenching too, I'll not deny. But here, what good am I? If I break wind in the backhouse, I have to look over my shoulder lest some listening spy call it treason. It's not the kind of life I care to lead: worrying before I move, not daring even to think."

Gerin understood that well enough, for much the same sense of oppression weighed on him. But Van was still talking: "I was all set to take my leave of you this morning—head north again, I suppose. But then I got to thinking"—he suddenly grinned—"and I decided that if any boy-loving Imperial Hand doesn't like the way I speak, why, I'll carve the son of a pimp into steaks and leave him by the side of the road to warn his scurvy cousins!"

Elise laughed in delight and kissed him on the cheek.

"I think you planned this whole thing just to get

that kiss," Gerin said. "Come on, you hulk, quit holding up the works."

"Bastard." Still grinning, Van pitched his gear into the wagon.

The morning was still young when they splashed through the chilly Langros river. Though not as great as the Niffet or the mighty Carastos which watered much of the plain of Elabon, its cold current ran swift as it leaped down from the Kirs toward the Greater Inner Sea.

The water at the ford swirled icily around Gerin's toes and welled up between the wagon's floorboards. Most of the travelers' belongings were safe in oiled leather sacks, but half the journeybread turned to slimy brown paste. Gerin swore in disgust. Van said, "Cheer up, captain, the stuff wasn't worth eating anyhow."

When they stopped to rest and eat, Van turned to Gerin and said quietly, "Thanks for not pushing me this morning. You might have made it hard for me to stay."

"I know," Gerin said. Neither of them mentioned the matter again.

They made good progress that day, passing small farms in the foothills and then, as the land began to level out, going by great estates with splendid manorhouses set well back from the raod. When shadows lengthened and cool evening breezes began to blow, they camped by the roadside instead of seeking an inn. Gerin fed and watered the horses as the sun set. In the growing darkness the ghosts appeared, but their wails were somehow muted, their cries almost croons.

Elleb's thin crescent soon followed the sun, like a small boy staying close to his father. That left the sky to the stars and Math, whose gibbous disk bathed the land beyond reach of the campfire in pale golden light. As the night went on, she was joined by Tiwaz, whose speedy flight through the heavens had taken him well past full. And, when Gerin's watch was nearly done, Nothos poked his slow-moving head over the horizon. The baron watched him climb for most of an hour, then gave the night to Van.

The next day gave every promise of rolling along as smoothly as had its predecessor. The promise was abruptly broken a bit before noon. A manor-holder had decided to send his geese to market. The road was jammed by an endless array of tall white birds herded along by a dozen or so men with sticks. The geese honked, cackled, squabbled, and tried to sneak off the road for a mouthful of grain. They did everything, in fact, but hurry. When Gerin asked their warders to clear a way so he could pass, they refused. "If these blame birds get into the fields," one said, "we'll be three days getting them all out again, and our lord'll have our heads."

"Let's charge right through," Van suggested. "Can't you see the feathers fly?"

The thought of a goose stampede brought a smile to Gerin's lips, but he said, "No, these poor fellows have their job to do too, I suppose." And so they fretted and fumed while the birds dawdled along in front of them. More traffic piled up behind.

As time dragged on, Van's direct approach looked better and better. The whip twitched in Gerin's hand. But before he used it, he noticed the road was coming to a fork. The geese streamed down the eastern path. "Can we use the western branch to get to the capital?" he called.

"You can that," one of the flock-tenders answered, so the Fox swung the wagon down the new way.

New? Hardly. Gerin noticed that none of the others stalled behind the geese used the clear road. Soon

enough, he found out why. The eastern branch of the
highway was far newer. After it was complete, evi-
dently nobody had bothered with the other one again.
The wagon jounced and rattled as it banged over gaping holes in the roadbed. On one stretch, the paved
surface vanished altogether. There the blocks had
been set, not in concrete, but in molten lead. Locals
had carried away blocks and valuable mortar alike as
soon as imperial inspectors no longer bothered to protect them. The baron cursed the lout who had sent
him down this road. He hoped he could make it without breaking a wheel.

The district had perhaps once been prosperous, but
had decayed when its road was superseded. The farther they went, the thicker the forest grew, until at
last its arms clasped above the roadway and squirrels
flirted their bushy gray tails directly overhead.
Soon the very memory of the road would be gone.

Finding a village in the midst of such decline
seemed divine intervention. The villagers fell on
Gerin and his friends like long-lost relatives, plying
them with food and a rough, heady country wine and
listening eagerly to every word they brought of the
world outside. Not a copper would they take in pay-
ment. The baron blessed such kindly folk, and blessed
them doubly when they confirmed that the road did
in fact eventually lead to the capital instead of sinking
into a bog.

"You see, captain? You worry too much," Van said.
"Everything will work out all right."

Gerin did not answer. He could not *let* things work
out all right; he had to *make* them do so. Backtracking
would have cost him a day he could not afford to
spend.

The villagers insisted on putting up their guests for
the night. Gerin's host was a lean farmer named
Badoc son of Tevis (the baron hid a shiver). Other

villagers, just as anxious for news, claimed Elise and Van.

The benches round Badoc's table were filled to overflowing by the farmer, his plump, friendly wife Leunadra, the Fox, and a swarm of children. These ranged in age from a boy barely able to toddle to Badoc's twin daughters Callis and Elminda, who were about seventeen. Gerin eyed the striking girls appreciatively. They had curly hair, sparkling brown eyes, and cheeks rosy under sun-bestowed bronze; their thin linen tunics clung to young breasts. As subtly as he could, the baron turned the conversation in their direction. They hung on his every word . . . so long as he was talking about Van. To his own charms they remained sublimely indifferent.

"I wish your friend could stay here," one of the twins mourned; Gerin had forgotten which was which. They both babbled on about Van's thews, his armor, his rugged features, his smile . . . and on and on, until Gerin began to hate the sound of his comrade's name. Badoc's craggy face almost smiled as he watched his guest's discomfiture.

At last the ordeal was over. The baron, quite alone and by then glad of it, went to his bed. His feet hung over the end, for Badoc had ousted one of his younger sons to accommodate the Fox. Gerin was tired enough that it fazed him not a bit.

A woman's cry woke him around midnight. Another followed, then another, long and drawn out: *"Evoi! Evoiii!"* The baron relaxed; it was only the followers of Mavrix, the Sithonian god of wine, out on one of their moonlight revels. Gerin was a bit surprised Mavrix's cult had spread to this out-of-the-way place, but what of it? He went back to sleep.

The next morning he discovered the considerate villagers had not only curried his horses till their coats gleamed, but also left gifts of fresh bread, wine, cheese, onions, and bars of dried fruit and meat in the back of the wagon. A troop of small boys followed him south until their parents finally called them home.

"I almost hate to leave," Van said. Gerin studied him: was he still wearing the traces of a satisfied grin? *What if he is, witling?* the baron asked himself. *Do you begrudge him his good fortune? Well, yes, a little,* his inner voice answered.

The road was a bit better south of the village; at least it never disappeared. Under the trees the air was cool and moist, the sunlight subdued. Gerin felt more at home than he had since leaving Ricolf's keep. He was not alone. He heard Elise softly humming a song of the north country. She smiled when she saw him watching her.

They came to a clearing almost wide enough to be called a meadow, hidden away deep in the forest. The Fox squinted at the sudden brightness. A doe which had been nibbling at the soft grass by the forest's edge lifted its head at the wagon's noisy arrival and sprang into the woods.

"Pull over, will you?" Van said. The outlander reached for Gerin's bow and quiver. Though he disdained archery in battle, he loved to hunt and was a fine shot. He trotted across the clearing and vanished among the trees with grace and silence a hunting cat might have envied.

Sighing, Gerin threw down the reins and stretched out full-length on the sweet-smelling grass. Sore muscles began to unkink. Elise stepped down and joined him. The horses were as glad at the break as the people; they cropped the grass with as much alacrity as the deer had shown.

Minute followed minute, but Van gave no sign of returning. "He's probably forgotten which end of the arrow goes first," Gerin said. He rose, went to the wagon, and emerged with Van's spear. "Carrying this, I shouldn't wonder." Every time he touched it, he marveled at his friend's skill with such a heavy weapon.

He practiced slow thrusts and parries to while away the time, more than a little conscious of Elise's eyes on him. Showing off in front of a pretty girl was a pleasure he did not get often enough. More and more he resented the wound that had kept him from courting this particular pretty girl.

It was not that he lacked for women. If nothing else, a baron's prerogatives were enough to prevent that, though he was moderate in his enjoyment of them and never bedded a wench unwilling. But none of his partners had roused more than his lusts, and he quickly tired of each new liaison. In Elise he was beginning to suspect something he had thought rare to the point of nonexistence: a kindred soul.

He had just dispatched another imaginary foe when a crackle in the bushes on the far side of the clearing made him raise his head. *Van back at last*, he thought; he filled his lungs to shout a greeting. It died unuttered. Only a thin whisper emerged, and that directed at Elise: "Do just what I tell you. Walk very slowly to the far side of the wagon, then run for the woods. Move!" he snapped when she hesitated. He made sure she was on her way before loping into the middle of the clearing to confront the aurochs.

It was a bull, a great roan, shaggy shoulders higher than a tall man's head. Scars old and new crisscrossed its hide. Its right horn was a shattered ruin, broken in some combat or accident long ago. The other curved out and forward, a glittering spear of death.

The aurochs' ears twitched as it stared at the puny man who dared challenge it. The certainty of a charge lay like a lump of ice in Gerin's belly: any aurochs would attack man or beast, but a lone bull was doubly terrible. Drago's grandfather had died under the horns and stamping hooves of just such a foe.

Quicker even than the Fox expected, the charge came. The beast's hooves sent chunks of sod flying skyward. There was no time to throw Van's spear. Gerin could only hurl himself to his left, diving to the turf. He had a glimpse of a green eye filled with insane hatred. Then the aurochs was past, the jagged stump of its horn passing just over him. The rank smell of its skin fought the clean odors of grass and dirt.

Gerin was on his feet in an instant. But the aurochs was already wheeling for another charge, faster than any four-footed beast had any right to be. The Fox hurled his spear, but the cast was hurried and high. It flew over the aurochs' shoulder. Only a desperate leap saved Gerin. Had the bull had two horns, he would surely have been spitted. As it was, he knew he could not elude it much longer in the open.

He sprang up and sprinted for the forest, snatching the spear as he ran. Behind him came the drumroll of the aurochs' hooves. The small of his back tingled, anticipating the horn. Then, breath sobbing in his throat, he was among the trees. Timber cracked as the aurochs smashed through brush and saplings. Still, it had to slow as it followed his dodges from tree to tree.

He hoped to lose it in the wood, but it pursued him with a deadly patience he had never known an aurochs to show. Its bellows and snorts of rage rang loud in his ears. Deeper and deeper into the forest he ran, following a vague game trail.

That came to an abrupt end: some time not long before, a forest giant had toppled, falling directly across the path. Its collapse brought down other trees and walled off the trail as thoroughly as any work of man's might have done. Gerin clambered over the dead timer. The aurochs was not far behind.

The Fox's wits had been frozen in dismay from the moment the aurochs appeared in the clearing. They began to work again as he leaped down from the deadfall. Panting, "I can't run any farther anyway," he jabbed the bronze-clad butt of Van's spear deep into the soft earth, then blundered away into the forest, having thrown his dice for the last time.

Ever louder came the thunder of the aurochs' hooves, till the Fox could feel the ground shake. For a terrible moment, he thought it would try to batter through the dead trees, but it must have known that was beyond its power. It hurled its bulk into the air, easily clearing the man-high barrier—and spitted itself on the upthrust spear.

The tough wood of the spearshaft shivered into a thousand splinters, but the leaf-shaped bronze point was driven deep into the aurochs' vitals. It staggered a couple of steps on wobbling legs, blood spurting from its belly. Then a great gout poured from its mouth and nose. It shuddered and fell. Its sides heaved a last time, then were still. It gave the Fox a reproachful brown bovine stare and died.

Gerin rubbed his eyes. In his dance with death out on the meadow, he had been sure the beast's eyes were green. His own hand came away bloody. He must have been swiped by a branch while dashing through the forest, but he had no memory of it. *Shows how much I know*, he thought. He wearily climbed back over the deadfall.

He had not gone far when Van came crashing down the game trail, drawn bow in his hands. Elise was right behind him. The outlander skidded to a stop, his jaw dropping. "How are you, captain?" he asked foolishly.

"Alive, much to my surprise."

"But—the aurochs . . . Elise said . . ." Van stopped, the picture of confusion.

Gerin was just glad Elise had had the sense to go after his friend instead of showing herself to the aurochs and probably getting herself killed. "I'm afraid I'll have to buy you a new spear when we get to the capital," he said.

Van hauled himself over the barrier. He came back carrying the spearpoint; bronze was too valuable to leave. "What in the name of the trident of Shamadraka did you do?" he asked.

The baron wondered where Shamadraka's worshipers lived; he had never heard of the god. "Climbing those trunks took everything I had left," he said. "The beast was hunting me like a hound—I've never known anything like it. He would have had me in a few minutes. But by some miracle I remembered a fable I read a long time ago, about a slave who was too lazy to hunt. He'd block a trail, set a javelin behind his barrier, and wait for the deer to skewer themselves for him."

Elise said, "I know the fable you mean: the tale of the Deer and Mahee. In the end he's killed by his own spear, and a good thing, too. He was a cruel, wicked man."

"You got the idea for killing the brute out of a book?" Van shook his head. "Out of a *book*? Captain, I swear I'll never sneer at reading again, if it can show you something that'll save your neck. The real pity of it is, you'll never have a chance to brag about this."

"And why not?" Gerin had been looking forward to doing just that.

"Slaying a bull aurochs singlehanded with a spear? Don't be a fool, Gerin: who would believe you?"

Van had killed his doe while the baron battled the aurochs. He dumped the bled and gutted carcass into the wagon and urged the horses southward. None of the travelers wanted to spend the night near the body of the slain aurochs. Not only would it draw unwelcome scavengers, but the spilled blood was sure to lure hungry, lonely ghosts from far and wide, all eager to share the unexpected bounty of the kill.

When the failing light told them it was time to camp, the deer proved toothsome indeed. Van carved steaks from its flanks. They roasted the meat over a fire. But despite a full belly, the outlander was unhappy. He grumbled, "I feel naked without my spear. What will I do without it in a fight?"

Gerin was less than sympathetic. "Seeing that you've brought a mace, an axe, three knives—"

"Only two. The third is just for eating."

"My apologies. Two knives, then, and a sword so heavy I can hardly lift it, let alone swing it. So I think you'll find some way to make a nuisance of yourself."

A nuisance Van was; he plucked a long straw from Elise's hand, leaving the short one—and the first watch—for Gerin. The Fox tried not to hear his friend's comfort-filled snores. His sense of the basic injustice of the universe was only slightly salved when Elise decided not to fall asleep at once.

Gerin was glad of her company. Without it, he probably would have dozed, for the night was almost silent. The sad murmurs of the ghosts, heard with the mind's ear rather than the body's, were also faint: the lure of the dead aurochs reached for miles, leaving the surrounding countryside all but bare of spirits.

For some reason the Fox could not fathom, Elise thought he was a hero for slaying the aurochs. He felt more lucky than heroic. There was precious little glory involved in running like a rabbit, which was most of what he'd done. Had he not plucked what he needed from his rubbish-heap of a memory, the beast would have killed him. "Fool luck," he concluded.

"Nonsense," Elise said. "Don't make yourself less

than you are. In the heat of the fight you were able to remember what you had to know and, more, to do something with it. You need more than muscle to make a hero."

Not convinced, Gerin shrugged and changed the subject, asking Elise what she knew of her kin in the capital. Her closest relative there, it transpired, was her mother's brother Valdabrun the Stout, who held some position or other at the Emperor's court. Though he did not say, Gerin found that a dubious recommendation. His imperial majesty Hildor III was an indolent dandy, and the baron saw little reason to expect his courtiers to be different.

To hide his worry, he talked of the capital and his own two years there. Elise was a good audience, as city life of any sort was new to her. He told a couple of his better stories. Her laugh warmed the cool evening. She moved closer to him, eager to hear more.

He leaned over and kissed her. It seemed the most natural thing in the world to do. For a moment, her lips were startled and still under his. Then she returned the kiss, at first hesitantly, then with a warmth to match his own.

You do have a gift for complicating your life, he told himself as she snuggled her head into his shoulder. *If things go on the way they've started, not only will Wolfar want to cut out your heart and eat it (a project he's been nursing quite a while anyhow), but your old friend Ricolf will be convinced—note or no note—you ran off with his daughter for reasons having very little to do with taking her to her uncle. And what is she thinking? She's no peasant wench, to be honored by a tumble and then forgotten. And further . . .*

A plague on it all, he thought. He kissed her again.

But when his lips touched her soft white throat and his hands moved to slide inside her tunic, she asked him softly, "Was it for this, then, you decided to bring

me south? Have I traded one Wolfar for another?"
She tried to keep her tone light, but hurt and disappointment were in her voice. They stopped him effectively as a dagger drawn, perhaps more so. She slipped free of his encircling arm.

Breath whistled through his nostrils as he brought his body back under mind's rein. "I would never have you think that," he said.

"Nor do I, in truth," she replied, but the hurt was still there. The time to remember he was man and she maid might come later, he thought. It was not here yet, despite the cool quiet of the night and the moonlight filtering through the trees.

She was silent so long he thought her still upset, but when he framed further apologies, she waved them away. They talked of inconsequential things for a little while. Then she rose and walked to the wagon for her bedroll. As she passed him, she stooped; her lips brushed his cheek.

His mind was still thought-filled long after she had fallen asleep. Elleb's thick waxing crescent was well set and the nearly full Math, bright as a golden coin, beginning to wester when he woke Van and sank into exhausted slumber.

His dreams at first were murky, filled now with the aurochs, now with Elise. He remembered little of them. He rarely did, and thought strange those who could recall their dreams and cast omens from them. But then it was as if a gale arose within his sleeping mind and blew away the mists separating him from the country of dreams.

Clear as if he had been standing on the spot, he saw the great watchfires flame, heard wild music of pipe, horn, and harp skirl up to the sky, saw tall northern warriors gathered by the fires, some with spears, others with drinking-horns in their hands. *This is no common dream*, he thought, and felt fear, but he could not leave it, not even when black wings drowned his sight in darkness.

Those proved to be the edges of the wizard's cloak Balamung wore. The sorcerer stepped back a pace, to be silhouetted against the firelight like a bird of prey. Only his eyes were live things, embers of scarlet and amber set in his gaunt face.

The barbarian mage was only too aware of the Fox. He turned a trifle and bowed a hate-filled bow, as if the baron had been there in the flesh. The light played redly off his hollow cheeks. He said, "Lord Gerin the Fox, it's no less than a nuisance you are to me, no less, so I pray you'll forgive my costing you a dollop of sleep to show you what's waiting in the northlands whilst you scuttle about the filthy south. Would I could be drawing the black-hearted soul of you from your carcass, but there's no spell I ken to do it, what with you so far away."

No spell Gerin knew could have reached across the miles at all. He was nothing, not even a wraith, just eyes and ears bound to see and hear only what Balamung chose to reveal.

The Trokmoi danced round the fires, tossing swords, spears, aye, and drinking-horns, too, into the air. The baron's disembodied spirit was less terrified than it might have been; the dance was one of those Rihwin had performed atop Ricolf's table. It seemed an age ago. But Balamung surely knew the baron expected him to arm for war. What else had he been summoned to see?

Balamung called down curses on the Fox's head. He hoped they would not bite deep. On and on the wizard ranted, until he paused to draw breath. Then he went on more calmly, saying, "Not least do I mislike you for costing me the soul of a fine fighting man this day. Like a wee bird I sent it flitting out, to light in the body of the great aurochs. Sure as sure I was he'd stomp you to flinders and leave you dead by the side of the road. Curse your tricky soul, how did you escape him? His spirit died trapped in the beast, for I could not draw it free in time. And when it flickered away, his body was forfeit too, poor wight."

No wonder the bull had trailed him with such grim intensity! Maybe he'd been right when he thought its eyes were green, there in the meadow; that might have been some byproduct of Balamung's magic. He had been lucky indeed.

"But sure and I'll have my revenge!" Balamung screamed. Behind him, the music had fallen silent. The dancers stood motionless and expectant.

The spell the mage used must have been readied beforehand, for when he cried out in the harsh Kizzuwatnan tongue a stout wicker cage rose from the ground and drifted slowly toward the fire. Gerin's spirit quailed when he saw it; he knew the Trokmoi burned their criminals alive, and in this cage, too, a man struggled vainly to free himself.

"Die, traitor, die!" Balamung shouted. All the gathered warriors took up the cry. Horror rose in Gerin, who suddenly recognized the condemned prisoner. It was Divico, the Trokmê chieftain whose life he had spared at Ikos. He wished sickly that he had let Van give the northerner a clean death. "Have a look at what befalls them who fight me," Balamung whispered, "for your turn is next!" His voice was cold as ice, harsh as stone.

And while he spoke, the cage entered the blaze. Some minor magic had proofed the wicker against flame; no fire would hold on it. But wherever a tongue licked Divico, it clung, flaring as brightly as if his body were a pitch-soaked torch.

Held there by Balamung's wizardry, Gerin watched in dread as the flames boiled Divico's eyeballs in his head, melted his ears into shapeless lumps of meat that sagged and ran against his cheeks, then charred the flesh from those cheeks to leave white bone staring through. Fire cavorted over the Trokmê's body, but Balamung's evil magic would not let him die. He fought against the unyielding door until his very tendons burned away. His shrieks had stopped long before, when flames swallowed his larynx.

"He was a job I had to rush," Balamung said. "When it's you, now, Fox, falling into my hand, I'll take the time to think up something truly worthy of you, oh indeed and I will!" He made a gesture of dismissal. Gerin found himself staring up from his bedroll, body wet with cold sweat.

"Bad dream, captain?" Van asked.

Gerin's only answer was a grunt. He was too shaken for coherent speech. Divico's face, eaten by flames, still stood before his eyes, more vivid than the dimly lit campsite he really saw. He thought he would never want to sleep again, but his weary body needed rest more than his mind feared it.

The sounds of a scuffle woke him. Before he could do more than open his eyes, strong hands pinned him to the ground. It was still far from sunrise. Did bandits in the southland dare the darkness, or was this some new assault of Balamung's? He twisted, trying to lever himself up on an elbow and see who or what had overcome him.

"Be still, or I'll rend thee where thou liest." The voice was soft, tender, female, and altogether mad. More hands, all full of casual deranged strength, pressed down his legs. They tugged warningly. He felt his joints creak.

All hope left him. After he had escaped Balamung's forays, it seemed unfair for him to die under the tearing hands of the votaries of Mavrix. Why had the wine-god's orgiastic, frenzied cult ever spread outside his native Sithonia?

Moving very slowly, the baron turned his head, trying to see the extent of the disaster. Perhaps one of his comrades had managed to get away. But no: in the moonlight he saw Van, his vast muscles twisting and knotting to no avail, pinned by more of the madwomen. Still more had fastened themselves to Elise.

The maenads' eyes reflected the firelight like those of so many wolves. That was the only light in them. They held no human intelligence or mercy, for they were filled by the madness of the god. The finery in which they had begun their trek through the woods was ripped and tattered and splashed with mud and grime, their hair awry and full of twigs. One woman, plainly a lady of high station from the remnants of fine linen draped about her body, clutched the mangled corpse of some small animal to her bosom, crooning over and over, "My baby, my baby."

A blue light drifted out of the forest, a shining nimbus round a figure . . . godlike was the only word for it, Gerin thought. "What have we here?" the figure asked, voice deep and sweet like the drink the desert nomads brewed to keep off sleep.

"Mavrix!" the women breathed, their faces slack with ecstasy. Gerin felt their hands quiver and slip. He braced himself for a surge, but even as he tensed the god waved and the grip on him tightened again.

"What have we here?" Mavrix repeated.

Van gave a grunt of surprise. "How is it you speak my language?"

To the Fox it had been Elabonian. "He didn't—" The protest died half-spoken as his captors snarled.

The god made an airy, effeminate gesture. "We have our ways," he said . . . and suddenly there were two of him, standing side by side. They—he— gestured again, and there was only one.

As well as he could, Gerin studied Mavrix. The god wore fawnskin, soft and supple, with a wreath of grape leaves round his brow. In his left hand he bore an ivy-tipped wand. At need, Gerin knew, it was a weapon more deadly than any mortal's spear. Mavrix's blond curls reached his shoulder; his cheeks and chin were shaven. That soft-featured, smiling face was a pederast's dream, but for the eyes: two black pits reflecting nothing, giving back only the night. A faint odor of fermenting grapes and something else, a rank something Gerin could not name, clung to him.

"That must be a useful art." The baron spoke in halting Sithonian, trying to pique the god's interest and buy at least a few extra minutes of life.

Mavrix turned those fathomless eyes on the Fox, but his face was still a smiling mask. He answered in the same tongue: "How pleasant to hear the true speech once more, albeit in the mouth of a victim," and Gerin knew his doom.

"Are you in league with Balamung, then?" he growled, knowing nothing he said now could hurt him further.

"I, friend to some fribbling barbarian charlatan? What care I for such things? But surely, friend mortal, you see this is your fate. The madness of the Mavriad cannot, must not be thwarted. Were it so, the festival would have no meaning, for what is it but the ultimate negation of all the petty nonfulfillments of humdrum, everyday life?"

"It's not right!" Elise burst out. "Dying I can understand; everyone dies, soon or late. But after the baron Gerin"—the Fox thought it a poor time to rhyme, but kept quiet—"singlehanded slew the aurochs, to die at the hands of lunatics, god-driven or no—"

Mavrix broke in, deep voice cracking: "Gerin slew a great wild ox—" The god's smile gave way to an expression of purest horror. "The oxgoad come again!" he screamed, "but now in the shape of a man! Metokhites, I thought you slain!" With a final despairing shriek, the god vanished into the depths of the woods. His followers fled after, afflicted by his terror—all but the lady of rank, who still sat contentedly, rocking her gruesome "baby."

Still amazed at being alive, Gerin slowly sat up. So did Elise and Van, both waring bewildered expression. "What did I say?" Elise asked.

Gerin thumped his forehead, trying to jar loose a memory. He had paid scant attention to Mavrix in the past, as the god's principal manifestations, wine and the grape, were rare north of the Kirs. "I have it!" he said at last, snapping his fingers. "This Metokhites was a Sithonian prince long ago. Once he chased the god into the Lesser Inner Sea, beating him about the head with a metal-tipped oxgoad: Mavrix always was a coward. I suppose he thought I was a new—what would the word be?—incarnation of his tormentor."

"What happened to this Metokhites fellow?" Van asked. "It's not the smartest thing, tangling with gods."

"As I remember, he chopped his son into bloody bits, being under the impression the lad was a grapevine."

"A grapevine, you say? Well, captain, if I ever seem to you to go all green and leafy-like, be so good as to warn me before you try to trim me."

At that, the last of the maenads lifted her eyes from the ruined little body she dandled. There was a beginning of knowledge in her face, though she was not yet fully aware of herself or her surroundings. Her voice had some of the authority of the Sibyl at Ikos when she spoke: "Mock not Mavrix, lord of the sweet grape. Rest assured, you are not forgotten!" Gathering her rags about her, she swept imperiously into the woods. Silence fell on the camp.

VII

Taking advantage of the quiet of the ghosts, Gerin decided to leave at once, though he knew mere distance was even less guarantee of safety from Mavrix than from Balamung. No thunderbolt smote him. Before too much time had passed, the rising sun turned Tiwaz and Math to a pair of pale gleams hanging close together in the southern sky.

So full of events had the previous day been that the Fox took till mid-afternoon to remember his dream, if such it was. By that time they were on the main road again, three more corpuscles among the thousands flowing toward the Empire's heart. "So that's why you woke with such a thrash!" Van said. Then the full import of the baron's words sank in. "You're saying the scrawny son of nobody knows where we are and what we're up to?"

Gerin rubbed his chin. "Where we are, anyway."

"I'm not sure I like that."

126

"I know damned well I don't, but what can I do about it?"

The Fox spent a gloomy, watchful night, fearing a return visit from Mavrix. The oracular tones of the god's half-crazed worshiper had left him jittery. The watch was lonely, too. Van fell asleep at once, and Elise quickly followed him.

That day on the road, she had hardly spoken to the baron. She spent most of her time listening to Van's yarns; he would cheerfully spin them for hours on end. She gave Gerin nothing more than cool courtesy when he tried to join the conversation. At length he subsided, feeling isolated and vaguely betrayed. The left side of his mouth quirked up in a sour smile; he knew only too well that his ill-timed ardor was what made her wary.

The new morning began much as the day before had ended: Gerin and Elise cautious and elaborately polite while Van, who seemed oblivious to the tension around him, bawled out a bawdy tune he had learned from the Trokmoi. So it went till they reached the Pranther River, another of the streams that rose in the foothills of the Kirs and ended by swelling the waters of the Greater Inner Sea.

The road did not falter at the Pranther, but sprang over it on a bridge supported by eight pillars of stone. The span itself was of stout timbers, which could be removed at need to slow invaders. This bridge was no flimsy magician's trick—it looked ready to stand for a thousand years.

Van gazed at it with admiration. "What a fine thing! It beats getting your backside wet, any day."

"It's probably the most famous bridge in the Empire," Gerin told him, grinning; the bridge over the Pranther was one of his favorite places in the south. "It's called Dalassenos' Revenge."

"Why's that, captain?"

"Dalassenos was Oren the Builder's chief architect. He was the fellow who designed this bridge, but Oren wanted only his own name on it. Being a Sithonian, Dalassenos didn't have much use for the Emperor in the first place, and that was too much to bear. So he carved his own message into the rock, then put a coat of plaster over it and chiseled Oren's name in that. After a few years, the plaster peeled away and—well, see for yourself." He jerked a thumb at the pylon.

"It's only so many scratches to me. I don't read Sithonian, or much else, for that matter."

Gerin thought for a moment. "As near as I can put it into Elabonian, it says:

'The plaster above? 'Twas nought but a farce,
And as for King Oren, he can kiss my arse.' "

Van bellowed laughter. "Ho, ho! That calls for a snort." A blind reach into the back of the wagon brought him his quarry—a wineskin. He swigged noisily.

Dalassenos' flip insolence also earned the Fox a smile from Elise; her appreciation was worth more to him than Van's chuckles. "What happened to Dalassenos when the plaster wore off?" she asked. The friendly interest in her voice told Gerin he had been forgiven.

"Not a thing," he answered. "It lasted through Oren's life, and he died childless (he liked boys). His successor hated him for almost bankrupting the Empire with all his building, and likely laughed his head off when he learned what Dalassenos had done. I know he sent Dalassenos a pound of gold, tight though he was."

As they passed over the bridge, Gerin looked down into the Pranther's clear water. A green manlike shape caught his eye. It was so close to the surface that he could easily see the four scarlet gill-slits on either side of its neck.

The Pranther held the only colony of rivermen west of the Greater Inner Sea. Dalassenos had brought the reptiles here from their native Sithonian streams. The canny artificer knew stones and sand propelled by the Pranther's current would eventually scour away the riverbottom from under his bridge's pilings and bring it tumbling down. Hence the rivermen: they repaired such damage as fast as it occurred.

In exchange, the Empire banned humans from fishing in the Pranther, and gave the rivermen leave to enforce the prohibition with their poisoned darts. It was also said that Dalassenos had hired a wizard to put a spell of permanent plenty on the fish. The baron did not know about that, but the rivermen had flourished in the Pranther for more than three hundred years.

Gerin heard the screech of an eagle overhead. Shielding his eyes from the sun, he looked up into morning haze until he found it. It wheeled in the sky, sun strking sparks from its ruddy plumage. Its feathers, he mused, were red as a Trokmê's mustache.

Sudden suspicion flared in him as he realized what he'd thought. "Van, do you think you can bring me down that overgrown pigeon?" he asked, knowing his friend's mighty arms could propel a shaft farther than most men dreamed possible.

The outlander squinted upward, shook his head. "No more than I could flap my arms and fly to Fomor."

"Fomor, is it?"

"Tiwaz, I mean. Whatever fool name you give the quick moon."

"Two years with me, and you still talk like a Trokmê." Gerin sadly shook his head.

"Go howl, captain. What's in your mind?"

The Fox did not answer. He pulled the wagon off the road. The eagle gave no sign of flying away, nor had he expected any. He had never seen a red eagle, and was convinced it was some creature of Balamung's, a flying spy. He climbed down from the wagon and began to root among the bushes by the roadside.

"What are you looking for, Gerin?" Elise asked.

"Sneezeweed," he answered, not finding any. He muttered a curse. The plant was a rank pest near Fox Keep; it grew everywhere in the northlands, even invading wheatfields. When it flowered, those sensitive to its pollen went into a season-long agony of wheezing, sneezing, runny eyes, and puffy faces. The dried pollen was also a first-rate itching powder, as small boys soon learned. The Fox remembered a thrashing his brother Dagref had given him over a pair of sneezeweed-impregnated breeches.

At last he found a ragged sneezeweed plant huddling under two bigger bushes, its shiny, dark green leaves sadly bug-eaten. He murmured a prayer of thanks to Dyaus when he saw a spike of pink flowers still clinging to it. It would serve for the small magic he had in mind.

He ran the spell over and over in his head, hoping he still had it memorized. It was simple enough, and one all 'prentices learned—a fine joke on the unwary. At the Sorcerers' Collegium, one quickly learned not to be unwary.

He held the spray of sneezeweed flowers in his left hand and began to chant. His right hand moved through the few simple passes the spell required. It took less than a minute. When it was done, he looked up and awaited developments.

For a moment, nothing happened. He wondered if he had botched the incantation or if it simply was not strong enough to reach the high-flying eagle. Then the bird seemed to stagger in mid-flight. Its head darted under its wing to peck furiously. No longer could it maintain its effortless rhythm through the air, but fought without success to maintain altitude. It descended in an ungainly spiral, screaming its rage all the while, and flopped into the bushes about twenty paces from the wagon. Van put an arrow through it. It died still snapping at the shaft.

Much pleased with himself, the Fox trotted over to collect the carcass. He had just brought it to the wagon when Elise cried out in warning. Two more red eagles were diving out of the morning sky, stooping like falcons. Van had time for one hasty shot. He missed. Cursing foully, he snatched up the whip and swung it in a terrible arc. It smashed into one bird with a sound like a thunderclap. Feathers flew in a metallic cloud. The eagle gave a despairing screech and tumbled to the roadway.

The other one flew into Gerin's surprised arms.

It fastened its claw on the leather sleeve of his corselet, seeming to think the garment part of its owner. The Fox plunged his free hand at its shining breast, trying to keep its bill from his eyes. It screamed and bucked, buffeting him with vile-smelling wings.

There was a crunch. Van drove the butt end of the whip into the eagle's head, again and again. The mad gleam in its golden eyes faded. Gerin slowly realized he was holding a dead weight. Blood trickled down his arm; that leather sleeve had not altogether protected him.

A gleam of silver caught his eye. The bird wore a tiny button at its throat, held on by a fine chain. The button bore only one mark: a fylfot. "Balamung, sure enough," Gerin muttered.

Van peered at it over his shoulder. "Let me have a closer look at that, will you?" he said. Gerin slipped the chain from the dead eagle's neck and passed it to him. He hefted it thoughtfully. "Lighter than it should be." He squeezed it between thumb and finger, grunting at the effort. "Gives a little, but not enough." He brought down a booted foot club-fashion.There was a thin, hissing wail. Gerin gagged. He thought of latrines, of new-dug graves fresh uncovered, of scummed moats, of long slow evils fermenting deep in the bowels of swamps and oozing upwards to burst as slimy bubbles.

The body in his arms writhed, though he knew it was, knew it had to be, dead. He looked down, and dropped his burden with an exclamation of horror. No longer was the corpse that of an eagle, but of a Trokmê, his head battered to a pulp, fiery locks soaked in blood. But ... the broken body was no bigger than the bird had been. Grim-faced, he and Van repeated the grisly experiment twice more, each time with the same result.

As he buried the three tiny bodies in a common grave, the pride he had felt in his sorcerous talent drained away like wine from a broken cup. What good were his little skills against such power as Balamung possessed, power that could rob men of their very shapes and send them winging over hundreds of miles to slay at his bidding?

Elise said, "It will take a mighty southern mage indeed to overcome such strength." Her voice was somber, but somehow her words, instead of depressing the baron, lifted his spirits. They reminded him he would not, after all, have to face Balamung alone. More and more, their conflict was assuming in his mind the nature of a duel between himself and the northern wizard, a duel in which the Trokmê owned most of the weapons. But why was he here in the southlands, if not for allies?

"You have a gift for saying the right thing," he told

her gratefully. She shook her head in pretty confusion. He did not explain. As the day wore on, he felt better and better. True, Balamung had tried to slay him from afar, but twice now his efforts had come to nothing, and every hour put more miles between him and his quarry.

Late in the afternoon, Van pointed to a hand-sized roadside shrub not much different from its neighbors and said, "You know some plant-lore, Gerin—there's another useful plant for you."

"That?" the Fox said. "It looks like any other weed to me."

"Then you Elabonians don't know what to do with it. It grows out on the plains of Shanda, too. The shamans there call it 'aoratos,' which means it lets you see a bit of the unseen when you chew the leaves. Not only that, they help keep you awake on watch. Like I said, a useful plant."

"What do you mean, 'it lets you see a bit of the unseen'?"

"That's the only way I can explain it, captain. Hold up a moment, and I'll let you see for yourself." Van uprooted the little bush and returned to the wagon. Gerin studied the plant curiously, but it was so nondescript he could not say whether he had seen its like before.

He got to test its properties soon enough, for he drew first watch that night. The leaves were gritty and bitter. Their juice burned as he swallowed. Little by little, he felt his tiredness slip away. As he sat sentinel, the night came alive around him.

The sky seemed to darken; Elleb, just past first quarter, shone with spectral clarity. So, when she rose, did Math, a day past full. The stars also seemed very bright and clear.

But that was the least effect of the aoratos plant. The Fox found he could tell with certainty where

every live thing lurked within a hundred yards of the
fire. No matter how well concealed it was, its life
force impinged on him like a spot of light seen in the
back of his mind.

He understood why Van had had trouble talking
about the experience—it seemed to use a sense his
body did not normally employ. He was even able to
detect strange patterns of radiance within the ghosts,
though their flickering shapes remained indistinct as
ever.

The extra perception gradually faded, and was gone
well before midnight. On the whole, he decided, he
approved of the aoratos plant. If nothing else, it made
ambushes nearly impossible. "Aye, it does that," Van
nodded when Gerin told him of his feelings, "but you
have to use near half the plant at every dose. The
gods know when we'll see another here. I never did
find one in the northlands, you know."

Nor did they find another aoratos bush the following day, or the next, or the next. The last of its leaves
stripped, the little plant was tossed away and all but
forgotten. As the road swung east, down into the great
plain whose heart was Elabon's capital, Gerin found
he had more important things to think about. The dry
warmth of the south, the quality of the sunlight pouring down from the sky, and the bustling people of the
ever more numerous towns were calling forth a side
of his nature he had had to hide on the frontier, a
gentler side his vassals would only have construed as
weakness.

Drago or Rollan could never have understood his
open admiration of a sunset; his search for verses
from Lekapenos appropriate to its beauty; his easy,
friendly dealing with merchants and innkeepers, men
at whom they would simply have barked orders. He
felt like a flower, half of whose petals were seeing the
sun for the first time in years.

The presence of Elise beside him was a pleasant pain. She unsettled him more than he was willing to admit, even to himself. He was too conscious of her as a woman to bring back all the ease of talk they had once enjoyed. She stayed warm and friendly, but deftly avoided anything truly personal, seeming content with the inconclusive status quo. Her warmth extended farther than the Fox, too; her laughing responses to Van's outrageous flirtation grated on Gerin's nerves.

Two days out from the capital, the travelers found lodging at a tavern in a little town called Cormilia. The lass who served them there was short, dark, and, though a bit plump, quite pretty; a tiny mole on her right cheek made her round face piquant.

Something about her struck the Fox's fancy. When he raised an eyebrow at her, she winked back saucily. He was not surprised when she tapped at his door later that night. While her thighs clasped him, she seemed hot-blooded enough for any man's taste. But her ministrations, immensely pleasant in the moment, somehow left him less than satisfied after she slipped away.

He knew he had pleased her. Her adoring manner the next morning spoke of how much. But the coupling only showed him the emptiness within himself. He was preoccupied and curt, and breakfasted without much noticing what he ate.

When he and Van went out to the stable to hitch up the horses, he blurted, "You know, when Dyaus created women he must have been in a fey mood. You can't live with them and sure as sure can't live without them."

Though surmise gleamed in Van's eye, he said nothing to that. He knew Gerin was a man who had to work things through in his own mind and often thought advice interference.

A briny breeze from the Greater Inner Sea blew all day. They might have made the capital by evening. But Gerin did not relish trying in the dark to find his old friend Turgis' inn; the great city's maze of streets was bad enough by day.

The coming parting with Elise also wrenched him more each mile he traveled. He was far from eager to speed it unduly. He decided to camp just in front of the last low ridge shielding the capital from sight. As darkness fell, the city's lights put a glow on the eastern horizon and bleached fainter stars from the sky.

In an area so densely peopled, night travel was no longer unthinkable. A brightly lit convoy of wagons and chariots rumbled past the campsite every few minutes, often with a mumbling priest to help ward off the spirits.

Of this Van heard nothing, for he fell asleep almost instantly. But Gerin did not pass his watch in lonely contemplation. For the first time since the night Mavrix appeared, Elise decided to stay up a while and talk. The reason soon became clear: she was bubbling over with excitement and curiosity about the capital and the family in it she had never seen.

She gushed on for a time, then stopped, embarrassed. "But this is terrible! What a loon I am! Here I play the magpie over all I'll see and do in the city, and not a word of thanks to you, who brought me here safe through so many troubles. What must you think of me?"

The answer to that had been slowly forming in the baron's mind ever since he helped her slip from Ricolf's keep. Her rhetorical question but served to bring it into sharper focus. He replied hesitantly, though, for fear of her thinking he was abusing the privilege their companionship had given him. "It's simple enough," he said at last, taking the plunge—

the thought of losing her forever filled him with more dread than any Trokmê horde. "After Balamung and his woodsrunners are driven back to the forests where they belong, nothing would make me happier than coming south again so I can court you properly."

He did not know what reaction he had expected from her—certainly not the glad acceptance she showed. "As things are now, I cannot say as much as I would like," she said, "but nothing would please me more." Her lips met his in a gentle kiss that gave him more contentment than all his sweaty exertions the night before in Cormilia. She went on, "Foolish man, did you not know I cried last year when I learned your wound would keep you from coming to my father's holding?"

He held her close, his mind filling with a hundred, a thousand foolish plans for the future. The rest of the watch flew by like a dream, as it would have for any lover who suddenly found his love returned. If Balamung's gaunt figure stood like a jagged reef between him and his dreams, on this night he would pretend he did not see it.

Elise fought sleep until Math rose to add her light to that of Elleb, whose nearly full disc rode high in the south. The baron watched her face relax into slumber, murmured, "Sleep warm," and kissed her forehead. She smiled and stirred, but did not wake.

When Gerin told Van what he had done, the outlander slapped his back, saying, "And what took you so long?"

The Fox grunted, half annoyed his friend had been able to follow his thoughts so well. Something else occurred to him. "We need to start right at sunrise tomorrow," he said.

"What? Why?" Van did not seem to believe his ears.

"I have my reasons."

"They must be good ones, to make a slugabed like you want an early start. All right, captain, sunrise it is."

They topped the last rise just as the sun climbed over the eastern horizon. It flamed off the Greater Inner Sea and transformed the water to a lambent sheet of fire, dazzling to the eye. Tiny black dots on that expanse were ships: merchantmen with broad sails billowing in the fresh morning breeze and arrogant galleys striding over the waves like outsized spiders on oared legs.

Elise, who had never seen the sea, cried out in wonder and delight. She squeezed Gerin's hand. The Fox beamed, proud as if he'd created the vista himself. Van also nodded his appreciation. "Very nice, captain, very nice," he told the baron.

"If that's all you can find to say, you'd likely say the same if Farris herself offered to share your bed."

"She's your goddess of love and such things?" At Gerin's nod, Van went on, "I'll tell you, Fox, that reminds me of a story—"

"Which I'll hear some other time," Gerin said firmly. Straight ahead, on a spur of land thrusting out into the sea, lay Elabon's capital. All his attention centered there.

A thousand years before, he knew, it had been nothing but a farming village. Then the Sithonians came west across the Sea, and the infant city, now a center for Sithonian trade with the folk they deemed barbarous westerners, acquired its first wall. Its inhabitants learned much from the Sithonians. Little by little it extended its sway over the fertile western plain, drawing on ever greater reserves of men and resources. Soon it swallowed up the Sithonian colonies on the western shore of the Greater Inner Sea.

Nor could the Sithonians come to the aid of those colonies, for Sithonia itself, divided into rival confederacies led by its two greatest city-states, Siphnos and Kortys, fell into a century of bloody civil war. All the while, Elabon waxed. No sooner had Kortys at last beaten down her rival than she had to face the army of Carlun World-Bestrider, whose victory ended the Elabonian League and began the Empire of Elabon. A great marble statue of him, ten times as high as a man, still looked east from the shore. It was easy to spy, silhouetted against the bright sea.

Not far away from Carlun's monument stood the Palace Imperial. Gleaming like an inverted icicle, it shot a spearpoint of marble and crystal to the sky. An eternal fire burned at its apex, a guide from afar to ships on the Inner Sea. Round it was a wide space of well-trimmed gardens, so the palace itself almost seemed a plant grown from some strange seed.

Near the palace was the nobles' quarters; their homes were less imposing by far than the Emperor's residence, but most were far more splendid than anything north of the Kirs.

To Gerin's mind, though, the rest of Elabon was the Empire's true heart. Men of every race and tribe dwelt there; it boiled and bubbled cauldron-wise with the surge of life through its veins. There was a saying that you could buy anything in Elabon, including the fellow who sold it to you.

The Fox could have gazed on the city for hours, but from behind a gruff bass voice roared, "Move it there, you whoreson! Do you want to diddle the whole day away?" The speaker was a merchant, a loudly unhappy one.

Gerin waved back at him. "This is the first time I've seen Elabon in eight years," he apologized.

The merchant was not appeased. "May it be your last, then, ever again. You stand gawking, you boy-loving booby, and here I am, trying to make an honest living from tight-fisted nobles and little bandit lordlings, and all my thirty wagons are piling into each other while you crane your fool neck. I ought to set my guards on you, and it's a mark of my good temper and restraint that I don't. Now move it!"

Gerin twitched the reins and got the horses moving. Van chuckled. "Fellow sounds like a sergeant I knew once."

Like any town south of the mountains, Elabon had its ring of crucifixes. Because of the city's size, the crosses made a veritable forest. Bright-winged gulls from off the Inner Sea squabbled with ravens and vultures over the dead meat on them. The stench was overpowering. Elise produced a wisp of scented cloth and pressed it to her nose. Gerin wished for one of his own.

Expanding through long years of security, the capital had outgrown three walls. Two had vanished altogether, their bricks and stones going to swell the growth. Only a low ridge showed where the rammed-earth core of the third had stood.

Gerin took the wagon down the city's main street. The locals affectionately called it the Alley; it ran due east, arrow-straight, from the outskirts of the capital to the docks, and was filled with markets and shops from one end to the other. The Fox drove past the Lane of Silversmiths (a trade Kizzuwatnans dominated), the pottery mart where Sithonians and Elabonians cried their wares, odorous eateries serving the fare of every nation subject or neighbor to the Empire, the great canvas-roofed emporium where wheat imported from the northern shore of the Inner Sea was sold, a small nest of armorers and smiths (the baron had to promise Van they would come back later), and so much else he began to feel dizzy trying to take it all in at once.

Beggars limped, prostitutes of both sexes jiggled and pranced, scribes stood at the ready to write for illiterate patrons, minstrels played on every corner, and, no doubt, thieves lurked to despoil them of the coins they earned. Running, shouting lads were everywhere underfoot. Gerin marveled that any of them lived to grow up. He pricked up his ears when he heard one shouting, "Turgis!" His head swiveled till he spied the boy.

"Snatch him, Van!" He steered toward his target, talking the horses to calm in chaos.

"Right you are, captain." Van reached out and grabbed up a ragamuffin whose first beard was just beginning to sprout.

"You can lead us to Turgis?" Gerin demanded.

"I can, sir, and swear by all the gods and goddesses no finer hostel than his exists anywhere."

"Spare me the glowing promises. I'm known to Turgis. Tell me, lad, how is the old butterball?"

"He's well enough my lord, indeed he is, and generous of food, though sparing of praises. You turn left here, sir," he added.

Within moments, Gerin was lost in the maze of the capital. He did not think Turgis' hostel had formerly been in this district; the old fraud must have moved. His guide, who called himself Jouner, gave directions mixed with shrill abuse directed at anyone who dared block the narrow, winding back streets. The abuse often came back with interest.

Jouner was also extravagantly admiring of his charges—especially Elise. She blushed and tried to wave him to silence, not recognizing that his manner was part professional courtesy. Still, the Fox heard sincerity in the lad's voice, too.

Most of the houses in this part of the city were two-storied, flat-roofed structures. Their whitewashed outer walls defined the twisting paths of its streets. Despite occasional obscenities scrawled in charcoal, from the outside one was much like another. But within the austerity, Gerin knew, would be courtyards bright with flowers and cheerfully painted statuary. Some, perhaps, would be enlivened further by floor mosaics or intricately patterned carpets woven by the Urfa.

Poorer folk lived in apartment houses: "islands," in Elabon's slang. Solid and unlovely, the brick buildings towered fifty and sixty feet into the air, throwing whole blocks of houses into shadow. More than once, jars of slops emptied from some upper window splashed down into the street, sending passersby running for cover. "Watch it!" Van bellowed up. An instant later, two more loads just missed the wagon.

"That's one of the first things you learn to watch for here," Gerin told him, remembering his own experience. "They hold the high ground."

When at last the travelers came to Turgis' establishment, the baron was agreeably surprised by the marble columns on either side of the entranceway and the close-cropped lawn in front of the hostel itself. "Go right in," Jouner said, scrambling down. "I'll see to your horses and wagon."

"Many thanks, lad," Gerin said as he descended. He gave the boy a couple of coppers, then helped Elise down, taking the opportunity to hug her briefly.

"Have a care with that Shanda horse," Van warned Jouner. "He snaps."

The boy nodded. As he began to head for the stable, Elise said, "A moment. Jouner, how do you live in this stench?"

Puzzlement crossed Jouner's face. "Stench, my lady? What stench? Travelers always complain about it, but I don't notice a thing."

Turgis met the travelers at the front door. His bald pate, brown as the leather apron he wore, gleamed in the sunlight. A smile stretched across his fat face, the ends of it disappearing into a thick graying beard.

"You appear to have come up in the world a mite," Gerin said by way of greeting.

"Crave pardon, sir? No, wait, I know that voice, though you've had the wisdom to hide your face in hair." Turgis' grin widened. "A cocky young whelp by the name of Gerin, badly miscalled the Fox, not so?"

"Aye, it is, you old bandit. Also Van of the Strong Arm and the lady Elise."

Turgis bobbed a bow. "You have a most lovely wife, Fox."

"The lady is not my wife," Gerin said.

"Oh? My lord Van—?"

"Nor mine." Van grinned.

"Oh? Ho, ho!" Turgis laid a finger alongside his nose and winked.

Elise spluttered indignation.

"Not that either," Gerin said. "It's a long story, and more complicated than I like."

"I daresay it must be. Well, it would honor me if you tell it."

"You'll hear it before the day is done, never fear. Turgis, it does my heart good to see you again, and to know you've not forgotten me."

"I, Turgis son of Turpin, forget a friend? Never!"

Gerin had hoped for that opening. "Then no doubt you recall just as well the promise you made the night I left the city."

The smile disappeared from Turgis' face. "What promise was that, lord Gerin? We both looked into our cups too often that night, and it was a long time ago."

"You won't wriggle out as easy as that, you saucy robber. You know as well as I, you gave me an oath if ever I came this way again I'd have my rooms for the same rate as I had them then!"

"What? You insolent whelp, this is a whole new building—or had your oh-so-perfect memory not

noticed that? Are you fain to hold me to a drunken
vow? May your fundament fall out! And the way
prices have risen! Why, I could weep great buckets
and your flinty heart would not be so much as—"

"An oath, damn your eyes, an oath!" Gerin said.
Both men were laughing now.

Turgis talked right through him."—softened. Think
of my wife! Think of my children! My youngest son
Egginhard would study wizardry, and for such school,
nothing less than which is his heart's desire, much
silver is needed."

"If he would be a conjurer, let him magic it up,
and not have his father steal it."

"Think of my poor maiden aunt!" Turgis wailed.

"When I was here last, your poor maiden aunt
ran the biggest gambling den in the city, you blood-
sucker. An oath, remember?"

"As my head lives, only a third more would satisfy
me—"

"On that your head would live entirely too well.
Would you be known as Turgis the Oathbreaker?"

"May all the grapes in every vineyard you own turn
sour!"

"Don't own any at all, truth to tell: too far north.
Is your memory jogged yet?"

Turgis hopped on one foot, hopped on the other
foot, plucked a gray hair from his beard, and sighed
heavily. "All right, I recollect. Bah! The innkeeping
trade lost a great one when you became a pirate or
baron or whatever it is you do. I'm sure you're a
howling success. Now go howl and let me lick my
wounds—or do you carry courtesy so far?"

"What do you think, Van?" Gerin said.

His comrade had watched the altercation with
amusement. "Reckon so, captain, if your friend can
fix me up with a hot tub big enough for my bulk."

"Who dares call Turgis son of Turpin a friend of

this backwoods bandit? Were I half my age and twice my size, I'd challenge you for that. As is, however, go down this corridor. Third door on the left. You might follow him, Gerin; even your name stinks in my nostrils at this moment. And for you, my lady, we have somewhat more elegant arrangements. If you would care to follow me . . . ?"

Turgis led Elise off to whatever facilities he had for making beautiful women more so. She seemed as much captivated by the innkeeper as was Gerin himself; though this was a new building, the same atmosphere of comfort and good cheer the Fox had always known was here. Other hostels might have had more splendid accommodations, but none of them had Turgis.

The bath-houses masseur was a slim young Sithonian with outsized hands, arms, and shoulders. His name was Vatatzes. As if by magic, he had two steaming tubs ready and waiting. He helped Van unlace his corselet. When the outlander shed his bronze-studded leather kilt, Vatatzes, true to the predilections of his nation, whistled in awe and admiration.

"Sorry, my friend," Van chuckled, understanding him well enough. "Gerin and I both like women."

"You poor dears," Vatazes said. His disappointment did not stop him from kneading away the kinks of travel as the hot water soaked off grime. Swathed in linen towels and mightily relaxed, Gerin and Van emerged from the bath to find Jouner waiting outside. "I've taken the liberty of moving your gear to your rooms," he said. "Follow me if you would, sirs." He also offered to carry Van's cuirass but, as usual, the outlander declined to be parted from it even for a moment.

The rooms were on the second floor of the hostel. They offered a fine view of the Palace Imperial. A door which could be barred on either side gave access from one to the other. "Don't bother to put things away," Gerin told Jouner. "I'd sooner do it myself— that way I know where everything is."

"As you wish, my lord." Jouner pocketed a tip and disappeared.

Gerin surveyed the room. If nothing else, it was more spacious than the cubicle he had called his own during his former stay in the capital. Nor would he sleep on a straw pallet as he had then. He had a mattress and pillow, both stuffed with goosedown, and two thick wool blankets to ward off night's chill. By the bed were a jug, bowl, and chamberpot, all of Sithonian ware fine enough to be worth a small fortune north of the Kirs. A footstool, chair, and stout oaken chest completed the furnishings. On the chest were two fat beeswax candles and a shrine to Dyaus with a pinch of perfumed incense already smoking away. Above it hung an encaustic painting of a mountain scene done by a Sithonian homesick for his craggy native land.

The baron quickly unpacked and threw himself onto the bed, sighing with pleasure as he sank into its soft stuffing. Van rapped on the connecting door. "This is the life!" he said when Gerin let him in. "I haven't seen beds so fine since a bordello I visited in Jalor. I don't know about you, Fox, but I'm all for sacking out for a while. It's been a long, hard trip."

"I was thinking the same thing," Gerin told him. Yawning, Van went back into his own room. The baron knew he should go down to see how Elise liked her chamber in the women's quarters. Enervated from the hot bath and massage and tired from many nights with little sleep, he could not find the energy. . . .

The next thing he knew, Jouner was knocking on the door. "My lord," he called, "Turgis bids you join him in the taproom for supper in half an hour's time."

"Thanks, lad. I'll be there." Gerin yawned and stretched. He heard Jouner deliver the same message to Van, who eventually grumbled a reply.

It was a bit past sunset. Tiwaz's razor-thin crescent, almost invisible in the pink in the west.

The Fox splashed water on his face, then went rummaging through his gear for an outfit that might impress Turgis and, not incidentally, Elise. After some thought, he decided on a maroon tunic with sleeves flaring out from the elbows and checked trousers of contrasting shades of blue. A necklace of gold nuggets and a belt with a bronze buckle in the shape of a leaping longtooth (Shanda work, that) completed the outfit. Wishing for a mirror, he combed his hair and beard with a bone comb. *I look the very northerner*, he thought: *well, fair enough, that's what I am.* He set out for the taproom.

Folk of every race filled the high-ceilinged hall. Three musicians—flautist, piper, and mandolin-player— performed on a small stage at one end, but they were all but ignored. Every man's attention was on Turgis' cook.

A dark, burly fellow with hooked noise, bushy beard, and black hair drawn back into a bun, he worked behind a great bronze griddle in the center of the room, and in his own way was more a showman than the musicians. He kept up a steady stream of chatter about every dish he was preparing, and knives were quicker in his hands than in those of any warrior Gerin had ever seen. Its gleam reflecting off his sweaty face, bronze danced as if alive, shining in the torchlight, dicing vegetables and slicing meat with a rhythm of its own. No, not quite; with a small shock, Gerin realized the knives were providing a percussion accompaniment to the music from the stage.

A waiter hovering by his elbow, Turgis sat at a quiet corner table. He surged to his feet and embraced

Gerin, who pointed to the cook and asked, "Where did you find him?"

"He's something, isn't he?" Turgis beamed. "He's good for business, too. Just watching him makes people hungry." He turned to the server, saying, "Bring me my special bottle. You know the one I mean. Bring some ordinary good wine, too, and—hmm—four glasses."

The Fox's eyes widened. "That can't be the same 'special bottle' you used to keep when I was here before?"

"The very same, and not much lower, either. Where would I get another? You know as well as I that it was salvage from a ship of some unknown land that wrecked itself down in the southeast on the Bay of Parvela's rocks. Aye, it's precious stuff, my friend— see, I still call you that, highway robber though you be—but then how often do we look upon friends thought lost forever?"

"Not often enough."

"Truth in your words, truth in your words."

The waiter returned. Careful not to spill even one drop, Turgis worked at the cork of the flask they had been discussing. Even that flask was special: small and squat and silvery, like no other glass Gerin had seen. "Here it is," Turgis said. "Nectar of the sun."

Gerin had a sudden terrible fear that when Van came down, he would loudly announce he had traveled with whole shiploads of the brew. By rights, there should be no more than this one miraculous bottle.

At Turgis' murmured invitation, the baron enjoyed the rare drink's rich fragrance. A silence fell over the hall. For a moment, Gerin thought his nose's pleasure had made him ignore his other senses, but the quiet was real. He looked up. There in the doorway stood Van, helm and armor gleaming, crimson cloak over his shoulders matching helm's crest. He was a splendid sight: indeed, too splendid, for Gerin heard a mutter of superstitious marvel. "Come in and sit down, you great gowk," he called, "before everyone decides you're a god."

Van's earthy reply sent relieved laughter echoing through the room. The outlander joined his friend and his host. He looked with interest at the bottle Gerin still held. "Never seen glasswork like that before," he said, and the Fox, too, knew relief.

A few moments later, Elise arrived. The buzz of conversation in the taproom again lowered, this time in appreciation. As Gerin rose to greet her, he realized once more how fair she was. He had grown used to her in battered traveler's hat and sturdy but unlovely clothes. Now, in a clinging gown of sea-green linen, she was another creature altogether, and startlingly beautiful.

Turgis' servitors had subtly enhanced the colors of her eyes and lips, and worked her hair into a pile of fluffy curls. The style became her; it was popular in Elabon this year, and several other women in the hall wore their hair thus. The baron saw more than one jealous glance directed at Elise, and felt proud to have earned the affection of such a woman.

Turgis was also on his feet. He bowed and kissed Elise's hand. "The sunshine of my lady's beauty brightens my hostel," he exclaimed. When he saw he had flustered her, he added with a wink, "What in Dyaus' name do you see in this predacious lout who brought you here?" Put at her ease, she smiled and sat. Turgis poured a drop or two of his nectar of the sun into each of the four glasses, then resealed the flask. He raised his glass. "To past friendships now restored and successes yet to come!"

Everyone drank. Gerin felt the brew caress his tongue like smooth silk, like soft kisses. He heard

Van's hum of approval and was glad his far-traveled friend had found a new thing to enjoy.

Turgis poured again, this time from the local bottle. As Gerin's stomach began to growl, the waiter returned, bringing dinner just in time, he thought, to save him from starvation. The first course was a delicate clear soup, made flavorful by bits of pork and chopped scallion. It was followed by what Turgis called a "meat tile," which convinced the Fox that Turgis' cook was a genius as well as a showman: simmered and sautéed pieces of lamb and veal in a spicy sauce which also featured pounded lobster tail and nutmeats. Whole lobster tails garnished the incredible creation; Gerin had never tasted anything so delicious in his life. He could hardly look at the fruits and spun-sugar confections that came after. All the while, Turgis made sure no glass stayed empty long.

The baron's head was beginning to spin when Turgis announced, "Now I will have the tale of your coming here."

All three travelers told it, each amplifying the others' accounts. Gerin tried to slide through the tale of his fight with the aurochs, but to his annoyance Elise made him backtrack and tell it in full.

Turgis looked at him shrewdly. "Still carrying your lantern with a hood on it, are you?" He turned to Elise: "My lady, here we have the most talented of men, the only one who does not know it being himself. He can sing a song, cut a purse (even mine, the unprincipled highwayman!), tell you what that fingerlong bug is on friend Van's cuirass—and the cure for its bite as well—"

Snarling an oath, Van crushed the luckless insect. "No need for that," the Fox said. "It was only a walkingstick, and it doesn't bite at all; its sole food is tree sap."

"You see?" Turgis said triumphantly. The wine had

flushed his face and loosened his tongue. "He can conjure you up an ever-filled purse—"

"Of mud, perhaps," Gerin said, wishing Turgis would shut up. The innkeeper's paean of praise made him nervous. Most plaudits did; as a second son, he'd seldom got them and never quite worked out how to deal with them. He knew his virtues well enough, and knew one of the greatest was his ability to keep his mouth shut about them. They were often of most use when employed unexpectedly.

Turgis was not about to be quiet. "Besides all that," he said, "this northern ruffian is as kind and loyal a friend as one could ever hope for"—Elise and Van nodded solemnly—"and worth any three men you could name in a brawl. I well recall the day he flattened three rascals who thought to rob me, though he wasn't much more than a stripling himself."

"You never told me that one," Van said.

"They were just tavern toughs," Gerin said, "and this fellow here did a lot of the work. He's pretty handy with a broken bottle."

"Me?" Turgis said. "No one wants to hear about me, fat old slug that I am. What happened after the aurochs was slain?" The hosteler howled laughter to hear how Mavrix had been thwarted. "Truly, I love the god for his gift of the grape, but much of his cult gives me chills."

The baron quickly brought the journey down to the capital: too quickly, again, for Elise. She said, "Once more he leaves out a vital bit of the story. You see, as we traveled we came to care for each other more and more, try though he would to hide himself behind modesty and gloom." She gave him a challenging stare. He would not meet her eye, riveting his attention on his glass. She went on, "And so it's scarcely surprising that when he asked if he might come south to court me when the trouble is done, I was proud to say yes."

"Lord Gerin, my heartiest congratulations," Turgis said, pumping his hand. "My lady, I would offer you the same, but I grieve to think of your beauty passed on to your children diluted by the blood of this ape."

Gerin jerked his hand free of the innkeeper's grip. "A fine excuse for a host you are, to insult your guests."

"Insult? I thought I was giving you the benefit of the doubt." Turgis poured wine all around. A sudden commotion drowned out his toast. Two men who had been arguing over the company of a coldly beautiful Sithonian courtesan rose from their seats and began pummeling each other. Three husky waiters seized them and wrestled them out to the street.

Turgis mopped his brow. "A good thing they chose to quarrel now. The could have broken Osnabroc's concentration—see, here he comes!"

A rising hum of excitement and a few spatters of applause greeted Osnabroc, a short, stocky man whose every muscle was so perfectly defined that it might have been sculpted from stone. He wore only a black loincloth. In his hand he carried a pole about twenty feet long; a crosspiece had been nailed a yard or so from one end.

A pair of young women followed him. They, too, wore only loincloths, one of red silk, the other of green. Both had the small-breasted, taut-bellied look of dancers or acrobats; Gerin doubted if either was five feet tall.

The musicians vacated the stage and Osnabroc ascended. More torches were brought. Each girl took one and set the rest in brackets. After a sharp, short bow to his audience, Osnabroc arched his back and bent his head backwards, setting the pole on his forehead. He balanced it with effortless ease. At his command, both girls shinnied up the pole, torches in their teeth. Once at the crosspiece, they turned somersaults, flips, and other evolutions so astounding Gerin felt his heart rise into his throat. All the while, the pole stayed steady as a rock.

One girl slid down headfirst, leaving the other hanging by her knees twenty feet above the floor. But not for long—she flailed her arms once, twice, and then she was upright again, going through a series of yet more spectacular capers. Despite her gyrations, the supporting pole never budged. A grimace of concentration distorted Osnabroc's face; sweat ran streakily down his magnificent body.

"Who do you think has the harder job?" Turgis whispered to Gerin: "Osnabroc or his girls?"

"I couldn't begin to tell you," the baron answered.

Turgis laughed and nodded. "It's the same with me. I couldn't begin to tell you, either."

Van, though, had no doubts: his eyes were only on the whirling girl. "Just think," he said, half to himself, "of all the ways you could do it with a lass so limber! She all but flies."

"Speak to me not of people flying!" Turgis said as the second girl slid down the pole to a thunderous ovation. She skipped off the stage, followed by her fellow acrobat and Osnabroc. He sagged now as he walked, and his forehead looked puffy.

Van tried to catch the eye of one of the girls, but with no apparent luck. Disappointed, he turned his attention back to Turgis. "What do you have against people flying?" he asked.

"Nothing against it, precisely. It does remind me of a strange story, though." He waited to be urged to go on. His companions quickly obliged him. He began, "You've told me much of the Trokmoi tonight; this story has a Trokmê in it too. He was drunk, as they often are, and since the place was crowded that night, he was sharing a table with a wizard. You know how some folk, when they go too deep into a bottle, like to sing or whatever. Well, this lad flapped his arms like he was trying to take off and fly. Finally he knocked a drink from the wizard's hand, which was the wrong thing to do.

"The wizard paid his scot and walked out, and I thought I'd been lucky enough to escape trouble. But next thing I knew, the northerner started flapping again, and—may my private parts shrivel if I lie—sure enough he took off and flew around the room like a drunken buzzard."

"A boozard, maybe," Gerin suggested.

"I hope not," Turgis said.

"What befell?" Elise asked.

"He did, lass, on his head. He was doing a fine job of flying, just like a bird, but the poor sot smashed against that candelabra you see up there and fell right into someone's soup. He earned himself a knot on the head as big as an egg and, I hope, enough sense not to make another wizard annoyed at him.

"This tale-telling gets to be thirsty work," Turgis added, calling for another bottle of wine. But when he opened it and began to pour, Elise put a hand over her glass. A few minutes later she rose. Pausing only to bestow a hurried but warm kiss on Gerin, she made her way to her room.

The three men sat, drank, and talked a bit longer. Turgis said, "Gerin, you're no fool like that Trokmê was. You're the last man I ever would have picked to make a sorcerer your mortal foe."

"It was his choosing, not mine!" The wine had risen to Gerin's head, adding vehemence to his words. "The gods decreed I am not to be a scholar, as I had dreamed. So be it. Most of my bitterness is gone. There's satisfaction in holding the border against the barbarians, and more in making my holding a better place for all to live, vassals and serfs alike. Much of what I learned here has uses in the north: we no longer have wells near the cesspits, for instance, and we grow beans to refresh the soil. And, though my vassals know it not, I've taught a few of the brighter peasants to read."

"What? You have?" Van stared at the Fox as if he'd never seen him before.

"Aye, and I'm not sorry, either." Gerin turned back to Turgis. "We've had no famines round Fox Keep, despite two bad winters, and no peasant revolts either. Wizard or no wizard, no skulking savage is going to ruin all I've worked so hard to kill. He may kill me— the way things look now, he likely *will* kill me—but Dyaus knows he'll never run me off!"

He slammed his glass to the table with such violence that it shattered and cut his hand. The pain abruptly sobered him. Startled by his outburst, his friends exclaimed in sympathy. He sat silent and somber, staring at the thin stream of blood that welled from between his clenched fingers.

VIII

After the Alley's hurley-burley, the calm, nearly trafficless lanes of the nobles' quarter came as a relief. Jouner had given the Fox careful directions on how to find Elise's uncle's home. For a miracle, they proved good as well as careful.

Valdabrun the Stout lived almost in the shadow of the Palace Imperial. Despite his closeness to the Empire's heart, the grounds of his home were less imposing than those of many nobles in less prestigious areas. No carefully trimmed topiaries adorned his lawns, no statuary group stood frozen in mid-cavort. Nor did the drive from the road wind and twist its way to his house under sweetly scented trees. It ran directly to his front door, straight as the Elabon Way. The dominant impression his grounds gave was one of discipline and strength.

The baron hitched the horses. Van gave both beasts feedbags, eluding a snap from the Shanda pony. He cuffed it, grumbling, "Poxy animal would sooner have my hand than its oats."

Valdanbrun's door-knocker was a snarling bronze longtooth's head. Gerin grasped a fang, swung it up, then down. He had expected the knock to set off sorcerous chimes. Many southern nobles liked such conceits. But there was only the honest clang of metal on metal. After a stir inside, a retainer swung open the door. "Sirs, lady, how may I help you?" he asked crisply.

The man's speech and bearing impressed Gerin: he seemed more soldier than servitor. "Is your master in?" the Fox asked.

"Lord Valdabrun? No, but I expect him back shortly. Would you care to wait?"

"If you would be so kind."

"This way, then." Executing a smart about-turn, the steward led them to a rather bare antechamber. He briefly saw to their comfort, then said, "If you will excuse me, I have other duties to perform." He left through another door; Gerin heard him bar it after himself.

A woman's voice, low and throaty, came from behind the door. Gerin could not make out her words, but heard the steward reply, "I know not, lady Namarra. They did not state their business, nor did I inquire deeply."

"I will see them," the woman said.

The bar was lifted. Valdabrun's man announced, "Sirs, lady, my lord Valdabrun's, ah, companion, the lady Namarra," and went off.

As Namarra entered, Van sprang to his feet. Gerin was only a blink behind. No matter what he felt toward Elise, Valdabrun's companion was, quite simply, the most spectacular woman he had every seen: tiny, catlike, and exquisite. The clinging silk she wore accented her figure's lushness.

Her hair, worn short and straight, was the color of flame. Like a fire, it seemed to give out more light than fell on it. Yet for all that incandescent hair, she was no Trokmê woman; her face was soft, rounded, and small-featured, her skin golden brown. Her eyes, a slightly darker shade of gold, were subtly slanted but rounded as if in perpetual surprise; the strange combination, more than anything save perhaps her purring name, made Gerin think her feline. She wore no jewelry—she herself was ornament enough, and more.

She studied the Fox with some interest, Van with a good deal more, and Elise with the wary concern one gave any dangerous beast suddenly found in the parlor. Out of the corner of his eye, Gerin saw Elise returning that look. He felt a twinge of alarm.

Namarra swept out a lithe arm to point at the baron. "You are—?"

He introduced himself and Van, and was on the point of naming Elise when he was interrupted: "And your charming, ah, companion?" Namarra used the same deliberately ambiguous intonation the steward had applied to her.

Voice dangerously calm, Elise replied, "I am Elise, Ricolf's daughter." The Fox noticed she made no claim of relationship to Valdabrun.

The name of Elise's father meant nothing to Namarra. She turned back to Gerin. "May I ask your business with my lord?"

The baron was not sure how to reply. He had no idea how much of the noble's confidence and trust his woman enjoyed. He was framing an equivocal answer when a door slammed at the back of the house. Seconds later, the steward reappeared, to announce his master's presence.

"Enough of this foolishness. Let me by," Valdabrun the Stout said as he surged into the antechamber.

Gerin hastily revised his notion of what the noble's sobriquet implied. Valdabrun was edging toward fifty, balding, and did in fact carry a considerable paunch, but the Fox was sure he would break fingers if he rammed a fist into it. Shaven face or no, here was a soldier, and no mistake. Hard eyes, firm mouth, the set of his chin all bespoke a man long used to command. Nor was he slow to see he faced two of his own breed.

The air in the room crackled as the three strong men took one another's measure. Each in his own way was a warrior to reckon with: Gerin supple, clever, always waiting for a foe to expose a flaw; Van, who fought with a berserker's delight and a drillmaster's elegance; and their host, who reminded the Fox of one of Carlun's or Ros' great captains: a man with scant polish or flair, but possessed of an almost brutal indomitability, the very concept of retreat alien to him.

The tableau held for long seconds. Elise shattered it, exclaiming "Uncle!" and throwing herself into Valdabrun's startled arms. The stern expression dropped from his face, to be replaced by one of utter bafflement.

Namarra's face changed, too. Her eyes narrowed; her lips drew back, exposing white, pointed teeth. A cat she was, and feral. She laid a hand on Valdarun's arm. "My lord—" she began.

"Be still, my dear," he said, and she *was* still, though restive. Gerin's respect for him grew. He untangled himself from Elise. "Young lady, you will explain yourself," he told her, still in that tone of command.

She was as matter-of-fact as he. "Of course. As I told your leman"—Namarra bristled, but held her tongue—"I'm Elise, daughter of Ricolf the Red—and your sister Yrse. My mother always said you would know this locket." She drew it up from between her breasts, freed it of its chain, and handed it to Valdabrun.

He examined it at arm's length; his sight had begun to lengthen, as it often does in the middle years. His face softened, as much as that craggy countenance could. "Yrse's child!" he said softly. This time, he folded her into a bearlike embrace.

Behind his back, Namarra's expression was frightening.

Elise introduced Gerin and Van to Valdabrun. "I've heard of you, sirrah," he told the Fox: "One of those who never pay their taxes, aye?"

"I pay them in blood," Gerin answered soberly.

Valdabrun surprised him by nodding. "So you do, youngling, so you do." He exchanged a bone-wrenching handclasp with Van that left both big men wincing, then announced, "Now I will have the tale of your coming here." He visibly composed himself to listen.

As they had the night before to Turgis, the three of them told their story. "I never thought that hare-brained scheme would work," Valdabrun observed when Elise spoke of her father's plan to find her a husband.

The noble proved a far more skeptical audience than Turgis had, firing probing questions at Gerin on Balamung's wizardry, politics in the northlands, Mavrix's cultists, and whatever else caught his interest.

"Well, well," he said at last. "The whole thing is so unlikely I suppose it must be true. Child, you are welcome to stay with me as long as you like." He told his steward to take her gear from the wagon, then turned to Namarra, who appeared less than delighted at his niece's arrival. "Kitten, show Elise around while I talk with these rogues."

"Of course. We can talk as we go. Come, child." In Namarra's red-lipped mouth, the word was poisonously sweet.

"That would be wonderful," Elise answered. "I've always wanted to talk to a woman of your, ah, experience." A tiny smile on her face, she kissed Van and Gerin, fiercely hugged the Fox, and whispered, "This will be hard. Hurry back, *please!*" She followed Namarra out. When the door closed behind her, Gerin felt the sunshine had left the day.

Valdabrun seemed oblivious to the byplay between the two women. That proved again to the baron that he was more used to the field than to the imperial court's intrigues. After his niece and mistress were gone, he said bluntly, "Fox, if half what you've said is true, your arse is in a sling."

"I'd be lying if I said I liked the odds," Gerin agreed.

"Advice from me would be nothing but damned impertinence right now, so I'll give you none. But I will say this: if any man is slippery enough to slide through this net, you may be that man. Yet you seem to have kept your honor too. I'm glad of it, for my niece's—how strange that seems!—sake." He shifted his attention to Van. "Could I by any chance persuade you to join the Imperial Guard?" His smile showed he knew the question foolish before he asked it.

Van shook his head; the plume of his helm swayed gently. "You're not like most of the popinjays here, Valdabrun. You seem a fighting man. So you tell me: where will I find better fighting than with the Fox?"

"There you have me," Valdabrun said. "Gentlemen, I would like nothing more than talking the day away over a few stoups of wine, but I must get back to the palace. The Eshref clan out of Shanda have forced a pass in the Skleros Mountains, and their brigands are plundering northern Sithonia. His imperial majesty thinks paying tribute will get them to leave. I have to persuade him otherwise."

"The Eshref?" Van said. "Is Gaykhatu still their chief?"

"I believe that was the name, yes. Why?"

"Send troops," the outlander said decisively. "He'll run. I knew him out on the plains, and he always did."

"You knew him on the plains . . ." Valdabrun shook his head. "I won't ask how or when, but I do give thanks for the rede—and when I talk with his imperial majesty, I'll term it 'expert testimony' or some such tripe. Dyaus, what drivel I've had to learn in the past year or so!"

As Van and Gerin drove away from Valdabrun's home, the baron was heavy-hearted over parting from Elise, necessary though he knew it was. Van, on the other hand, was full of lickerish praise for Namarra and lewd speculation on the means Valdabrun, who was certainly no beauty, used to keep her at his side. His sallies grew so unlikely and so comical that Gerin finally had to laugh with him.

"Where now?" Van asked as the Alley's turmoil surrounded them once more.

"The Sorcerers' Collegium. It's in the southwestern part of the city, near the apothecaries' district. I should know when to turn."

But he did not. He never learned whether the building he sought as a marker was torn down or if he had simply forgotten its looks in the eight years since he'd seen it last. Whichever, before long he knew he had gone too far west along the Alley. He turned to passersby for directions.

At first he got no responses save shrugs and a few vaguely pointing fingers. Realizing his mistake, he tossed a copper to the first halfway intelligent-looking fellow he spied. The man's instructions were so artfully phrased, accompanied by such eloquent gestures, that Gerin listened as if spellbound. He had all he could do to keep from applauding. Instead, he gave his benefactor another coin.

The man's thanks would have drawn an aurochs into a temple.

Unfortunately, the Sorcerers' Collegium was nowhere near where he claimed. Gerin expended more coppers and most of his patience before he finally found it.

There was nothing outwardly marvelous about the building that housed it, a gray brick "island" not much different from scores of others in the capital. But it was discreetly segregated from its neighbors by a broad smooth expanse of lawn. None of the nearby buildings had a window that faced the Collegium. They only gave it blank walls of stucco, timber, or brick, perhaps fearing the sorceries emanating from it.

Though the Collegium accepted students only from within the Empire, folk of various races called on it for services. Many odd vehicles and beasts were tied in front of it; to his horses' alarm, Gerin hitched the wagon next to a camel some Urfa had ridden up from the desert.

No sooner had he done so than three muscular individuals appeared and asked if the gentlemen in the wagon would pay them to watch it. "I'll see you in the hottest firepit in the five hells first," Gerin said genially. "You know as well as I, the Collegium has spells to keep thieves away from its clients."

The largest of the bravos, a fellow who would have been a giant beside anyone but Van, shrugged and grinned. "Sorry, boss," he said, "but the two of you looked such rubes, it was worth the chance."

"Now you know better, so be off with you." After exchanging a final good-natured insult with the baron, the ruffians ambled away, looking for less worldly folk to bilk. Gerin shook his head. "When I was a student the same sort of rascals were about, preying on strangers."

Inside the Collegium the ground floor was lit, mundanely enough, by torches. Some of them flared crimson, green, or blue, but that was the simplest of tricks, scarcely sorcery at all, merely involving the use of certain powdered earths. A greater magic kept the chamber free of smoke but let the nose detect the pinches of delicate incense burning in tiny braziers set along the walls and mounted on the sturdy granite columns that supported the Collegium's upper stories.

The procedures on the ground floor of the Collegium reminded Gerin of nothing so much as those of the Imperial Bank. Orderly lines of clients snaked their way toward young mages seated at tables along the north wall. Once there, they explained their problems in low voices. Most were helped on the spot, but from time to time a wizard would send one elsewhere, presumably to deal with someone more experienced.

Van bore queueing up with poor grace: "I don't fancy all this standing about."

"Patience," Van said. "It's a trick to overawe people. The longer you have to wait, the more important you think whoever you're waiting for is."

"Bah." Van made as if to spit on the floor, but changed his mind. It was too beautiful to soil: an abstract mosaic of tiny glass tesserae of silver, lilac, and sea-green, glittering in the torchlight.

The man in front of them finally reached a wizard and poured out his tale of woe like a spilled jug of wine, glug, glug, glug. At last the wizard exclaimed, "Enough! Enough! Follow this"—a blob of pink foxfire appeared in front of the startled fellow's nose— "and it will lead you to someone who can help you." He turned to Gerin and Van, said courteously, "And what my I do for you gentlemen? You may call me Avelmir; my true name, of course, is hidden."

Avelmir was younger than Gerin, his round, smoothly shaved face smiling and open. His familiar, a fat gray lizard about a foot long, rested on the table in front of him. Its yellow eyes gave back Gerin's stare unwinkingly. When Avelmir stroked its scaly skin, it arched its back in pleasure.

Gerin told his story. When he was done, Avelmir's smile had quite gone. "You pose a difficult problem, sir baron, and one in which I am not sure we can render timely assistance. Let me consult here . . ." He glanced down at a scrap of parchment. "We are badly understaffed, as you must be aware, and I fear we shall be unable to send anyone truly competent north of the Kirs before, hmm, seventy-five to eighty days."

"What!" Gerin's bellow of outrage whipped heads around. "In that time I'll be dead, with my keep and most of the northland aflame for my pyre!"

Avelmir's manner grew chillier yet. "We find ourselves under heavy obligations in the near future, the nature of which I do not propose to discuss with you. If you do not care to wait for our services against your barbarous warlock, hire some northern bungler, and may you have joy of him. Good day, sir."

"You—" Outrage choked the Fox.

The battle-gleam kindled in Van's eyes. "Shall I break the place apart a bit, captain?"

"I would not try that," Avelmir said quietly.

"And why not?" Van tugged at his sword. It came halfway free, then struck. He roared a curse. Avelmir's hands writhed through passes. When Gerin tried to stop him, the reptilian familiar puffed itself up to twice its size and jumped at him. He drew back, not sure if it was venomous.

Sweat started forth on Van's forehead, and an

instant later on Avelmir's. The outlander gained an inch, lost it again. Then more and more blade began to show. At last it jerked clear. With a howl of triumph, Van raised his sword arm.

Gerin grabbed it with both hands. For a moment, he thought he would be lifted off the floor and swung with the blade. But reason returned to Van's face. The outlander relaxed.

Avelmir had the look of a man who'd fished for minnows and caught a shark. Into the dead silence of the great chamber, he said, "We must see if a way can be found. Follow this."

A blue foxfire globe popped into being an inch in front of Gerin's nose. Startled, he took a step backwards. The foxfire hurried away, like a man on an important errand. Gerin and Van followed.

The ball of light led them down a steep spiral stairway into the bowels of the Collegium. Gerin's excitement grew; here, he knew, the potent sorceries were undertaken. When he was a student, he had been restricted to the upper floors. As the eerie guide led him down echoing corridors, he realized for the first time how much of the Collegium was underground— and how little he had understood its true extent.

He and Van passed doors without number. Most were shut; more than one bore runes of power to ensure it stayed so. Many of the open ones were innocuous: a smithy, a chamber in which glassblowers created vessels of curious shapes and sizes, a crowded library. But a winged, tailed demon thrashed within a pentacle in one room. It glared at the Fox with fiery eyes; its stench followed him down the hall.

"What do you suppose would happen if we didn't choose to follow our magical guide?" Van said.

"Nothing good, I'm sure."

The foxfire winked out in front of a closed door.

Gerin knocked; there was no reply. He lifted the latch. The door silently swung open.

The chamber was far underground and held no lamps, but it was not dark. A soft silvery gleam which had no apparent source suffused it. Behind a curiously carven ebony table sat an old wizard who looked up from some arcane computation when the privacy of his cubicle was breached. His amber silk robes rustled as he moved.

He nodded to Gerin and Van. "If you need a name for me, call me Sosper." That was clearly a pseudonym, for he was no Sithonian. Though his phrases were polished, he spoke with a western accent; he must have been born somewhere on the long peninsula that jutted into the Orynian Ocean.

He smiled at Van. "No need to keep hand on hilt, my friend. It will avail you nothing, as I am no child in shaping spells of sealing." The outlander, confident as always in his own strength, tried to draw. His sword was frozen fast. Gerin would have believed Sosper without test; the man radiated power as a bonfire radiates heat.

Gentle but overwhelmingly self-assured, Sosper cut off the baron when he began to speak. "Why do you question Avelmir's judgment? I can give you no aid, nor can the Collegium, until the time he specified. What happens among barbarians is of little moment to us in any event, and less now. You may perhaps be able to deduce the reason, having once studied here. No, look not so startled, my young friend: who knows the chick better than the hen?"

Trying to master his surprise, Gerin turned his wits to the problem Sosper had set him. He found no solution, and said so.

"Do you not? A pity. In that case, there appears to be no need for further conversation. Leave me, I pray, so I may return to my calculations."

"At least tell me why you will not aid me," Gerin said. "Balamung is no ordinary mage; he has more power than any I've seen here."

For the first time, Sosper spoke with a touch of asperity. "I am under no obligation to you, sir; rather the reverse, for you take me away from important matters. And as for your Trokmê, I care not if he has the Book of Shabeth-Shiri—"

"He has. You don't seem to have listened to a word I said."

"How can you know this? Have you seen its terrible glow with your own eyes?" Sosper was skeptical, almost contemptuous.

"No, but I spoke with a woodsrunner who has."

"You accept the untrained observations of a savage as fact? My good man, a hundred generations of scriers have sought the Book of Shabeth-Shiri—in vain. I doubt a barbarian hedge-wizard could have found it where they failed. No, lost it is and lost it shall remain, until the one no grave shall hold brings it back to the world of men."

Gerin had not heard that bit of lore before. It chilled him to the marrow. But his protests died unspoken. The old man before him had been right for so long, and grown so arrogant in his rightness, that now he could not hear anything that contradicted his set image of the world. He was talented, brilliant . . . and deafened by his own rigidity.

"Leave me," Sosper said. It was order, not request. Followed close by Van, Gerin left the chamber. Ice was in his heart. The door swung closed behind them of its own accord. Like a faithful servant, the foxfire ball reappeared to guide them back to its creator.

On their return, Avelmir looked to be considering some remark at their expense, but Gerin's stony visage and an ominous twitch of Van's great forearm muscles persuaded him to hold his tongue.

"What now, captain?" the outlander asked as they left the Collegium.

Gerin shook his head in dejected bewilderment. "Great Dyaus above, how should I know? Every move I make rams my head into a stone wall: the Sibyl, Carus, now this. Maybe Balamung was right. Maybe I can do nothing to fight him. Still, I intend to go on trying—what else can I do? And I can do one thing for myself right now."

"What's that?"

"Get drunk."

Van slapped him on the back, sending him staggering down the steps. "Best notion I've heard in days. Where do we find a place?"

"It shouldn't be hard." Nor was it. Not five minutes' ride from the Collegium stood a small tavern, set between an apothecary's shop and an embalmer— "Where the druggist sends his mistakes, I suppose," Gerin said. He read the faded sign over the tavern door. "'The Barons' Roost.' Hah! Anything that roosted here would come away with lice in its feathers."

"Someone doesn't seem to care." Van pointed to the matched blooded dapples and fine chariot tied in front of the tavern.

"He must be slumming." Gerin slid down and hitched the wagon next to the fancy rig.

The Barons' Roost had no door, only a splotchily dyed curtain, once perhaps forest green. Inside, it was dirty, dark, and close. Its few patrons, from the look of them mostly burglars, pimps, and other small-time grifters, gave Gerin and Van a wary once-over before returning to their low-voiced talk. "Hemp for smoking?" Gerin heard one say to another. "I can get it for you, of course I can. How much do you want?"

"What can I give you boys?" asked the fat man

behind the bar. His hard eyes gave the lie to the jovial air he tried to cultivate.

"Wine," Gerin said. "And quiet."

"The quiet's free. For the wine, I'd see your silver first."

Van laughed at that. "Show too much silver in a dive like this and half the jackals here'll decide they're wolves today."

"They don't seem to be troubling him, do they?" The taverner jerked a thumb at the noble slumped over the far corner of the bar. Three jars of various vintages stood before him; from his slack-jointed posture they were empty, or nearly so.

"For all I know, he's one of them, or their boss," Van said.

At that, the noble slowly swung round. A golden earring caught candlelight and glinted. "Who is it," he asked loftily, "who dares impute me a part of this place in any way save my location?" A swacked grin spread across his face as he focused on Gerin and Van. "As I live and breathe, the wench-stealers!"

"Rihwin! What are you doing here?" Gerin exclaimed.

"I? I am becoming preternaturally drunk, though if I can still say preter—pre—that word, I have not yet arrived. I shall be honored to stand you gentlemen a round: anyone filching so luscious a lass as Elise from Wolfar of the Axe deserves reward. Yet after she was gone, what point to my staying in the north—especially as my welcome had worn rather thin? So three days later, home I fared, and here I am."

Considering it, Gerin decided it was quite possible; Rihwin would have taken no side-trips to delay his journey. With his load of cares, the Fox was glad to see any face he knew. He answered, "You can buy for us if we can buy for you."

"Fair enough." Rihwin turned to the tapster. "A

double measure of Siphnian for my comrades, and quickly! They have considerable overtaking to do."

The wine the taverner brought had never seen Siphnos, and the amphora in which it came was a crude local imitation of Sithonian ware. At any other time, Gerin would have stalked out of the dive. Now he relished the warmth rising from his belly to his brain. When the vessel was empty he ordered another, then another.

No amateur toper himself, Rihwin watched in disbelief as Van poured down mug after mug of wine. "Heaven above and hells below!" he exlaimed. "I toast your capacity." The three men drained their cups.

"And I your fine company," Van said. The cups emptied again. Rihwin and Van looked expectantly at Gerin.

He raised his mug. "A murrain take all magicians." He drank.

Van drank.

"All but me," Rihwin said. He drank too.

"What's that?" Gerin was abruptly half sober.

"What's—arp!—what? Excuse me, I pray, I am not well." Rihwin's head flopped onto his arms. He slept. Gerin shook, prodded, and nudged him, to no avail. The southerner muttered and whimpered, but would not wake.

"We've got to get him out of here," the Fox told Van.

Van stared owlishly. "Who out of where?"

"Not you too!" Gerin snarled. "Before he flickered out, this candle said he was a wizard."

"A murrain take all wizards!" Van shouted. He drank.

The baron tried to whip his fuzzy wits into action. At last he smote fist into palm in satisfaction. "I'd wager you think you're quite the strong fellow," he said to Van.

"I am that," the outlander allowed between swigs. "And sober, too."

"I doubt it," Gerin said. "In fact, I'd bet you're too puny and too drunk even to carry this chap here"—he indicated the inert Rihwin— "out to the wagon."

"Go howl, captain." Van slung Rihwin over his shoulder like an empty suit of clothes and headed for the door. Gerin paid the taverner and followed.

Van slung Rihwin into the back of the wagon so hard Gerin hoped the noble was unhurt. "Will you own you were wrong?" he said.

"It seems I have to," Gerin answered, smiling inside.

"Pay up, then."

"Tell you what: I'll race you back to Turgis', double or nothing. You take the wagon and I'll drive Rihwin's chariot."

"Doesn't seem quite fair," Van complained.

Privately, Gerin would have agreed. He loaded his voice with scorn. "Not game, eh?"

"You'll see!" Van untied the wagon from the hitching rail, leaped aboard. He cracked his whip and was gone. Gerin was right behind him. Pedestrians fled every which way, tumbling back into shops and displays for their lives.

Rihwin's team was as fine as it looked, but the Fox still had trouble gaining on Van. The outlander, with more weight behind him, bulled through holes Gerin had to avoid. He also drove with utter disregard for life and limb, his own or anyone else's.

They were neck and neck when they reached the Alley. They stormed down it. And then, right outside the wheat emporium, they descended on a great flock of geese being driven to slaughter. Gerin doubted it was the flock which had delayed them on their way to the capital. That one still had to be on the road.

Van never slowed down. He had time for one bellowed "Gangway!" before he was into the middle of the geese, Gerin still a length or two behind. The Fox glimpsed blank despair on the face of one goose-tender. Then the air was full of terrified honking, squealing, cackling, defecating big white birds.

Some flew into the grain market. They promptly began to devour the wheat there. Swearing merchants tried to drive them back into the street, only to retreat in dismay as the birds fought back with buffeting wings and savage pecks and bites.

Half a dozen geese flapped their way through the second-story window of a bath-house. An instant later, four nude men leaped out the same window.

A dun-colored hound contested the right of two geese to a cartload of peaches. When five more birds joined the fray, the dog ran off, tail between its legs. Squawking contentedly, the victors settled down to enjoy their spoils.

Yet another goose seized a trollop's filmy skirt in its beak. The goose tore it from her legs and left her half naked in the roadway. Her curses only added to the turmoil.

Somehow or other, the racers got through. Any pursuit was lost in the gallinaceous stampede. Gerin took the lead for a moment, then lost it when Van, quite by accident, found a shortcut. The baron was gaining at the end, but Van pulled into Turgis' forecourt a few seconds in front.

Plucking a feather from his beard, he walked over to the Fox, broad palm out. "Pay up, if you please."

"You know, we forgot to set a stake. I owe you twice nothing, which, the subtle Sithonians assure us, remains nothing."

Van pondered this, nodded reluctantly. "Then we'll just have to race back," he declared. He took two steps toward the wagon and fell on his face.

The pound of galloping hooves brought Turgis out

his front door on the run. "What in the name of the gods is going on?" he shouted. "Oh, it's you, Gerin. I might have known."

The baron lacked the patience to trade gibes with him. He boiled with urgency. "Do you have a potion to sober up these two right away?" He nodded toward Van and Rihwin, whom he had lain beside his friend. The noble had stayed unconscious all through the wild ride.

"Aye, but they'll not be happier for it." Turgis vanished into the hostel. He returned a moment later with a small, tightly stoppered vial. He poured half its contents into Van, gave the rest to Rihwin.

As the drug took effect, the two of them thrashed like broken-backed things, then spewed their guts on the ground. Sudden reason showed in Rihwin's eyes. Wiping his mouth, he asked, "What am I doing here? Where, for that matter, is here? Who do you think you are, my good man?" he added when Van, still in pain, rolled up against him. His voice showed much of his usual cheerful hauteur.

The outlander groaned. "With any luck, I'll die before I remember. There's an earthquake in my brains."

Rihwin rose gingerly. He looked from Van, who stayed on the ground with head in hands, to Gerin, none too steady on his feet himself. "I congratulate you, my friends: practice has made you a superior pair of kidnappers. Tell me, which of you has wed Elise, and which intends to marry me? I confess, I have given little thought to my dowry."

"Go howl!" Gerin said. "Tell me at once: is it true you're a wizard?"

"Where did you learn that, in that horrid dive? How drunk was I? It were better to say I am all but a mage. I completed the course at the Collegium but never graduated, nor was I linked to a familiar."

"Why not?"

"Of what interest is this to you, may I ask?"

"Rihwin, you will have my story, I promise you," Gerin said. "Now tell me yours, before I throttle you."

"Very well. The fault, I fear, was my own. I learned all the required lores, mastered the spells they set me, met every examination, completed each conjuration with adequate results—which is to say, no fiend swallowed me up. And all this I accomplished on my own, for he who nominally supervised my work was so concerned with his own goetic researches that he had scant moments to lavish on his pupils."

"Not the wizard who styles himself Sosper?" Gerin asked.

"Indeed yes. How could you know that?"

"I've met the man. Go on, please."

"Came the night before I was to be consecrated mage, and in my folly I resolved to repay my mentor for all his indifference. He is a man who likes the good life, is Sosper, for all his sorcerous craft, and he dwells near the Palace Imperial. At midnight I essayed a small summoning. When the demon I evoked appeared, I charged it to go to my master's bedchamber, give his couch a hearty shake, and vanish instanter once he awoke. What I ordained, the demon did."

A reminiscent grin lit Rihwin's face. "Oh, it was a lovely jape! Even warlocks are muzzy when bounced from slumber, and Sosper, suspecting nothing other than a common earthquake, rushed in his nightshirt to the palace to inquire after the Emperor's safety. I would have given half my lands to see his face when he found the temblor his private property.

"But it takes a mighty wizard to befool such a man for long, and I, alas, had nowhere near the skill to maintain my appearance of innocence 'gainst his inquiry. Which leaves me here . . . almost a mage, and glad, I suppose, my punishment was no worse than expulsion."

Rihwin's tale was in keeping with the judgment Gerin had formed of him at Ricolf's holding: a man who would dare anything on the impulse of a moment, never stopping to consider the consequences—but one who would then jauntily bear those consequences, whatever they were.

Banking on that mercurial nature, Gerin plunged into his own tale. "And so," he finished, "I found I could get no proper mage, and was in despair, not knowing what to do. Meeting you in the tavern seems nothing less than the intervention of the gods—and on my behalf, for once. Fare north with me, to be my aid against the Trokmoi."

Rihwin studied him, wearing his usual expression of amused cynicism like a gambler's stiff face. "You know, I suppose, that I have every right to bear you ill-will for winning the love of a girl for whose hand I struggled over the course of a year?"

"So you do," Gerin said stonily.

"And you know I find your northern province uncouth, unmannered, and violent, nothing at all like this soft, smiling land?"

"Rihwin, if you mean no, say no and stop twisting the knife!"

"But my dear fellow Fox, I am trying to say yes!"

"What?" Gerin stared at him.

"Why do you think I traveled north a year ago, if not for the adventure of it, and the change? I was stifled by the insipid life I led here; were it not that I am in a bad odor up there, I doubt I should have returned at all."

Van struggled to his feet. "Good for you! Keep the same ground under your feet too long and you grow roots like a radish."

"But—what you said of Elise . . ." Gerin was floundering now.

"What of it? That I lost her was my own foolish fault, and none other's. I was not in love with her, nor she with me. Aye, she's a comely maid, but I've found there are a good many of those, and most of them like me well. I entered Ricolf's contest much more to measure myself against the other suitors than for her sake."

The last of his foppish mask slipped away, and he spoke with a seriousness the baron had never heard from him: "Lord Gerin, if you truly want my aid, I will meet you here in three days' time, ready to travel. I pray your pardon for not being quicker, but as I'm here, I should set my affairs in order before faring north again. Does it please you?"

Dumbfounded, Gerin could only nod. Rihwin sketched a salute, climbed into his chariot, and departed. His horses whickered happily at the familiar feel of his hands on the reins.

"What do you know?" Van said. "More to that fellow than he lets on."

Gerin was thinking much the same thing. It occurred to him that he had seen Rihwin only on a couple of the worst days of his life; now he began to understand why Ricolf, with longer acquaintance, had thought the southerner a fit match for Elise.

More than once over those three days, the Fox wondered if Rihwin would have second thoughts, but he was too busy readying his own return to waste much time on worry. Van acquired a stout ash spear ("A little light, but what can you do?") and four examples of another weapon Gerin had not seen before: flat rings of bronze with sharp outer edges. Their central holes were sized so they fit snugly onto the outlander's forearms.

"They're called chakrams," Van explained. "I learned the use of them in Mabalal. They're easier to throw straight than knives, and if I just leave them where they are, they make a forearm smash unpleasant for whoever's in the way."

When the baron paid Turgis, the innkeeper put an arm round his shoulder. "You're a good friend, Fox. I'm sorry to see you go. You remind me of the days when I still had hair on my pate. Please note, however, you brigand, I am not so sorry as to make you any rash promises. The last one cost me dear enough."

Rihwin arrived on the morning he had set, and as ready as he had vowed. Gone was his thin toga; he wore a leather tunic and baggy woolen trousers. A sword swung at his hip, armor and a quiver of javelins were stowed behind him, and he had set a battered bronze helm on his curls.

His left ear, though, still sported a golden ring. "It's possible to ask too much of me, you know," he said sheepishly when Gerin pointed at it.

"Rihwin, for all I care, you can wear the damned thing in your nose. Let's be off."

The baron drove the wagon up the Alley. Van stayed in the rear compartment, out of sight. Gerin did not want to be stopped by some irate merchant who'd had his goods smashed or scattered in the wild ride and now recognized one of its perpetrators. He was confident he was immune from being identified so; save for his northern dress, he looked like just another Elabonian. Thus it came as a small shock when someone waved frantically and called his name.

"Elise!" he said. "Great Dyaus above, what now?"

IX

Elise's story was simple enough, if unpleasing. Valdaburn's delight at guesting his unknown niece had faded. The fading quickened when he realized how cordially Elise and Namarra despised each other.

"It all blew up at dawn this morning in a glorious fight," Elise said. She reached into a pocket of her traveling coat and brought out a lock of Namarra's fiery hair. "Black at the roots, you'll notice."

"May I be of service, my lady?" Rihwin asked. "A spell for an enemy's ruin is easy when one has a lock of hair with which to work."

"I know enough magic for that myself," Gerin said, not wanting Rihwin to help Elise in any way at all.

"The hussy hardly merits being blasted from the face of the earth simply because she and I don't get along," Elise said. She asked Rihwin, "How is it you are in the city, and in Gerin's company?"

He briefly explained. She said, "When last I saw

you—and more of you than I wanted to, I'll have you
know—I would have thought you'd never want to go
back to the northlands again."

He flinched at that, but answered, "They hold no
terror for me, so long as I am not required to face
your father."

"Where shall I take you now?" Gerin asked Elise.
"You must have other kin here."

"I do, but I know none of them by name. Nor
would it do me much good if I did. My uncle is not
a man to use half-measures. He swore he'd make sure
I was no more welcome in any of their houses than
in his. That leaves me little choice but to travel north
with you."

Gerin realized she was right.

"Get moving, will you, and talk later," Van said
from his comfortless perch in the back of the wagon.
"I feel like an ostrich in a robin's egg."

Once they were out of the city, he emerged from
confinement and stretch till his joints creaked. "Let
me ride with you a while, Rihwin," he said. "I like
the bounce of a chariot under my feet."

"Do you indeed?" Rihwin said. He flicked the whip
over his matched dapples. They leaped forward, sending the light car bounding into the air whenever its
bronze-shod wheels struck a stone set an inch or two
higher in the roadbed than its fellows. Van was unruf-
fled. He shifted his weight with marvelous quickness,
not deigning to clutch at the chariot's handrail.

Rihwin gave up after a wild quarter of a mile, slowing his horses to a walk. As Gerin caught up, he asked
Elise, "Does he always act so?"

"I've rarely seen him otherwise. The day he came
to court me, he stepped down from his car, kissed
me, then kissed my father twice as hard! But he has
such charm and nonchalance that the outrageous

things he does don't grate as they would from some-one else."

"What, ah, do you think of him?" Gerin asked carefully.

"As a possible husband, you mean? I could have done much worse." She laid a hand on his arm. "But I could do much better, too, and I think I have."

Guard duty was easier to bear with three men to carry the load. Golden Math, a waning crescent, had been in the sky when Rihwin woke Gerin to stand the third watch. Elleb, three days past full, was near-ing the meridian; Tiwaz had just set.

"Tell me, how is it you know sorcery?" Rihwin asked. To Gerin, he seemed to be saying, *How could a backwoodsman like you hope to master such a subtle art?*

The baron had met that attitude from southerners too often during his first stay in the capital. Touched on an old sore spot, he said shortly, "Surprising as it may seem, I spent two years studying in the city, including a turn at the Collegium, though a short one."

"Did you really? What did you study besides mage-craft?" Far from being condescending, Rihwin showed eager interest.

"Natural philosophy, mostly, and history."

"History? Great Dyaus above, man, did you ever hear Maleinos lecture?"

"Yes, often. He interested me."

"What do you think of his cyclical notion of histori-cal development? I was so impressed by the perora-tion he always used that I memorized it: 'Peoples and cities now have great success, now are so totally defeated as no longer to exist. And the changing cir-cuit revealed such things before our time, and will reveal them again, and the revelations will not cease, so long as there be men and battles.' And he would stalk off, like an angry god."

"Yes, and do you know where he'd go?" Gerin said: "To a little tavern close by, to drink resinated wine—how do Sithonians stand the stuff?—for hours on end."

Rihwin looked pained. "You just shattered one of my few remaining illusions."

"I'm not saying he's not a brilliant man. I do think he presents his ideas too forcefully, though, and makes too little allowance for variations and exceptions to his rules."

"I can't quite agree with you there. . . ." All but oblivious to their surroundings, they fenced with ideas, arguing in low voices until Rihwin exclaimed, "Is it growing light already?"

They made good progress the next day, and the next, and the next, reaching the Pranther River at the end of the fourth day out of the capital. They camped near its southern bank.

The night was quiet, save for the river's gentle murmur. Pale clouds drifted lazily from west to east, obscuring now the pale thin waxing crescent of Nothos, now Tiwaz's bright full face, now rosy Elleb, which came into the sky halfway through the midwatch. Gerin, whose watch that was, endured the muttering of the ghosts for another couple of hours, then nudged Van.

His friend woke with a thrash. "Anything happening?" he asked.

"Not so you'd notice," Gerin said.

"Aye, it seems restful enough." Van looked down. "What's this? Look what I've been all but sleeping on, captain—another aoratos plant." He plucked it from the ground.

Gerin eyed it with distaste. "Now that I'm only standing one watch in three I don't need anything to keep me awake at night, and the leaves are so bitter they shrivel my tongue. Throw it away."

"I'd sooner not. I want to see if Rihwin knows of it."

"Suit yourself. As for me, I can hardly keep my eyes open."

It was still nearly dark when Van woke him. "Something moved over by the river, behind that stand of brush," the outlander whispered. "I couldn't quite make out what it was, but I don't like it."

"Let's have a look." Grabbing for sword and trousers, the baron slid out of his bedroll. He roused Elise and Rihwin, told them to give him and Van a few minutes and then to use their own judgment. Then he slipped on his helm and followed Van down toward the Pranther.

As always, the Fox marveled at Van's uncanny ability to pick his way through undergrowth. His own woodscraft was better than most, but once or twice an arm or shoulder brushed a branch hard enough to make it rustle. His comrade made never a sound.

Van froze when he came to the edge of the brush. A moment later Gerin eased up beside him, following with his eyes the outlander's pointing finger. "Trokmoi!" he hissed, hand tightening of itself on swordhilt.

A pair of the barbarians sprawled by the riverbank. Their attention seemed focused on the stream. Their tunics were not checked in the usual northern fashion, but were all over fylfots. These were Balamung's men!

But they did not move, not even when Gerin parted the curtain of bushes and walked toward them. His bafflement grew with every step. He came up close behind them, and still they were oblivious. Then he bent down and prodded one of them.

The Trokmê toppled. He was dead, his face an agonized rictus. In his throat stood an unfletched wooden dart, half its length stained with an orange paste. A matching dart was in his companion's unmoving chest. A fat green trout lay between the Trokmoi, bone hook still set in its mouth.

"What in the gods' holy names—!" Van burst out.

A grim smile formed on Gerin's face. "I do believe the rivermen have done us a good turn," he said. "Can you think of any reason Balamung would send men south, except to hunt us? And here, almost up with their prey, they stopped to do a little fishing—in the one river in all Elabon men don't fish." He explained how the rivermen had come to the Pranther.

Van shook his head. "Poor damned fools, to die for a trout. But it will make us a fine breakfast." He stooped to pick up the fish.

Gerin grabbed his arm and stopped him. A reptilian head was watching them from the river. No expression was readable in the riverman's unwinking amber eyes, but he held an envenomed dart ready to throw.

"All right, keep the blasted thing!" Van flung the trout into the Pranther. The riverman dove after it, surfacing a moment later with it in one webbed hand. A grave nod and he was gone.

"What's toward?" Riwhin called from the bushes. The baron was glad to see he'd had sense enough to don armor and to carry his bow with an arrow nocked and ready. He was a good deal less glad to see Elise behind Rihwin; he wished she wouldn't always run toward trouble. Frowning, he told them what had happened.

Rihwin said, "That Trokmê must hate you indeed, to work so hard for your destruction. Or perhaps he fears you."

Gerin laughed bitterly. "Why should he? I doubt I'm more than a pebble underfoot to him—a sharp pebble, aye, but a pebble nonetheless."

Hooves thuttered on the bridge called Dalassenos'

Revenge. Rihwin half drew his bow, expecting more Trokmoi. But it was only a dour courier in the black and gold of the Empire, a leather message pouch slung over one shoulder. He headed south fast as his lathered horses would take him. "Make way!" he shouted, though no one blocked him.

"Just once," Gerin said, "I'd like to see one of them have more to say than 'Make way!' It's no more likely than a wolf climbing trees, though."

The Fox disliked Elabon's courier corps. All the barons north of the Kirs saw it as part of the thin web binding them to the Empire, and they were right. The couriers carried news faster than anyone else, but only on imperial business.

Later that day another courier came south at the same headlong pace. Gerin called after him for news. He got none. They refused even to gossip, fearing it might somehow compromise them. Cursing, Gerin hurried his own northward pace.

Rihwin, as it happened, did not know of the aoratos plant or its uses. "And that is passing strange," he said, "for I thought surely the Collegium's herbalists were aware of the properties of every plant that grows within the Empire." He took the little bush from Van and studied it. "I must say it seems ordinary."

"Which is likely why no one's bothered with it here," Van said. "On the plains it stands out a good deal more."

"I must try it tonight," Rihwin said.

"The taste is foul," Gerin warned him.

"What if it is? If the effects are as interesting as claimed, I may be on the brink of discovering a whole new vice." He gave a voluptuary's leer, but spoiled it by winking.

"If you were half the carpet knight you pretend to be, you'd have debauched yourself to death years ago," Gerin said.

"And if you were as sour as you let on, you'd long since have pickled in your own juice," Rihwin retorted, a shot with so much justice that Gerin chuckled and owned himself beaten.

He stood first watch that night. By sunset he had grown so edgy that he decided to chew some aoratos leaves himself, regardless of their flavor. He felt fatigue flow away as the juice coursed through his veins. The curious extra sense the plant conferred showed him a squirrel asleep in its nest high in an aspen tree, a fox stalking a vole, a nightjar whipping after fluttering moths. The ghosts seemed troubled; thanks to his added perception, Gerin could almost make out the cause of their alarm, but in the end it eluded him.

He did not know whether he'd swallowed more leaves this time or this was a more potent aoratos, but its effects were still strong in him when he woke Rihwin. They made the baron reluctant to seek sleep at once. He was also curious to learn what the southerner would think of the plant.

"Pah!" Rihwin almost choked on the first mouthful, but choked it down. "A gourmet's delight it is not." He chewed more leaves. A few minutes passed. His breath began to whistle more quickly through his nostrils. His voice grew soft and dreamy. "How bright Tiwaz is, like polished silver!" After another moment: "Is that a ferret over there, Gerin?" He pointed into the darkness.

The baron felt his own mind reach out. "I think it is."

"Remarkable. And the ghosts—hear them wail!"

They talked idly for a while, trying with scant success to find some everday sensation comparable to that induced by the aoratos. "This is foolishness," Gerin said at last. "If there were half a dozen things like it, it would not be marvelous at all."

"Astutely reasoned," Rihwin answered, his tone mildly sarcastic. "From that, it would follow—" He paused in mid-sentenced, exclaimed, "The ghosts are gone!"

They were, fled away as suddenly and completely as if driven to shelter by the rising sun. The gloom outside the campfire's glow seemed somehow strange and flat. Surrounded by this great stillness, the cry of a hunting owl came shockingly loud.

Gerin's surprised senses were still groping for an explanation when Rihwin, now feeling the aoratos more strongly than did the baron, whispered, "I know why they fled. Look north."

Looking was not what was required, but Gerin understood. The blood froze in his veins as he sensed the approaching demon. Only the aoratos plant let him do so; without it, the flying monster would have stayed unseen, undetected, until it descended on the travelers like a hawk stooping on roosting fowl.

The huge demon drew swiftly nearer, like a stone hurled from a god's hand. Even with the aoratos, its shape was hard to define. Gerin was most reminded of the jellyfish that floated in the Greater Inner Sea, but the analogy was imperfect, for Balamung's sending—the baron had no doubt it was such—surveyed with three bright, pitiless eyes the landscape over which it sailed. For mouth it had a rasping sucker disk, set with hundreds of tiny curved teeth. The edges of its gross body blurred and wavered, like a stone seen through running water.

Still, while in this plane it had to be vulnerable to weapons, however fearsome its appearance. Though fear gripped him, Gerin strung his bow and set an arrow in it. His fingers worked more of themselves than under his conscious direction.

But the demon halted well out of bowshot. The baron's heart sank. He saw no way to lure it into range before it began a killing rush too swift to give him a good shot. Whistling tunelessly, Rihwin glanced from bow to demon.

The creature gave no sign of immediate attack. It seemed as uncertain as the men it faced. Words formed in the baron's mind: "How do you know of me? The man-thing who sent me forth promised easy meat, not warriors with weapons to hand."

For no reason Gerin understood, Rihwin was grinning. "Nor is that the only way in which your master deceived you," he said. He spoke softly to avoid waking Van and Elise, who could not sense the demon; it felt his ideas as he and Gerin perceived its.

"I name no man-thing master!" Its thought dinned in Gerin's head. More quietly, it asked, "And how else am I deceived?"

"Why, by thinking you can do us harm, when you cannot so much as touch us," Rihwin answered airily.

"How not?" the demon asked. Gerin was tempted to do the same. They had no protection against it, as it surely knew.

But Rihwin was not perturbed. "Consider," he said: "To reach us, you first must traverse half the distance, not so?"

"What of it?" the demon snarled.

"Then you will travel half the remaining interval, and then half of that, and half that, and so on forever. You may come as close as you like, but reach us you never will."

Gerin felt the demon muttering to itself as it pursued Rihwin's chain of logic. It did not seem very intelligent; relying on invisibility and ferocity, it had rarely needed much in the way of wits. At last it said, "You are wrong, man-thing, and my showing you this will be your death." Terrifyingly quick, it was twice as close as before. It halted for a moment. "Do you see?"

It halved the gap again, paused to show itself—and Gerin drove his arrow cleanly through its central eye.

It screamed like a woman broken on the rack and was gone, fleeing back to whatever plane Balamung had summoned it from. Gerin thought that agony-filled cry had to wake everything for miles, but only he and Rihwin seemed to hear it. Van and Elise slept on, and all was unchanged out in the darkness. No, not quite—the ghosts returned, their murmurs now far less fear-filled than before.

The baron picked up the denuded aoratos bush. He hefted it thoughtfully. "Thank the gods for this little plant," he said to Rihwin. "Without it, we'd've been nothing but appetizers for that devil."

"At the moment I am still too terrified to move, let alone think about anything so abstract as giving thanks. You have an unpleasant and powerful enemy, my fellow Fox."

"I've already told you that. Didn't you believe me before? As for fear, you handled yourself better than I did—I thought we were done for till you stalled the demon."

Rihwin shrugged. "That paradox always did intrigue me. I first heard a variation of it posed at the Collegium, purportedly to demonstrate that a longtooth could never catch its prey, even were the victim five times slower than it."

"It's logically perfect, but it can't be true. Where's the flaw?"

"I haven't the faintest idea, nor did my instructor. Your elucidation with the bow seemed as elegant as any."

Gerin tried to sleep. He was too keyed up to find rest quickly. He was still awake when Rihwin passed the watch to Van, and listened to his friend's sulfurous oaths at not having been waked to help fight the demon. Van was still grumbling complaints into his beard as his comrades at last gave in to slumber.

The next morning, Gerin let Elise drive for a while and tried to get more sleep in the back of the wagon. He knew Van had managed the trick on the way south. Now he wondered how. Every pothole was magnified tenfold when felt all along his body, and rumbling wheels and creaking axles did nothing to help his repose. Red-eyed and defeated, he came forward to take the reins again.

Traffic was light, for which he gave thanks. He wished Van had been able to buy a pair of Shanda horses instead of just the one. The shaggy little animal pulled magnificently. It seemed never to tire.

Its harnessmate the gray gelding was willing enough, but lacked the steppe beast's endurance. It exhaustedly hung its head at every rest stop. Gerin was afraid its wind would break if he pushed it much harder.

From the chariot Rihwin was sharing with him, Van pointed up the road at an approaching traveler and said, "Someone's coming in one awful hurry."

"Probably another whoreson of a courier," Gerin said. He reached for his bow nonetheless.

A courier it was, whipping his horses as if all the fiends of all the hells were after him. The beasts' scarlet, flaring nostrils and lathered sides said they had been used so for some time. "Way! Clear the way!" the courier shouted as he thundered past.

He was gone in the blink of an eye, but not before Gerin saw the long Trokmê arrow lodged in the crown of his broad-brimmed hat. North of the Kirs, the blow had fallen.

Rihwin stared blankly at the dismayed looks his friends wore; like Gerin, Elise and Van had recognized that arrow for what it was. Elise hid her face in her hands and wept. When the baron put an arm around her, he almost steered the wagon into Rihwin's chariot.

"Careful, captain," Van said.

Gerin's laugh was shaky. "Here I am trying to make Elise feel better, and look at me."

"Will someone please tell me what the trouble is?" Rihwin asked plaintively.

Gerin did, in a couple of curt sentences. Despite the gray gelding's exhaustion, he urged more speed from his horses.

"That's good thinking," Van called. "You can bet there's a mob a few hours or a day behind that courier, all of them hightailing it south as fast as they can go. Best make haste while the road's still clear."

"A pox! I hadn't even thought of that." Gerin added another worry to his list. He tried to comfort Elise, who was still sobbing beside him.

She shook his arm away. "I wish I had never left—I should be with my father." She cried even harder.

"I know," he said quietly. "But no one can change what you did, not god or man. All we can do now is wait to see how things are north of the Kirs and not borrow trouble till we know." *Wonderful*, he told himself, *you talk as if you thought you really could do it—and if your own guts knot any tighter, you can use them for lute strings*.

Despite his own doubts, his words seemed to reach Elise. She raised her tear-streaked face, trying without much success to smile. As the hours passed and the Kirs loomed ever taller on the horizon, a spurious calm came to the northbound travelers. They talked of life in the capital, legends from Kizzuwatna, swordfish-fishing on the Bay of Parvela south of Sithonia—anything except the Trokmoi and what was happening on the far side of the mountains.

As Van had guessed, they soon began meeting refugees fleeing the Trokmê invasion. The first one they saw brought a sardonic smile to Gerin's face: there stood Carus Beo's son, tall in his chariot. He used his whip with more vigor than the baron thought he still had. He shot passed Gerin's party without recognizing them.

The Marchwarden of the North was but the precursor of a steadily swelling stream of fugitives, many with better reasons to flee than his. The warriors who appeared had the look of defeated troops: they straggled south in small, dejected parties, and many were wounded. Now and again Gerin saw a minor baron among them, sometimes leading his family and a small party of retainers, more often alone, haggard, and afraid.

The Fox kept hoping to find a man he knew, so he could stop him and grill him at length. For two days he was disappointed. On the third, he spied a merchant who had been to Fox Keep two or three times, a man called Merric Forkbeard. The trader was still leading a string of donkeys, but their packsaddles were all empty. Gerin looked in vain for the two youths who had accompanied Merric in times past. When Merric heard the baron call his name, he pulled off the road to share what word he had. He took a skin of wine. His hands shook as he raised it to his lips. He had only a few more years on him than did Gerin, but looked to have added another ten in the past few days: his thin face, which Gerin remembered as full of quiet humor, was gray and drawn, his eyes haunted.

"I can't tell you as much as I'd like, Fox," he said, running fingers through thinning sandy hair. "Six days ago, I was on the road between Drotar's holding and Clain the Fluteplayer's—a good bit southwest of your keep, I guess that is—when I saw smoke ahead. It was the plague-taken woodsrunners, burning out a peasant village and acting as if not a soul in the world could stop them. I turned around and headed south—and ran into an ambush." He bit his lip. "That's when I lost my nephews. They died cleanly—I think."

Gerin tried to express his sympathy, but Merric brushed it aside. "It's done, it's done," he said tiredly. He took another pull at the wineskin, went on, "I will say you're the last man I ever expected to see south of the mountains."

"I was looking for help against the Trokmoi, though I didn't find much."

"Even if you had, it would do you little good."

"What? Why?"

"I came through the pass hours ago. Even then, officers and men were rushing about, making ready to seal it off. What use would your aid be, trapped on this side of the Kirs?"

Gerin stared at him, aghast. "Hours ago, you say?"

"Aye."

"Then I have no time to waste bandying words with you, I fear. The gods keep you safe, Merric, and may we meet again in happier times." The baron twitched the reins and got his wagon into motion. Van and Rihwin followed close behind in the northerner's chariot.

Merric watched them speed north. "I don't think I'm the one who needs the gods for my safety," he muttered to himself.

Now Gerin could show the gray gelding no pity. Once north of the Kirs, he might be able to replace it, but unless he forced an all-out effort from it now, all such problems would cease to matter.

The rich southern countryside flashed by in a blur. To the north, the Kirs grew ever taller. Their crowns of snow were smaller than they had been twenty days before. High summer was drawing near.

The stream of fugitives continued to thicken, clogging the road and stretching the baron's nerves tighter. Yet had that stream failed, all his hope would

have vanished with it, for he would have known the
pass was sealed.

He raced through the grimy town of Fibis, past its
crucifixes, and into the foothills, now cursing desperately at every slight delay. The gray began to fail. Its
nostril flared to suck in great gulps of air and its sides
heaved with the effort it was making, but it plainly
could not keep up the killing pace much longer. Gerin
felt its anguish as keenly as if it were his own. Strange, he
thought, how in the end all his hopes rode not on his own
wit or brawn, but on the stamina of a suffering beast.

Much too slowly, the pass drew near. Another party
of refugees appeared ahead, blocking the roadway and
forcing the Fox to the verge. No, these were not refugees—they were the garrison troops who had manned
the pass. They marched south in good order, spears
neatly shouldered. If they were pulling out, the pass
would be closed very soon. Even curses failed Gerin—
had he come so far to miss by so little?

At last the gap came into sight. The baron's heart
descended from his throat when he saw it was still
unblocked. But at his approach an officer stepped into
the road, backed by a double squad of archers. The
officer stepped forward with a salute, introduced himself as Usgild son of Annar. "I am most sorry, sirs,
lady. No travel is permitted beyond this point. We
are but minutes from ending contact with the north,
as it is under strong barbarian attack."

"I know—that's why I'm here." Gerin quickly out-
lined his need.

Having heard him out, Usgild shook his head. "I
cannot take the responsibility for delaying a measure
vital to the safety of my Empire." As if to underscore
his words, his archers nocked arrows.

"Can nothing persuade you?" Gerin asked, hearing
the finality in Usgild's voice. *Perhaps*, he thought frantically, *I can bribe him*. But he knew that had to be

futile. Usgild seemed honest. Even if he wasn't, Gerin did not have enough money to buy him.

Nonetheless, he rummaged through his pockets—and his fingers closed on the tiny bronze Imperial Hand the agent Tevis had left behind in Grizzard's tavern. He drew it forth and displayed it on his upturned palm. "Can nothing persuade you?" he repeated: "Not even this?"

He was afraid Usgild would doubt his right to the token, but the officer sprang to attention at the sight of the most potent official talisman the Empire knew. "My lord, I had no idea—"

"Never mind all that," Gerin said, determined to give him no chance to wonder. "Send a man at once to hold things up until we are through."

"Hanno!" the officer bawled. One of his archers raced for a chariot.

Gerin decided more, not less, effrontery would make him seem genuine. "My supplies are a bit low. I could use some field rations, and also" —he held his breath— "a fresh horse to replace this poor creature."

Usgild was beyond questions. "At once." Under his efficient direction, his men met Gerin's needs. A sturdy bay stallion replaced the gelding, which barely had the strength to be led away. Soldiers stowed square loaves of journeybread, salt beef, smoked sausages, and lumps of pale, hard cheese in the back of the wagon. They and their commander eyed the Fox with almost servile respect, doing his bidding as though they thought their lives were hanging in the balance. They probably did, Gerin thought sourly—an Imperial Hand was no one to trifle with.

He wondered why Tevis had seen fit to give him the emblem of his office. Could a Hand have realized the barons, in their way, served the Emperor too? It was hard to credit a southern man with such breadth of vision, but then Tevis, whatever else he had been, was no ordinary southerner.

Usgild broke into Gerin's thoughts. "My lord, may I ask your mission in the north?"

"I intend to seek out and slay the wizard who controls the Trokmoi." For the first time Gerin spoke simple truth, and for the first time Usgild looked unbelieving. The baron hardly blamed him, as he himself had no idea how to put an end to Balamung.

The soldier Hanno returned. Flicking a salute to Gerin, he said, "Imperial Hand or no, sir, if I were you I'd hustle down the pass. You've got some wizards mighty peeved at you. They were about halfway through their spells when I told them to hold up, and they're not what you'd call pleased about having to wait and start over."

A party like Usgild's must have been covering the northern end of the pass. The gap through the Kirs, so congested and noisy when Gerin had come south, was achingly empty and silent. The Empire's fortresses stared, empty-eyed, at wagon and chariot moving lonesomely where hundreds of men, beasts, and wains usually passed.

Half a dozen sorcerers paced the battlements of their sparkling, glassy towers. They too glowered down on the baron and his comrades. Though they were too high and too far for him to read their faces, the very snap of their robes in the breeze bespoke annoyance.

As soon as he was past, the wizards began their spells anew, moving in sharp, precisely defined patterns and chanting antiphonally. Their voices, thin and high in the vast quiet, followed Gerin a long way down the pass.

"I know that spell," Rihwin said, "but to think of using it on such a scale. . . ." His voice trailed away. He urged his dapples out in front of the wagon.

The commander of the pass had been no fool: to stop southbound traffic he had posted at the gap's northern outlet not a token force of archers but a solid company of spearmen and charioteers. They were needed. The road stretching north was full of fugitives, shouting, begging, threatening, gesticulating, but leaderless and not quite daring to rush the orderly ranks of gleaming spearheads standing between themselves and the southland. The din was dreadful.

Or so Gerin thought for a moment. Then the earth shook beneath the wagon. The sub-bass roar of endless tons of cascading stone left his ears stunned and ringing. A dust-filled blast of wind shrieked out of the pass behind him. It caught a couple of birds and sent them tumbling through the air. Guardsmen and refugees cried out in terror, but no sound from a merely human throat could pierce the avalanche.

"Looks like I'm home for good," Gerin said. No one could hear him either, but what did that matter? The fact itself seemed clear enough.

X

As inconspicuously as he could, Gerin made his way through the shaken solidery. No one tried to stop him. If any of the imperial troops had, he would have shown them the Hand. He was glad he did not have to. He did not want to find out how they would react to the symbol of a regime which had just marooned them on the wrong side of the moutains.

Those who had fled their homes and lands in the face of the Trokmê onslought now parted before Gerin, stepping aside like wolves in the presence of a longtooth. Any man going north of his own free will had to be of superior stuff, not to be hindered by the likes of them.

Rihwin let the baron catch up to him, then said, "You will surely need a fighting tail later. Why not start collecting it now?"

Gerin shook his head. "These are the ones who ran first and fastest. I might be able to shame some into coming with me, but they'd likely disappear again at the first sign of a red mustache."

"Right you are, captain," Van said. "Later we'll run into some who got honestly beat: bushwhacked like poor Merric, or just too many woodsrunners and not enough of them. That bunch will be aching for revenge, or a second chance, or what have you. They'll be the ones we take along."

"The two of you make good sense," Riwhin said, adding thoughtfully, "There's more to this business than meets the eye."

They rolled through Cassat not long before nightfall, fighting heavy southbound traffic all the way. The town was nearly deserted. Most of its soldiers and the folk who catered to them must have fled with Carus Beo's son. Looters prowled through abandoned shops and taverns, seeking valuables, drink more potent than water, or perhaps just shelter for the night.

At most times, Gerin would have been after them sword in hand. To his way of thinking, they were worse than Trokmoi: scavengers, preying off the misfortunes of others. Now he had more important concerns. He drove by, wanting to put as much distance as he could between the rats' nest Cassat had become and his camp for the night.

Only Nothos' crescent was in the sky when the sun went down. Math was a day and a half past new and lost in the glow of sunset. Tiwaz would not rise till midnight, and ruddy Elleb less than two hours before the next sunrise.

"Strange, not to have the Kirs staring us in the face," Elise remarked.

Her three companions round the campfire nodded. To Gerin, it was not only strange but wonderful. For the past couple of days, the mountains and the sealing of the pass had loomed over him like a death sentence. Now he felt reprieved. Tomorrow he would need to start thinking of Balamung and the Trokmoi again but, as he drew in a deep breath of cool night air made flavorful by the fire's smoke, he deliberately suppressed such worries.

Some responsibility, though, had to stay with him. "We need to be really careful on watch tonight," he said. "Some of the fools on the run will be more afraid of the Trokmoi than the ghosts. They'll likely be on the move tonight. And who knows? The woods-runners may be this far south already."

Travelers in the night there were, but no Trokmoi and no problems, at least during the baron's watch. But when he woke the next morning to the sound of Rihwin's fervent cursing, he knew something had gone wrong. "What now?" he muttered, groping for his sword.

"The plague-taken wine's gone sour!" Rihwin said. "It's no better than vinegar."

"Great Dyaus above, from the howl you raised I thought it was Balamung come in person. Worse things have happened than sour wine, my friend."

"So have better ones. You cannot know what torment my year at Ricolf's was, away from the sweet grape."

"Aye, and look at the trouble you got into, once you had it back," Van said.

Rihwin ignored him. "By the gods, I'd thought a year's separation long enough, but here I am, bereft again."

"If you *must* have you precious wine," Gerin snapped, "are you not mage enough to call it back from vinegar? If not, why did I ask you to come with me?"

Rihwin refused to notice the expasperation in Gerin's voice, but eagerly seized on his idea. "Your wits are with you, my fellow Fox! I learned that spell—"

("Naturally," Elise murmured, so low only Gerin heard) "and it's easy to cast."

As usual, the southerner was quick to fit action to thought. He rummaged through his gear, producing a packet of grayish powder and a minor grimoire. Gerin was relieved to see him checking the spell before he used it, but still felt a gnawing sense of unease. Things were moving too fast, and out of his control.

Rihwin fed tinder to the nearly dead embers of the fire, coaxing them back into flame. He sprinkled a few drops of the turned wine onto the fire, chanting an invocation in Sithonian. The gray powder followed. It produced an aromatic cloud of smoke. Rihwin chanted on: ". . . and to thee, O great Mavrix—"

Gerin's unease became alarm, but too late. With a whistling hiss, the summoned god, in all his effeminate finery, stood before Rihwin. "So!" Mavrix screeched, bouncing with wrath. "You are in league with this miscreant, and have the gall to seek my aid?" The furious deity pointed a finger at Gerin; somehow it did not seem strange that the digit should lengthen till it thumped the baron's chest.

"I will never help you, wizard! Never! Never!" Mavrix shouted, dancing around the little fire in a sort of war-dance. "And you shall never have the chance to ask my aid again. Mortal wretch, now and forevermore you have forfeited your right to work sorcery, and be thankful I leave you the remainder of your pustulent life!

"Take that, ox-goad!" the god added for Gerin's benefit. He stuck out a long pink tongue like a frog's, made a gesture street urchins often used in the capital, and vanished.

"What was all that in aid of?" Rihwin asked, white-faced.

"I told you before, the god and I had a disagreement not long ago."

"Disagreement forsooth! The next time you have a disagreement with a god, my dear Gerin, please let me know in advance so I can take myself elsewhere— *far* elsewhere." Rihwin tried to resume his interrupted spell, stopped in confusion. "A pox! The pestilential godlet did it! I still know every spell I ever knew, but I can't use them. No wine, no magic . . ." He seemed ready to burst into tears.

So, for the moment, was Gerin. He had gone south with high hopes, and returned with—what? A suddenly useless wizard and some sour wine. *No, fool, wait*, he told himself before his mood altogether blackened—*there's Elise, and she's worth troubles a dozen times worse than these*. His gloomy side added: *or she will be, if troubles no worse than these at all don't kill you first*.

The Elabon Way continued packed with refugees. They fled south toward a safety that no longer existed, carrying on their backs or in handcarts such pitiful belongings as they had salvaged. Pushing north against them was so slow that at last, much against his will, Gerin decided to leave the highway and travel on back roads. Though less direct, he hoped they would also be less traveled.

His hopes were justified most of that day. He made better progress than he had since he'd first seen that accursed imperial courier. But as the first cool evening breezes began to blow, what must have been the whole population of two or three farming villages jammed the narrow track on which he was traveling.

The peasants had their women, children, and meager possessions in ramshackle carts driven by oxen or asses. They drove their flocks of cattle and sheep before them. When the baron tried to tell them the way through the Kirs was blocked, they listened in dull incomprehension, as if he were speaking some foreign tongue, and continued on their way.

The same thing happened three more times in the next two days. Gerin's pace slowed to a crawl. Once more he had the feeling the whole world was against him. He was brusque even with Elise, and so churlish toward Rihwin and Van that the outlander finally growled, "Captain, why don't you shut up and do us all a favor?" Shame-faced, the Fox apologized.

Later that day, Gerin heard a commotion ahead, but thick woods and winding road kept its nature hidden. He, Van, and Rihwin reached for their weapons. But when the path opened out into a clearing, they put them down—there would be no fighting here. Instead of Trokmoi, they had come upon yet another group of peasants taking flight and the local lordlet trying to talk them out of it. Or so Gerin thought at first. A moment's listening showed him the noble had given up on that and was telling them what he thought of them for going.

"You cheese-faced, goat-buggering, arse-licking whores' get—" The noble's command of invective was marvelous; even Van listened in wide-eyed admiration. The fellow's appearance complemented his delivery. He was a solidly made man of about thirty-five; he had a fierce red face with one eye covered by a leather patch, thick brows, and a tangled black beard. He wore a bearskin cape over broad shoulders and massive chest, and carried a brace of scabbardless swords on his belt. "Lizard-livered, grave-robbing sodomites—"

The abuse rolled off his tenants like water from oiled leather. They were going whether he liked it or not. Despite the three troopers and two chariots he had at his back, there were at least twenty men in the exodus, each with scythe, mattock, or pitchfork close at hand. Gerin wished they would have been as ready to take up arms against the Trokmoi.

As the peasants began to move, the minor baron noticed Gerin. "Who in the five hells are *you*?" he growled. "Why aren't you on the run like these pissweeds here?"

Gerin named himself and his friends. He asked, "Are the woodsrunners so close, then, to send your villeins flying?"

"Close? I've yet to see one of the pox-ridden bandits, for all they've sent these dungheaded clods a-flying, aye, and most of my fighting men too. I've seen partridges with more heart in 'em than *they* showed." He spat in utter contempt and slowly began to calm. "I'm Nordric One-Eye, in case you're wondering— lord hereabouts, not that I look to have much left to be lord over."

"Friend Nordric," Rihwin said, "would it please you to fare north with us and take vengeance on the barbarians who have caused such chaos?"

Nordric lifted an eyebrow at the southerner's phrasing, but the notion of hitting back at the Trokmoi was too tempting for him to resist. "Please me? Great Dyaus above, I'd like nothing better! Those sheep-futtering, louse-bitten woodsrunning robbers—"

He rumbled on for another couple of angry sentences. Then he and one of his men climbed aboard one chariot and the other two soldiers into the second. His driver, Gerin learned as they began to travel, was Amgath Andar's son; one of the last pair was Effo and the other Cleph, but the Fox was not sure which was which. Neither of them said much. Nor, for that matter, did Amgath.

That did not surprise Gerin. Nordric talked enough for four. Not only that, he kept peppering his speech, even on the most innocuous subjects, with fluent, explosive profanity.

Rihwin steered close to Gerin. "It's as well for him he's short an eye—otherwise they'd surely style him Nordric Swillmouth."

The baron grinned and nodded. He was still glad to have Nordric along. He did not think the foul-mouthed baron would shrink from a fight, or his men either. Facing Trokmoi in battle had to be less terrifying than confronting an angry Nordric afterwards.

Though armed, Nordric and his men carried few provisions. Gerin had resupplied from imperial stores at the pass, but he knew what he had would not feed eight people long. The food would go even faster if he gathered more followers. That meant spending time hunting instead of traveling, something he resented but whose necessity he recognized.

More companions, though, also meant more men to stand watch. Freed from the need to break his sleep with a watch in three, Gerin spent the early evening sitting by the fire with Rihwin. He studied the southerner's grimoires with a desperate intensity that he knew was almost surely futile. Still, he persisted. The vengeful Mavrix had taken Rihwin's power to work magic, but not, it seemed, his ability to pass on what he knew.

"Here." Rihwin pointed to an incantation written in the sinuous Kizzuwatnan script. "This is another spell for the destruction of one's enemies when a bit of their spittle, hair, or nail parings is in one's possession."

"How does it differ from the more usual one, the one I would have set on the fair Namarra?"

"It has the advantage of needing no elaborate preparation, but is more dangerous to the caster. Unless perfectly performed, it will fall on his head rather than the intended victim's."

"Hmm." The spell looked simple enough, involving only a couple of genuflections and some easy passes with the left hand. But as Gerin studied its verbal element, his first enthusiasm faded: the Kizzuwatnan text was one long tongue-twister, full of puns, subtle allusions to gods he barely knew, constantly shifting patterns of rhyme and rhythm. He almost passed at once to the next charm. Then, stung by the challenge and artistry of the ancient versicle, he stopped and read it again and again, until it was fairly well lodged in his mind.

"I have it," he said at last, adding, "I think. What's next?"

"Here is one I've always found useful. It keeps horses' hooves sound and strong, and helps prevent all sorts of lameness."

"Yes, I can see where that would be a good thing to know. Ah, good, it's in Sithonian, too. Let me have a closer look—" And soon the veterinary magic was also stored in the baron's capacious memory.

The next day dawned luminously clear. The sun leaped into a sky of almost southern clarity and brilliance. The fine weather pleased Gerin less than it might have under other circumstances. In such heat, armor became an itchy, sweaty torment, but trouble was too close to chance removing it.

Thus the baron, longing for relief from the sweltering day, was glad to hear the rush of river water ahead. But almost at the same instant, he became aware of other sounds rising above the stream's plashing: the clash of bronze on bronze, the deep battle cries of Elabonian fighting men, and the higher, wilder yells of the Trokmoi.

Van was driving Rihwin's chariot. When he caught the noise of combat, his head jerked up like that of a dog suddenly taking a scent. "A fight!" he shouted, his voice pure glee. "The gods beshrew me, a fight!"

He sent the light car bounding forward with such a rush that he almost pitched the startled Rihwin into the roadway. Nordric and his driver were right behind, the stocky baron swearing sulfurously. On his heels were his liegemen, leaving Gerin to bring up the rear.

The Fox cursed as fervently as Nordric, but for a different reason. The last thing he wanted was to expose Elise to the risks of war, but he had no choice. "For Dyaus' sake, stay in the wagon and don't draw attention to yourself." He handed her his bow and quiver. "Use them only if you have to."

Black willows grew along the riverbank. Under their low spreading branches a grim drama was under way, with seven southerners battling twice as many Trokmoi. The Elabonians had accounted for four woodsrunners, but three of their own number were down and the survivors desperately fighting back to back at the water's edge when unexpected rescue arrived.

The Trokmoi shouted in dismay as Gerin's band leaped from chariots and wagons and loosed murder among them. Van was a thunderstorm, Gerin and Rihwin a pair of deadly snakes, striking and flickering away before being struck in return. Nordric's men fought with dour competence, but the petty baron himself brought the worst terror to the barbarians.

At last come to grips with the foes who had turned his life upside down, he went berserker-mad, his ruddy features darkening to purple, incoherent cries of raw rage roaring from his throat, spittle flecking his beard with white. Swinging a sword in each meaty hand, he rampaged through the Trokmoi, oblivious to his own safety as long as he felt flesh cleave and bones shatter beneath his hammerstrokes. The Trokmoi broke and ran after half of them had fallen. All but one were cut down from behind by the vengeful Elabonians. An arrow from the wagon brought down the last of them, who had outdistanced his pursuers— Elise once more proving her worth.

The onslaught was so sudden and fierce that Nordric's man Cleph was the only Elabonian badly hurt. He had a great gash in his thigh. Gerin washed it with wine and styptics and bound it up, but the bleeding would not stop. Cleph was pale and clammy, and seemed partly out of his wits.

"You're going to have to tie off his leg," Van said.

"I hate to," Gerin answered. "If I leave the tie on for more than a few hours the leg may go gangrenous, and if I take it off he'll probably start bleeding again."

"Look at him, though. He'll damn well bleed out on you right now if you don't do something in a hurry," Van said. Shaking his head, Gerin applied the tourniquet. The flow of blood slowed to a trickle, but Cleph remained semi-conscious, muttering curses under his breath against demons only he could see.

Nordric's battle-demon, on the other hand, deserted him after the fight was done. A man in a daze, he wandered across the small field of combat, staring at the results of his own butchery. "Dip me in dung and fry me for a chicken," he grunted, apparently not much believing what he saw.

"Friend Nordric, must your every phrase have an oath in it?" Rihwin asked.

"That's not so—" Nordric began, but his driver Amgath interrupted him.

"I fear it is, my lord," he said. "Remember what happened when Holgar the Raven bet you a goldpiece you couldn't go a day without saying something vile? 'You son of a whore, you're on!' you said, and forfeited on the spot."

The four footsoldiers Gerin and his comrades had saved were glad to take service with him. Two of them had lost brothers to the Trokmoi and another a cousin. They were all burning to retaliate. "The worst thing about dying here," said one, "would have been knowing we'd only taken a woodsrunner apiece with us."

Elise found herself less troubled over the Trokmê she'd slain than she had been at Ikos, which in turn troubled her. That evening she said to Gerin, "I don't understand it. He was only running away, and the driver back at the Sibyl's shrine was trying to kill us, but the first death left me sick for days, and now I feel almost nothing: only that I did what I had to do."

"Which is nothing less than true," the Fox said, though he knew it did not help much.

He stood a late watch, and a strange one in that no moons were in the sky: Tiwaz was new that night, Elleb a thin crescent, golden Math a fatter one, and pale, slow-moving Nothos just past first quarter. By an hour past midnight it was cool, quiet, and amazingly dark. Countless dim stars the baron had never seen before powdered the sky with silver, their light for once not drowned by the moons.

Cleph died early the next day. He had never really come to himself after the shock of the wound, and whenever the tourniquet was loosened it began to bleed again. They hastily buried him and pressed on.

Two men joined them that day, half a dozen more on the next, footsoldiers all. Of necessity, Gerin was reduced to a pace a walking man could keep. He wondered it the added numbers were worth the delay, and considered moving ahead with chariots alone. Van and Nordric were all for it. Rihwin advised caution. Events soon proved him right.

The baron's fighting tail was emerging from forest into cleared fields when a wild shout from ahead made them all grab for weapons. Just out of bowshot waited a force of Trokmoi of nearly the same makeup as their own: four chariots and a double handful of retainers afoot. About half the northerners wore plundered Elabonian armor. The others were in their native tunics and trousers, except for one tall, gaunt barbarian who was naked but for shield and weapons.

Gerin heard a growl go up behind him. He knew the men at his back were wild to hurl themselves against the Trokmoi. But he did not want to fight at this moment, against this foe. The little armies were too evenly matched. Even if he won the battle, he would be defenseless against the next band of woods-runners he happened across.

The Trokmê seemed to have similar thoughts, which puzzled the baron. Most northerners fought first and questioned later. He watched, bemused, as the chief winded a long, straight horn. He was no trumpeter, but Gerin recognized the call he had blown: parley.

He waved an agreement, got down from the wagon, and walked alone into the field. He ignored the scandalized murmurs of his men. Those stopped abruptly when Van announced, "The next one of you who carps will be carp stew." His huge right fist, fingers tight round the sweat-stained leather grip of his mace, was a persuasive argument.

The northerner met Gerin halfway between their men, empty hands outstretched before him. Plump for a woodsrunner but cat-courteous, the Trokmê bowed low and said, "I am Dagdogma the son of Iucharba, who was the son of Amergin the great cattle-thief, who was the son of Laeg the smith, who was . . ." Gerin composed himself to wait out the genealogy, which, if it was like most others, would go back ten or twelve generations to a god.

Sure enough, Dagdogma finished, ". . . who was the son of great Fomor himself." He waited in turn.

Gerin did not think it wise to reveal his true name to the barbarian. "Call me Tevis," he said, picking the first name he thought of. Like Dagdogma, he spoke in Elabonian.

"The son of—?" Dagdogma prompted politely.

"Nobody, I fear."

"Ah well, a man's a man for all he's a bastard, and a fine crew you have with you. Not that we couldn't deal with them, but I'm thinking 'twould be a shame and a waste of my lads and yours both to be fighting the now."

Gerin studied Dagdogma, suspecting a trick. Things he had not noticed at first began to register: the Elabonian women's rings the Trokmê had jammed onto his little fingers, the gleaming soft leather boots he wore instead of the woodsrunners' usual rawhide, the booty piled high in his chariots. The baron suddenly understood. This was no northern wolf, just a jackal out to scavenge what he could with as little effort as possible.

The Fox was filled with relief and contempt at the same time. His talk with Dagdogma went quickly and well since, each for his own reasons, neither man had any stomach for fighting. The Trokmê trotted back to his men. He moved them off along a forest track running west, clearing the way north for Gerin and his troop.

But Gerin's own warriors were unhappy he had talked his way past the Trokmoi instead of hewing through them. "I came in with you to kill the whoresons, not pat 'em on the fanny as they go by," said one of the men who had joined just that day. "If you're going to fight your fool war like that, count me out. I'd sooner do it right."

He stamped away, followed by four more footsoldiers of like spirit. Van looked questioningly at Gerin, asking with his eyes whether to bring them back by force. The baron shook his head. He had no use for unwilling followers.

In turn, he eyed Nordric curiously; he'd expected the hot-tempered lordlet to leave him the moment he ducked a confrontation. Nordric spat. He said. "That was just a pig in a red mustache, and scarce worth

the slaughter. There'll be real fighting soon enough—
I think you draw bloodspilling like honey draws
flies."

Just what I need, Gerin thought, but he had the
uneasy feeling Nordric was right.

As he and his band moved north the next day, signs
of the devastation the Trokmoi were working became
more frequent: corpses by the roadside (some Elabonian warriors, some woodsrunners, and all too many
serfs hacked down for the sport of it), empty peasant
villages (some abandoned; others gutted, smoking
ruins), livestock wantonly slaughtered and now rotting
in the sun, fields of wheat and oats trampled into ruin
or torched, and a good many keeps overthrown. A
couple of castles now flew northern banners. Some of
the Trokmoi, at least, had come to stay.

Their raiding parties were everywhere—bands of
half a dozen men or so, under no real leadership, out
more for the joy of fighting and the hope of booty
than for Balamung or the conquest of the world. The
Trokmoi seemed surprised to see a sizable party of
Elabonians under arms. They gave them a wide berth.

The farther north Gerin went, the fewer refugees
he came across. Most of those who had fled had
already fallen to the barbarians, perished on the road,
or made their way south. The few fugitives he did
encounter could tell him little. They had been skulking in the woods for days now. None wanted to join
him.

His homeland's agony brought torment to the Fox.
How could he alleviate it even if he beat Balamung?
"Twenty years of peace will hardly repair this," he
said bitterly that night, "and when has the border ever
known twenty years of peace?"

Only the moons, almost evenly spaced across the
sky, were above all strife. Nothos had been nearly due
southeast at sunset, Math a day past first quarter,

Elleb just at it. Rushing toward his three slower siblings, Tiwaz was now a fat waxing crescent. As twilight deepened, the fourfold shadows they cast spread fanwise from men, chariots, and trees. The ghosts began their senseless night whispers.

Although Gerin's troop was still traveling by back roads, Elise began to recognize the cast of the land the next morning. Pointing to a keep crowning a hillock ahead, she said, "That holding belongs to Tibald Drinkwater, one of my father's vassals. We must be less than a day from home!"

The Fox had not dared hope he could come this far unscathed. An unfamiliar confidence began to grow in him. It was rudely dashed when he drew closer to Tibald's keep and discovered it had been abandoned and looted and its palisade torn down.

A little later, the path they were following merged with the Elabon Way. Without hesitation, Gerin led his band onto the highway. They sped north for the castle of Ricolf the Red. Van left Rihwin's chariot and joined the Fox. He took over the driving; Elise, despite her protests, was relegated to the rear of the wagon. If they traveled openly through country held by their foes, they had to do so in battle order; one of the new footsoldiers took Van's place with Rihwin.

As Van tested the edge of one of his chakrams with a callused forefinger, he said softly, "Captain, if Ricolf's holding has fallen, you'll look a right fool coming up on it in the open like this."

"If Ricolf's holding has fallen, I'll be in too much trouble to care how I look."

The last time Gerin traveled this stretch of road, it had been too dark and he was going too fast to pay much attention to landmarks. By now, though, Elise was on land she had known since birth. "As soon as we round this next bend, we'll be able to see the keep," she said.

"Aye, there it is," Van said a moment later, "and the red banner still flying, too. But what's all that folderol around the moat—tents and things?" He drew up the wagon. Gerin waved the rest of his little force to a halt.

"It's a Dyaus-accursed siege camp, that's what it is," the baron said. "Who would have thought it from the Trokmoi? Freeze, blast, and damn Balamung! Still, though, I think we may be able to give them a surprise." He climbed down from the wagon and talked briefly with his men. They nodded and readied themselves.

The Trokmoi had set up their perimeter just out of bowshot from the ramparts of Ricolf's castle, intending to starve it into submission. A scallop in the outer edge of the moat showed where they had tried to hurry matters by filling it and storming the walls. That, plainly, had failed.

No one raised an alarm as Gerin and his men drew close. As the baron had noticed, the woodsrunners did not seem to think an armed party could belong to anyone but themselves. But sooner than the Fox hoped, a sharp-eyed Trokmê raised a shout: "Esus, Taranis, and Teutates! The southrons it is!"

Quick as he was, he was too late. Gerin's men were already rushing forward, foot and chariotry alike. A flight of fire arrows sent trails of smoke across the sky. The arrows landed on the woolen fabric of the Trokmê tents. A second flight followed the first; a couple of archers had time for a third release before they had to reach for spear and sword to defend themselves from the barbarians, who came rushing from the siege line to meet this new threat.

The Trokmoi hurled themselves into battle with their usual ferocity. These were no fainthearts like Dagdogma and his crew, but Gerin's attack cast them into confusion. And after the first few moments, they had no leader to direct their courage. Van took care of that. He sent a chakram spinning into the throat of a gilded-helmed noble. It cut him down in the midst of a shouted order.

"What fine things chakrams are!" Van told Gerin as he readied another knife-edged quoit. "I can cast them and drive at the same time." As he had in the capital, he handled the wagon as if it were a chariot. The baron, who had both hands free, felled two barbarians with well-placed arrows.

Battle madness seized Nordric harder now than it had by the river. Disdaining even his sword, he leaped from his chariot, seized a Trokmê, and broke him over his knee like a dry stick. An instant later he was down himself, caught in the side of the head by the flat of a northerner's blade. Three Elabonian footsoldiers held off the Trokmoi until he was on his feet and fighting again.

Leaderless or no, the woodsrunners badly outnumbered Gerin's men. He was beginning to wonder if he'd bitten off more than he could chew when, as he'd hoped, their camp began to blaze. Many of them pulled out of the fight in dismay. They tried to fight the flames or salvage what belongings and booty they could.

Then Ricolf's drawbridge thudded down. He and his men fell on the barbarians from the rear. Ricolf and a few of his followers had harnessed their chariots. Their arrows spread destruction through the northerners.

The battle was suddenly a rout. The Trokmoi fled singly and in small groups, turning to loose an occasional arrow but not daring to stand and fight. Ricolf and his charioteers rode a short distance in pursuit, but had no real mass of fugitives to chase. They soon reined in.

Then the men from the besieged castle were all

over Gerin's troopers. They squeezed their hands, pounded their backs, and yelled congratulations and thanks. But their jubilation faded as they recognized first Rihwin and then Gerin and Van. Curiosity replaced it. That grew tenfold when Elise stuck her head out of the wagon. Many shouted happily to see her, but as many seemed confused.

Ricolf returned from the hunt. His jaw dropped when he caught sight of Rihwin, who was having a hurt arm attended to. "What are *you* doing here?" he growled. Rihwin flinched. He started to stammer a reply, but Ricolf paid no heed. He had just seen Gerin, Van, and his daughter.

Gerin waited in some apprehension, not sure what the older baron's reaction would be. Ricolf got down from his chariot, speechless and shaking his head. He folded Elise into his arms, then turned to the Fox. "I might have known trouble would lure you back, kidnapper," he said; Gerin was relieved to hear no anger in his tone. "Your timely return has an explanation, I'm sure?"

"Would you hear it now?"

"This very instant. If any man is entitled, I am."

Having recovered some but not quite enough of his usual aplomb, Rihwin suggested, "Perhaps to cool his throat after his exertions, my fellow Fox could use a cup of wine—" He stopped abruptly. The glare Ricolf turned on him was frightening.

"Rihwin, you are a fine young man in many ways," Ricolf said, "but if ever I hear the word 'wine' in your mouth again, I vow it will have my fist there for company."

So, unmoistened, Gerin plunged into the tale. His comrades did not let him tell it unhindered, but he controlled the flow of it, and it went well. He saw Ricolf's men, many of whom had given him hard looks when he began, coming round as he spoke. When he was done, Ricolf stayed silent a long time. He finally said, "Do you know, I believe you. No one would make up such an unlikely story."

"The last person who said something like that was Valdabrun," Gerin told him.

"From what I remember of my brother-in-law, he has trouble believing the sun comes up each morning. He misses a good deal of the juice in life." A twinkle in his eye, Ricolf asked Elise, "Do you mean to tell me you'd rather have this devious wretch than a forthright warrior like Wolfar?"

She kissed the Fox by way of answer.

Ricolf turned to Gerin. "Frankly, Fox, I thought you had more sense than to get involved in a tangle like this one."

"Frankly, so did I."

"Hmm. A year ago I had Elise's wedding plans firmly in hand, and now I seem to have very little to say about them. As I recall, Gerin, you said something about 'a mind of her own.' You were right, the gods know. This, though, I say and mean: I think you will make my daughter a good husband, but there will be no rushed wedding for fear of what the future may bring. If it should bring ill, such a wedding had better never happened. When the Trokmoi are driven away, that will be time enough."

"I can't quarrel with you," Gerin said. He saw disappointment cross Elise's face, but Ricolf's demand was only just under the circumstances.

Van said, "Ricolf, would you put a fist in *my* face if I asked for a mug of ale?"

"In your face?" Ricolf laughed. "You're like the thousand-pound thrush in the riddle, who perches where he pleases. Things are a bit tight—the damned barbarians have been sitting outside for some days.

We're a long way from being starved out, though. Come along, all of you. We'll see what we can do."

"You spoke of Wolfar in jest a moment ago," Gerin said. "What happened to him after I, ah—?"

"Left suddenly? When he woke up (which wasn't soon; you're stronger than you think), he tried to beat down the door of my chamber and have me send all my men after you at once. I'd have done it, too, were it not for the note Elise left behind," Ricolf said.

Elise looked smug. Gerin pretended not to notice.

Ricolf went on, "When I said no, things grew unpleasant. Wolfar called me an oathbreaker and worse. He said he'd pull my castle down around my ears for me. After that, I told him he could take his carcass away while he still had ears of his own. I see what you meant about him, Gerin: he can be mild as milk when it suits him, but cross him and he raves."

"It's the streak of wereblood in him," Gerin said. "It runs thinly in many families on both sides of the Niffet, you know, but strong in his." He told Ricolf what had happened to Wolfar when Nothos and Math were full together.

The older baron frowned. "I had not heard of that. If I had, I'd never have asked him here. Lucky such conjunctions are rare."

For all their joy over driving away the Trokmoi, neither Gerin's men nor Ricolf's could work up much revelry. The day was drawing to a close. Both bands were exhausted. Even Van, as dedicated a roisterer as was ever born, contented himself with little more than the single mug of ale he had asked of Ricolf. Men gnawed at smoked beef and hard bread, cheese and sun-dried fruit. Then they sought bedrolls or fell asleep where they sat. Gerin woke in Ricolf's great hall at sunrise the next morning, still holding the same half-empty cup over which he'd dozed off.

The day passed in watchful waiting. Everyone

expected the Trokmoi to try to restore their siege. But the morning slipped by with no sign of the barbarians. Tiwaz rose at noon, overlooking only peace. Elleb followed a couple of hours later. He was trailed at hourly intervals by Math and pale Nothos, and all was still quiet.

"I think you may have driven them away for a while," Ricolf said to Gerin. The Fox pointed to heaven, wishing Ricolf's words into the ear of Dyaus.

As men began to realize the woodsrunners would not be back at once, they began the celebration they'd been too worn to unleash the night before. Gerin and Ricolf quickly saw they could not stop it: the warriors needed release. The barons did what they could, ordering a few reliable men to stay sober and stand sentry lest the Trokmoi dare a night attack.

Among the troopers Gerin chose was Amgath Andar's son, Nordric One-Eye's driver. Nordric himself happened to be close by. He reinforced the Fox's orders: "Keep your eyes open, you son of an unwed she-moose, or I'll wear your family jewels on a necklace."

"Does he always use his men so?" Ricolf whispered to Gerin.

"No. Usually he's worse."

Someone by the main gate got out a mandolin and began to play. Gerin thought fleetingly of Tassilo and Rihwin, and of how a couple of foolish drunks had changed his life. Leaving Elise tomorrow, he thought, would be harder in its own way than facing the Trokmoi: that he had done many times. But only once had he left the woman he'd come to love, and then in hands he thought safe. Now, even behind Ricolf's sheltering walls, Elise was in nearly as much danger as he.

When one of Ricolf's men passed him an earthen jug of ale, he gave it back still corked. He knew drink would only lower his spirits further. He watched as Van came up with his clay flute to accompany the mandolin-player. The man who had offered Gerin ale soon joined them with one of the long horns the Trokmoi favored. That surprised the Fox; few Elabonians played the northern instrument. The music was loud and cheery, but powerless to expel Gerin's gloom.

The sun sank and was forgotten. Most of the men in the holding gathered by the gate. Song followed bawdy song. Sentries shouted refrains from the stations on the wall. When too many throats grew dry at once, Van spun things along with a tale of his days on the plains of Shanda, a story of high daring and higher obscenity. Then the soldiers roared into another ballad.

To escape the gaiety he could not share, Gerin wandered into the castle's great hall. Dyaus' altar had no offering before it now, nor were the benches crowded with feasters. One warrior snored atop a table. His head rested in a puddle of dark, sticky ale. In a corner, another trooper was kissing the bare breasts of a serving maid. Neither he nor his partner paid the Fox any mind.

Gerin walked through the dark hall, kicking at rushes and bones. Once in the corridor beyond, he stopped and looked about: which sconce's torch, he wondered, had he used to flatten Wolfar? Was it the one by that much-scarred wooden door, or its neighbor a few feet down the hallway? Unable to recall, he turned a corner—and almost ran into Elise.

Later he realized he must have been trying to find her, searching for the one happiness he'd found in a collapsing world. At the moment, no thoughts intruded. She was warm in his arms. Her lips and tongue met his with the same desperation he felt. "Where—?" he whispered, stroking her hair.

"Follow me."

It was, he thought, the chamber in which he'd slept on his way south. That seemed fitting, somehow. He chuckled under his breath. Elise made a questioning sound. He shook his head. "It's nothing, love."

The straw of the matress rustled as he drew her down. She softly cried out beneath him, three times: first in pain, then in wonder, and then, at last, in joy.

When she rose to leave, the pain of separation was nearly more than Gerin could bear. She bent down for a last kiss, said softly, "Come back to me," and was gone. He was sure he would toss for hours after the door closed behind her. Almost at once, though, he fell into a deep and dreamless sleep.

XI

It was nearly noon the next day before the Fox and his companions began the last leg of their journey. He left the wagon behind. Ricolf lent him his own stout three-man chariot, and with it a lean, weathered man named Priscos son of Mellor, his driver and shieldman.

Gerin suspected Ricolf guessed what had happened the night before, why he'd left the celebration so early. It showed in no overt way but, as the Fox made small talk with the older man while getting ready to leave, he felt an acceptance, a closeness between them of a different sort from their earlier friendship. He was glad. Ricolf's good opinion mattered to him.

Elise's farewell was wordless. He tasted tears on her lips as they kissed goodbye. He, Van, and Priscos climbed into Ricolf's chariot; Nordric and Amgath were beside them, as were Rihwin and Effo, the survivors of the fighting tail the Fox had recruited along the way, and a few volunteers from Ricolf's holding. They were twenty-two in all, with four three-man and five two-man chariots.

Priscos clucked to the horses. The little army started to move. The gatekeepers lowered the drawbridge. One of them caught Gerin's eye as he passed. "What are you running off with this time, my lord?" he asked.

"Nothing you don't see, Vukov," the Fox answered, pleased he remembered the fellow's name. He doubted the gatekeeper had had a happy time the morning after Elise left. He turned for a last glimpse of her, but the cramped confines of the gatehouse already blocked his view.

Priscos was a man of few words, most of them about horses. "You don't see many Shanda beasts hereabouts," he remarked. "Where did you come by this one?"

"What's the name of that town in the mountains, Gerin?" Van asked.

"Cassat."

"Aye. That's where I picked him up. Cheap, too— the clod of a horse-trader didn't know what he had. He's been a rare worker."

"They're ornery, I hear," Priscos said. He went on, more to himself than Gerin or Van, "Reckon I can handle that, though." Gerin was sure he could. Priscos had an air of quiet competence he liked.

As the sun sank, they camped by what had been the border station between Ricolf's land and Bevon's. Now the square wooden building which had housed Ricolf's guardsmen was only charred ruins. *One more debt to pay*, the baron thought, *among so many*.

The ghosts were strange that night. Their keenings and wailings were more intense, and also more nearly understandable, than the Fox had ever heard. One in particular flitted round him as if drawn like moth to flame. For all its efforts, he could neither make sense of what it would tell him nor recognize its pallid form in the flickering firelight.

"That is an uncanny thing," Rihwin said, watching the wraith's frantic but vain efforts to communicate.

"Likely it's like a Shanda spirit, seeking to lure you away from the light so it can drink your blood," Van said.

Gerin shook his head. "I feel no harm in it, even if I can't understand what it would say. Besides, Van, every ghost in the north country must have had a glut of blood by now."

To that the outlander had no reply but a grave nod.

Remembering the fraternal strife tearing Bevon's barony even before the Trokmoi invaded, Gerin wanted to cross it in a single day if he could. He did not want to camp inside it: if he could expect night marauders anywhere, Bevon's tortured land would be the place.

And tortured it was. The Fox's band passed two battlefields before the sun was high in the southeast. The woodsrunners had plundered both fields, but all the bloated, naked corpses seemed to be Elabonians. Here brother had fought brother, and fought with a hate greater than they turned against the Trokmoi.

As he surveyed the second meadow filled with bodies, Gerin's face was stony and full of bitterness. "Poor fools," he said. He wondered if his words were not an epitaph for all the northland.

Whichever brother had won the war, he had not enjoyed victory long. A lot of the keeps still standing were held by small bands of Trokmoi. They hooted in derision as they saw Gerin's force go by, but did not move against it. "They think us beneath contempt," the Fox said to Van, "and perhaps we are."

"Honh! The next time I care what a woodsrunner thinks will be the first."

A bit more than halfway through Bevon's barony, they passed a roadside holding destroyed in a way Gerin had never imagined before. The timbers of one whole wall of the palisade lay like jackstraws in the bailey, as if kicked in by a monster boot. The stone keep itself was a pile of broken rubble.

Something white stuck out from under one limestone slab. As the baron drew closer, he saw it was the skeleton of a human hand and arm, picked clean of flesh by scavengers. No one, Elabonian or Trokmê, garrisoned this keep.

"This is the work of your Balamung?" Rihwin asked.

"He's not mine. I wish with all my heart I'd never heard of him," Gerin said, but he had to nod as he spoke. His warriors eyed the shattered keep with awe, fear, and wonder. Hand-to-hand fighting against the Trokmoi was all very well, but how could they hope to hold against sorcery like this? Even Nordric was grim and quiet.

"I wonder why such powerful wizardry has not been used further south," Rihwin said. "Few castles could stand against it, yet here, so close to the Niffet, is the first sign we've had of anything more than a simple barbarian invasion."

"What difference does it make?" Gerin said bleakly, staring once more at the blasted holding.

"Maybe none, maybe a great deal. One explanation I can think of is that your northern mage may have so much trouble trying to lay low one particular keep—I name no names, mind you—that he has had little leisure to help his men elsewhere."

Gerin gave him a grateful look. The line of hope the southerner had cast him was thin, but he was all but drowning in despair. Anything that buoyed his spirits was welcome.

His renewed optimism and his hope of crossing

Bevon's lands in one day both collapsed not long after noon. His band came to the top of a low rise. There they stopped in horror and dismay. For the next three or four miles, the Elabon Way and most of the surrounding landscape had been brutally wiped out of existence. All that was left was a ruined expanse of raw-edged muddy craters, some a hundred feet across and twenty deep. They overlapped one another in the mangled earth, as if the same giant who had pulverized the keep had then amused himself by pelting the ground with thousands of huge boulders. But there were no boulders, no visible explanation of how the devastation had been committed.

Chariots were not built to cross such terrain. Twice Gerin and his band had to stop to mend wheels battered by half-buried fragments of roadbed and tree-trunk, and once more to fix the axle of Nordric's car when it broke.

Van repaired it with bronze nails, leather lashings, and a large measure of hope. He said, "It may hold, and then again it may not. All we need now is for a horse to break a leg in this mess."

Gerin's fingers moved in a protective sign. "May the ears of the gods be closed to you."

They barely managed to escape the ruined land before the sun set. All four moons were low in the east, slow-moving Nothos being most nearly full and Tiwaz still closest to first quarter.

That night the ghosts were louder and more insistent than Gerin had over known them. Again, one in particular tried to deliver some message to him; again, he did not understand. Although he failed, something in him responded to the ghost, as if it was the shade of someone he had once known well. Irked by the riddle he could not solve, he pored over Rihwin's grimoires until sleep overtook him.

He and his men came on another band of desolation

not far into the lands of Palin the Eagle. This was worse than the one before: the ravaged area held several streams and ponds. Their water made the trek a nightmare of slimy, clinging mud.

In some places, chariots sank axle-deep in the muck. The warriors had to get out and slog through it on foot to lighten the load enough to let the horses move the cars at all. Men and beasts alike were filthy and exhausted when at last they reached flat, solid ground. To his disgust, Gerin found several fat leeches clinging to his legs.

Though some daylight was still left, the Fox decided to camp when he came to an unfouled creek in which to wash. Most of his men, spent by the day's exertions, collapsed into slumber almost at once.

Only Rihwin kept any semblance of good cheer. That surprised Gerin. He had expected the southern dandy to be dismayed at his present unkempt state.

"Oh, I am, my fellow Fox, I am," he said with a grin when Gerin asked, "but what, pray, can I do about my plight save laugh? Moreover, I truly begin to think Balamung has wreaked all this havoc for no other purpose than sealing aid away from your lands. Did you not tell me a mage was warding your keep?"

"Aye, or so I hope, at any rate: Siglorel Shelofas' son. He's southern-trained, true, but I don't know how long he can stand against one such as Balamung. For one thing, he drinks too much."

"By your reckoning, so do I, yet did it keep you from bringing me along on this mad jaunt? Also, never forget that while crisis makes cravens of some, in others it burns away the dross and leaves only their best."

"From your mouth to Dyaus' ear," Gerin said, touched again by Rihwin's efforts to reassure him. What the southerner was saying held just enough sense to keep him thoughtful, too: maybe Balamung did have some unknown reason to fear him. *And maybe*, he told himself, *I'll do as Van says and flap my arms and fly to Fomor*. Neither was likely.

Despite the gift of fowls' blood, the ghosts were a torrent of half-seen motion, a clamorous murmur of incomprehensible voices. The spirit which had visited Gerin on the two previous nights returned once more. He coud see its ill-defined features writhing in frustration as it failed again to impart its tidings.

"You know, captain," Van said, "I may be daft, but I think the poor wraith even looks a bit like you." Gerin shrugged. For one thing, though the ghosts were extraordinarily immanent of late, they remained cloudy and indistinct. For another, the Fox, like most folk in the Empire and the lands it knew, had only a vague idea of his features. Mirrors of polished bronze or silver were uncommon and expensive; even the best gave images of poor quality. He probably had not seen his own reflection more than a dozen times since taking over his father's barony.

The holding of Raff the Ready, Palin's vassal who had guested Gerin and Van on their way south, was only a burnt-out shell. The little pond beside it was rubble-choked and fouled with the bodies of men and beasts. Gerin viewed the ruins with sadness, but little surprise. Too many years of peace had led Raff to neglect his walls. He could not have put up much of a fight, not in his dilapidated keep.

Late that afternoon, the Fox passed from Palin's land and entered his own once more. The roadside guardhouses on either side of the border were deserted, but had not been burnt. The borderstone itself had been uprooted by the Trokmoi. Gerin cursed when he saw its moss-covered runes effaced by fylfots chipped into the rock, as if Balamung was claiming the land for his own.

So, perhaps, he was. Gerin and his band had not gone far before they tripped some sorcerous alarm the wizard had planted. A misty image of the black-robed sorcerer appeared in the road before them. "Back, are you, Fox, in spite of it all? Well, you'll have no joy of it. My lads will see to that, and soon." With a scornful laugh, the projection vanished.

"The spell your enemy placed here was plainly set to react to you and no one else," Rihwin said. "In which case—"

Gerin finished for him: "—there's sure to be another charm in action now not far away, telling a few hundred woodsrunners to come down and make an end of me. Well, what can I do but go on? Balamung has thrown away the advantage of surprise in his vainglory, for whatever that's worth."

Arms at the ready, they moved ahead as the sun sank low in the west. As they passed a tiny crossroads, a whoop from behind some brush told them they had been seen. Archers nocked arrows; spearmen tightened grips on their weapons.

They did not have long to wait. Chariots and infantry together, a veritable army thundered down the cross road toward them. At its head was Wolfar of the Axe. His hairy features split in a bloodthirsty grin when he recognized the Fox. "What luck! It's the wench-stealing sodomite himself!" he roared to his men. Then, to Gerin: "I'll make a capon of you, to keep you from having such thoughts again!"

Had Wolfar's rancor against the Fox driven him into the arms of the Trokmoi? Gerin would not have thought that even of his western neighbor, yet here he was.

There was scant time for such thought. Gerin shot at Wolfar but missed. His arrow tumbled one of the men behind Wolfar out of his chariot. Rihwin and the other bowmen let fly too, dropping a couple of other men and sending a chariot down in crashing ruin as one of its horses was hit. But to stand and fight was madness, for Wolfar had easily ten times Gerin's force.

"North!" the Fox shouted to his followers. "We'll outrun the footsoldiers, at least, and meet him on more even terms."

North they fled in the gathering dusk. Wolfar howled hatred close behind. Arrows flew up. Almost all went wide—the jouncing chariots made poor shooting platforms.

"Captain," Van shouted in Gerin's ear, "what in the five hells is that up ahead?"

Only his will kept the baron from hysterical laughter. Whatever else Wolfar was, he was shown to be no traitor. "What does it look like? It's the wizard's bully-boys, come to finish us off. We're on the horns of a dilemma, sure enough, but maybe, just maybe, they'll gore each other instead of us."

The leader of the Trokmoi was an immensely tall, immensely fat blond barbarian who filled most of a three-man chariot by himself. He stared in dismayed amazement at the force of chariotry bearing down on him. Instead of the small band he'd expected, this looked like the leading detachment of an army as large as his own.

He frantically reined in, shouting, "Deploy, you spalpeens! Don't be letting 'em get by you, now!" The Trokmoi shook themselves out into a wide line of battle, some afoot, others still in their cars.

But Gerin did not intend to take evasive action. He and his men stormed toward the center of the Trokmê line, hoping to slash through and then let the northerners and Wolfar's men slaughter each other to their hearts' content. But the Trokmoi were too many and too quick to be broken through so easily. They swarmed round the Fox's chariots, slowing the momentum of his charge and stalling him in their midst.

Their huge leader left his car to swing a great bludgeon

with deadly effect. He crushed the skull of Rihwin's chariot-mate, then lashed out at Priscos. Gerin's driver took the blow on his shield. It all but knocked him from the chariot. The baron chopped at the Trokmê with an axe. The barbarian, quicker than his girth would have suggested, ducked the stroke.

A horse shrieked as a woodsrunner drove a dagger into its belly.

For a moment, Rihwin was close by Gerin. "We've got to get out of here!" he cried.

"If you have any notion how, I'd love to hear it," Gerin said.

A barbarian tried to climb into his chariot. Van hit the man in the face with a chakram-braceleted forearm. He screamed through a torn, blood-filled mouth and fell away.

Then, suddenly, the pressure of the woodsrunners on Gerin's beleaguered band slackened as Wolfar hurled himself into the sea of Trokmoi after the man he hated. "He's mine, you arse-lickers! He's mine!" he roared.

The barbarians turned to meet this new and much more dangerous threat. Gerin tried to extricate his men from the now three-cornered battle. It was not easy. The Trokmoi had not forgotten them, and to Wolfar's men the woodsrunners were only obstacles blocking the way to their real target.

Unnoticed by anyone in the melee, the sun sank below the horizon. As it set, the four moons rose within seconds of one another, all of them full. The last time that had happened had been close to three centuries before Elabon's capital was founded.

Huge tides swamped low-lying coastal areas, drowning small towns and wrecking great ports. Prophets the world around cried doom.

And in those lands where the taint of wereblood ran through a folk, no moons at quarter or crescent counteracted the pressure to change shape exerted by the light of a full moon's disk. Those with only the thinnest, most forgotten trace of wereness were now liable, indeed compelled, to take beast form.

Hills off to the east briefly shielded the battlefield from the rays of the rising moons. Then they topped the low obstacle and washed the fighters in their clear, pale light. Gerin was trading axe-cuts with a scrawny, green-eyed Trokmê who fought without armor when his foe dropped his weapon, bewilderment and alarm on his face.

The Fox had no idea what was happening to him, but was not one to let any advantage slip. His stroke was true, but the northerner ducked under it with sudden sinuous ease. The Trokmê's body writhed, twisted . . . and then the baron was facing no Trokmê, but rather a great wildcat. It spat fury and leaped at him.

He had no time to wonder if he had lost his mind. Razor-sharp claws tore at the bronze facing of his shield, snarling jaws full of jagged teeth snapped at his arm. He brought his axe crashing down between the mad eyes of the cat, felt its skull splinter under his blow. Hot blood spattered his arm. The carcass lay still a moment, twitching.

Gerin stared in disbelief. The awful wound he had inflicted healed before his eyes. Bones knit, skin and fur grew together as he gaped. The wildcat's eyes opened and caught sight of him. It yowled, gathered itself for a second spring—and was bowled over and spun to the ground by an outsized wolf. They rolled away, locked in a snarling, clawing embrace.

The battlefield was a world gone mad. At first the Fox thought some spell of Balamung's, intended for his destruction, had gone awry. He soon realized the chaos was far too general for anything of that sort.

Then, quite by accident, he saw the four full moons.

Understanding came, but brought no relief, only terror. Nearly half the fighting men had gone were, in one beast-shape or another. The field was littered with corselets, greaves, and helms they escaped when the change came over them. The were-creatures fought former friends, foes, and fellow beasts with an appalling lack of discrimination.

A bellow of red rage from beside Gerin made him whip his head around, fearful lest Van too was falling under the influence of the moons. Not so: the outlander, in dispatching one of Wolfar's men who had remained both human and combative, had taken a cut on his forearm.

More and more, those who kept their human form left off fighting one another and banded together against the ravening werebeasts. At the baron's side were three Trokmê foot soldiers, but neither they nor he had any leisure in which to quarrel.

The werebeasts were so lithe and fast, they found it easy to slip through the quickest human guard and fasten claws or fangs on flesh. Even when they were killed, men gained only momentary respite from their onslaught. Within seconds of taking the most ghastly wounds, they grew whole once more.

Men caught away from their fellows were for the most part quickly killed. One pair of exceptions was Nordric One-Eye and his driver Amgath. Their chariot had foundered in the middle of the field when Van's repairs failed at last and the car's axle broke beneath it.

The werebeasts made short, dreadful work of their horses, but Nordric was in full berserker rage, and fast and savage as any shape-changer. With one mighty stroke of his sword he cut a leaping werewolf in two, then seized its tail and hurled the spouting hindquarters far away. "Live through *that*, you backscuttling demons' get!" he shouted.

Still, had the werebeasts not battled each other with the same ferocity they gave those who had not changed, they would have made short work of them all. As it was, boar stomped and tusked wolf, a pair of wildcats sprang at a stag. The stag tossed one away with a wicked swipe of its antlers, but went to its knees as the other reached its back. Then the were-wolf was beset in turn by a gigantic badger.

The shape-changers, Gerin noted, seemed to keep the same body weight they had possessed as men. A couple of hawks far too heavy to fly stumped about the battlefield. Their cruel beaks gaped as they screamed challenge to all and sundry. Nor were they long without foes. A wolf attacked one, a fox the other. Between beaks, talons, and battering wings, both soon had cause to regret it.

The majority of the werebeasts were wolves, foxes, or wildcats, but deer, boar, bear, badger, and wolverine were all commonly represented. Along with these mundane creatures, though, were several oddities. One of Wolfar's men must have had some Urfa blood in his past, for a miniature but combative were-camel, moaning, snorting, and spitting, struck shrewd blows with its forefeet at the carnivores assailing it.

Off to one side lay a tremendous salmon, a corselet still round the middle of its body. It flopped and gasped in the air it could not breathe. It could not die, either, because of the vitality of its wereblood.

In the convulsions of the field, two transformed creatures stood out. One was the wolf which had been Wolfar. His passion against Gerin was so fierce that he kept it in beast shape. He fought to force his way through the press and close his jaws on the Fox's throat. His howls of fury held almost understandable curses buried within them.

Yet even the were-Wolfar gave way before a great tawny longtooth which, from its bulk, must have been the animal shape of the swag-bellied Trokmê commander. It flailed its way through the imbroglio with hammerlike blows of its paws, blows that sent even werebeasts reeling back, stunned.

The monster cat came up to the stalled chariot in which Nordric and his driver still held out. Amgath snapped his long lash at it, hoping to keep it at a distance. It squalled in pain and anger but, instead of being repulsed, ran at him. He dropped the whip and grabbed a short thrusting-spear. Too late. A single cuff crushed his face and broke his neck.

The longtooth's rush overturned the chariot and tumbled Nordric among the ravening werebeasts. Gerin was sure he was doomed. In an instant, though, he was on his feet, a sword in either hand. His curses pierced the cacophony of beast-noises around him. He seemed to face every way at once, flashing blades keeping death at bay. He drove off one werebeast after another. Trokmoi and Elabonians shouted together.

Their cheers turned to groans as he went down, a wildcat clinging to his back. Van leaped from the chariot and ran to his rescue. The wolf that had been Wolfar bounded toward him, slavering jaws agape, yellow eyes blazing hatred.

The outlander was ready when it sprang. A blow of his spiked mace shattered its skull. The wereflesh healed with unnatural speed, but Van was past by the time the wolf regained its feet. He kicked the cat away from Nordric. It lashed out at the first thing it hit, another, even bigger, wildcat. While they tried to gut each other with raking claws, Van hauled Nordric erect. Side by side, they fought their way back to the chariots.

Nordric was battered and bleeding, but still full of fight. Gerin and Van had to hold him back from throwing himself once more against the were-longtooth that had killed Amgath.

"There's no vengeance to gain against a beast you cannot kill," Gerin said. "He'll be in human shape again, you know—maybe you'll meet him then." Nordric let himself be persuaded, a true measure of the punishment he had taken.

Wolfar's chief lieutenant, Schild Stoutstaff, had not gone were. Now he began to rally to himself such of his overlord's men as were left. The Trokmoi, too, gravitated toward a pair of their nobles.

Gerin thought it a good time to vanish discreetly from the field. Followed by all his surviving men—Rihwin and Nordric in the former's chariot and three more warriors in another car—he edged toward the cover of the woods.

Their departure went unmarked by still-struggling men, but one werebeast saw. The wolf that was Wolfar bayed angrily and started to lope after them. Before he could clear the battlefield, the longtooth knocked him down from behind. It tried to bury its fangs in were-Wolfar's neck. The werewolf tried to twist free, but his foe's great weight held him down.

Wolfar writhed, wriggled, and clamped his teeth on one of the longtooth's forelegs. Bones crunched. The longtooth screamed. It tore at the wolf's belly with its hind feet. Wolfar let go, but only to snap at the longtooth's throat. Any greater purpose was forgotten in the fighting madness now gripping him. Outmatched physically, he was nearly the longtooth's match because of the fury that drove him.

Gerin thanked the gods he and the poor handful of followers left him had made good their escape. Giving quiet directions to Priscos, he guided them north through a web of tiny trails. No one who had not lived in the barony could have followed them in the dark.

At last he judged it safe to stop. The din of battle had long since died behind him, but the night was far from still. More than the usual number of animals ranged the woods. Many were men caught in the open by the werenight and now running wild, bloodlust in their souls.

That led to another thought: what hell was the werenight playing in keeps under siege—especially in Castle Fox (always assuming it had not fallen)? "Don't worry about it, captain," Van said when Gerin spoke aloud. "Whatever's going on inside, it's just as bad out, and that you can bet on. Balamung or no, the Trokmoi'll be in no shape to take advantage of things tonight. Maybe a weresnake will swallow the cur and solve our problem for us."

"Such happy endings happen more often in romances than in fact, I fear," Gerin said, but the outlander had heartened him.

Something else occurred to Rihwin: "Great Dyaus above! I wonder what's happening south of the mountains?" The Fox shied away from that idea. With even a small part of its populace turned were, the capital's narrow, winding streets and dark alleys would be a worse jungle than any forest through which he'd pass. He thought of Turgis and hoped the innkeeper was safe.

Not so the Sorcerers' Collegium. He started to send a curse down on its head, then stopped, suddenly ashamed of himself. "Now I understand why the southern wizards offered me no help!" he exclaimed. "They must have known this was coming, and been making ready to meet it. Sosper as much as told me so. No wonder they needed to keep every man they had in the southlands."

Despite exhaustion, Gerin found sleep hard to come by. So did his men: they were all in pain from wounds taken fighting the Trokmoi, Wolfar's warriors, or the werebeasts.

Also, the light of the four full moons seemed to allow the ghosts fuller access to this plane than at more normal times. They floated round the campfire, sometimes darting up to one or another of the men to try to give such advice as each thought important. Thanks to the moons, they were sometimes able to make themselves understood, but that understanding did not always make their listeners see why the wraiths deemed their news important.

"What possible difference does it make to me that the price of barley in the capital dropped two coppers a bushel three days ago?" Rihwin demanded. The spirit that told him did not explain.

The ghost that had been straining for days to get through to Gerin drifted toward him again. "Captain, I take oath it looks like you," Van said. "Face a little wider, maybe, but leave out that and what looks like a broken nose and it could be your twin—"

"Father Dyaus above!" Gerin whispered. "Dagref, is it you?" He moved to embrace his slain brother's shade, but it was like trying to hold a breeze.

The ghost withdrew a few paces, slowly and sadly shaking its head. Gerin recalled that gesture well. His older brother had always used it when the Fox did something foolish.

The memory brought sudden tears to the baron's eyes, though he and Dagref had not always been close. Dagref was half a dozen years older, while Gerin, as he approached manhood, found the soldier's life Dagref took to so naturally did not suit him at all. *Or so I thought then,* Gerin said to himself: *here I am living it.*

The lips of Dagref's ghost were moving, but the Fox still could not make out any words. He heard his brother's voice in his mind, but so windblown and blurred by echoes that he could not grasp Dagref's meaning. "Once more," he begged.

The wraith grimaced in exasperation, but started over. This time its meaning, or a sentence of it, was clear: "You still don't keep the stables as clean as our father would have liked," Dagref's ghost said. It shook its head again in the gesture so familiar to Gerin, then, satisfied it had finally got across what was necessary, disappeared into the darkness, leaving Gerin more bewildered than before.

"What did it say?" Van asked. Gerin told him. Van tugged at his beard, gave the Fox a quizzical look. "It's hounded you for days to let you know you're a scurvy excuse for a housekeeper? Tell me, captain, was your brother crack-brained?"

"Of course not." The news Dagref's ghost had given was plainly important to it. Gerin cursed himself for failing to see why. He turned the ghost's enigmatic words over and over in his mind, but came no closer to understanding them.

Half a night's sleep brought no new insight. He was glad, though, when he woke, to see the sun shining through the trees to the east and all the moons gone from the sky.

"You look like death warmed over," Van said. "There's dried blood all over your face."

The baron scrubbed with his fingers, saying, "I must have done enough tossing and turning to open up a cut or two." He pounded left fist into right palm. "Damn everything, what was Dagref trying to tell me?"

He got no good answer to that, either from his own wits or from his comrades when he put the riddle to them. "Perhaps he wants you to have a good storage place for my cheap barley," Rihwin suggested. Gerin glared at him, but it made as much sense as anything else.

Not long after they left camp, they came upon the mangled and partially eaten carcass of a brown bear.

Beside it slept a naked Trokmê. Awakened by their approach, he leaped up and fled into the woods, red hair streaming behind him.

Rihwin stared in disbelief. "No man could—"

"And no man did," Van said grimly. "Look at the tracks: bear and wildcat. It shouldn't have been too hard. In were shape, the woodsrunner would have taken no hurt. Then he had his feast, curled up afterwards—and changed back when the moons set."

The forest path was punctuated by random death: another bear, horribly torn; a Trokmê with his throat ripped out; a pair of Elaboninan warriors so mutilated as to appall even Gerin's hard-bitten crew; a crofter's cottage, its flimsy door torn from leather hinges, a blackened puddle of blood luring flies at the threshold. Gerin did not need to look to be sure no one was alive inside. He hoped the deaths there had been quick.

Live Trokmoi still lurked in the woods. An arrow from hiding grazed the side of Gerin's helm. He and Rihwin shot blindly into the undergrowth. The sniper, unhurt, let fly again, hitting Priscos' left arm just below the shoulder. The driver cursed and tore out the arrow, then ripped at his tunic for cloth to bandage the wound.

The rest of the Elabonians jumped from their chariots. They ran for cover, then stalked the barbarian sharpshooter. The Trokmê, no fool, held his well-concealed position until he had what he thought was a good shot at Van. But in his cramped quarters he could not draw bow to his ear, only to his chest. The outlander's stout cuirass turned his shaft.

Van shouted in rage and rushed at the thicket from which the arrow had come. The Trokmê fled. A blow of Van's mace felled him from behind before he had taken ten strides. Like a charging longtooth, the outlander was deadly quick in a short rush.

He surveyed the sniper's corpse without a hint of remorse. "A pity the craven bushwhacker didn't die slower," he said. "If he wanted to fight, he should have come at us like a man."

Gerin had planned and executed enough ambushes in his time to keep a discreet silence.

When they returned to the chariots, Priscos was matter-of-fact. "Did you get him?" he asked. At Gerin's nod, he said, "Good," and jerked the reins to get the horses moving north again.

They returned to the Elabon Way no more than a couple of hours' journey south of Fox Keep. Gerin was sickly aware he was returning without even the ragtag army which had set out from Ricolf's holding. The werenight had seen to that. His main hope now was that it had disrupted Balamung's men more than the Elabonians.

Then that hope died too. A shout rang out from the flanking forest: "Here's more o' the buggers!" A score and more of footsoldiers charged from the woods, spears ready to cast, swords bared.

But the Fox was still reaching for his bow when he realized the cry had been in his own tongue, not the woodsrunners'. And when the onrushing warriors spotted him (or more likely spied Van and his distinctive armor), they stopped so abruptly that one man stumbled and fell to his knees. Then they came on again, but now in friendship and joy, raising a cheer to chill the heart of any Trokmê in earshot.

Gerin recognized them as Drago the Bear's men; their commander was one of Drago's chief retainers, Fedor the Hunter. The Fox did not know Fedor well. He usually stayed behind at Drago's keep as deputy when his overlord went to Castle Fox. But Gerin had never been gladder to see anyone than this heavyset, scar-faced warrior.

Fedor led his men up to the Fox. "We thought you

dead, my lord," he said accusingly. "The Trokmoi and their cursed wizard claimed you were, when they tried to get me to yield the Castle of the Bear to them."

"Drago's holding stands?" Gerin said. "You beat back an attack the wizard led himself? Great Dyaus, Fedor, how? His magic has leveled more keeps than I can count."

"Oh, he tried to shake the holding down after I said no to him, so he did. Fires and smokes and flying demons and I don't know what all. But the Castle of the Bear is good and solid, and it sits on bedrock. As for the rest"—he shrugged with the same stolidity Drago would have shown—"we were inside and they were outside, and that's the way it stayed. The wizard's lightnings blasted one breach, but no woodsrunners came through it alive. They paid a lot more than half the butcher's bill, my lord. After a while, they'd had enough and went away."

Listening to the bald report, Gerin decided Fedor had not had the imagination to see he had no chance. And, going on phlegmatically where a more perceptive man would have despaired, he had endured. *Something to be said for dullness after all*, the Fox thought.

But Fedor was not yet done. "You need not look so surprised, my lord. Fox Keep still holds too, you know."

The baron's heart gave a great bound within him. "No," he said softly. "I did not know."

"Aye, it does." Fedor seemed oblivious to the impact his news had on the Fox. "They're under siege, true, but they managed to sneak a messenger to us through the woodsrunners' lines: some trick of your wizard Siglorel, I understand. Sixty men set out from the Castle of the Bear two days ago, but after last night—" He shrugged again. "For a while I thought

I'd lost my wits, but I was too busy staying alive to worry about it."

"Weren't we all?" Gerin said.

Thanks to the footsoldiers, the final approach to Fox Keep was slower now, but Gerin would not have traded them for all the treasures of Ikos. A final fear gripped him: that the keep had fallen after its messenger went out. Then Van pointed north. "Right on the skyline, captain—the very tip of your watchtower. And I think" —he squinted— "aye, I think it's your banner atop it."

As his men exulted, Gerin tried to follow his friend's pointing finger. He had to say, "Your eyes are better than mine." But that Van saw what he claimed, the baron had no doubt. He had surmounted every stumbling block now, save the last . . . putting an end to the mightiest mage the world had seen in two thousand years. And even as he quickened his pace toward his castle, he realized he still had no idea how to do that.

XII

Castle Fox had taken a fearful beating, Gerin saw as he and his men sped toward it. Part of one wall had fallen, to be replaced by a lower, makeshift bulwark of timbers and earth. For some reason, the logs of the palisade were painted a sour dark green. Though the watchtower still stood, gaps had been bitten into some of the upper stonework of the keep.

Still, on the whole the Trokmê investment was a shabby job. Mighty sorcerer or no, Balamung was only a woodsrunner when trying to besiege a holding his magic could not flatten. He knew nothing of engines or stratagems, but had to rely on the ferocity of his troops—and ferocity counted for little against a fortress with determined defenders. Broken bodies littered the ground below the palisade. Here as at the Castle of the Bear, their bravery and inexperience were making the Trokmoi pay more than their share of blood.

But what ferocity could do, it would. Just out of bowshot from the palisade, Balamung harangued his men, nerving them to yet another charge against out-wall and gate. Despite the repeated maulings the Elabonians had given them, despite the horrors of the werenight just past, they waved their weapons and cheered at his speech, for all the world like so many outsized, destructive children.

The Fox's men on the palisade caught sight of Gerin before the Trokmoi did. Their yells made Balamung pause in mid-word. He looked up. An evil orange glow lit his eyes. His voice sounded inside the Fox's head, scornful and exasperated at the same time: "It's infernally hard to kill that you are. Well, so long as you're here, you can watch your fine castle die, for I'm fresh out of patience with your puppydog of a wizard, indeed and I am."

The lean sorcerer gave quick orders to his men. Fifty or so loped toward the Fox ("Just to make sure you don't joggle my elbow, now," Balamung said). The rest advanced on the palisade. The baron found their discipline remarkable—and alarming. He'd hoped his sudden advent would draw all the barbarians from the walls and free his men inside to sally against them.

The first arrow hissed past his head. Another found the breast of one of Rihwin's proud dapples. The southerner's chariot slewed, flipped over. He and Nordric, both veterans of such mishaps, landed lightly. They were on their feet at once to face the oncoming Trokmoi.

More arrows flew past. The Fox shot a couple in return. Then he yelled to Priscos, "We'd all better get down. The horses will just have to take their chances."

The driver chewed his lip, unhappy at the thought of abandoning the beasts but knowing not all spills ended so luckily as Rihwin's. He pulled to a halt, his long face doleful. Sword in hand, he followed Gerin and Van to the ground.

He ran to the horses. Evading a snap from the Shanda pony, he slashed through their traces and slapped both beasts' rumps with the flat of his blade. They galloped away, leather straps trailing. Priscos gave Gerin a wintry grin. "All right, my lord, I expect I'm ready now."

The baron had no time to answer—the Trokmoi were upon them. He glimpsed a hurled stone just in time to flick up his shield and knock it aside. A wild-haired northerner, naked but for a helm and one greave, thrust at his legs with a short pike. He skipped aside.

Van rammed his own, longer, spear into the Trokmê's belly. He jerked it free with an expert twist. Bloody entrails came with it.

At first, progress toward Fox Keep was not hard. Though outnumbered almost two to one by the Trokmoi Balamung sent to hold them off, the Elabonians had better weapons and armor than their foes. But soon the lack of order the baron had looked for before began to cost his relieving force. More and more Trokmoi gave up the attack on the palisade and ran toward the hand-to-hand fighting they loved so well. Their wizard leader cursed shrilly and tried to bend them to his will again, but had little luck. Wizard or no, leader or no, he could not change the habits of the proud, wild folk he led.

A tall noble in brightly burnished scale-mail confronted the Fox. "It's Dumnorix son of Orgetorix son of—" he began. He got no farther, for an arrow—a Trokmê arrow, by its length and fletching—suddenly sprouted in his throat and sent him spinning to the ground.

Then the baron was facing a woodsrunner who must have learned his swordplay from an Elabonian.

Forsaking the usual slashing style of the Trokmê, he thrust wickedly at Gerin's face, belly, and face again. His wrist was quick as a snake. But Rihwin sprang to Gerin's side. His slim blade darted at the Trokmê. Unable to stand against two such swordsmen, the barbarian sprang back among his comrades.

Both sides slowed to a brief, panting halt. Not fifteen feet from the Fox, a sweaty barbarian leaned on his spear. He was picking his teeth with a gory forefinger. He caught Gerin's eye and grinned. "Good fighting." And in truth, that was all the twisted corpses, the gashed limbs, the terror and agony meant to him: a sport, something to enjoy and at which to excel.

Gerin wearily shook his head. Too many on both sides of the border felt thus.

Someone threw a stone. Someone else cast a spear. The heat of battle again grew to a boil. Shouting like men struck mad, a wedge of Trokmoi slammed into the middle of Gerin's thin line, splitting his force in two.

The larger half, led by Nordric, made for the repaired breach in the palisade. That, thought Gerin, was largely because his berserker comrade saw more Trokmoi there than anywhere else. Nordric and his companions fought their way into range of covering arrows from the palisade. Its defenders cheered their every forward step.

For his own fragment, which included Van, Rihwin, and Priscos, the baron had another goal: Balamung himself. The black-robed mage, hood flung back to show his face, stalked menacingly round the palisade. Under one arm he carried the Book of Shabeth-Shiri. The codex was bound in light, fine-grained leather, perhaps tanned human hide.

No arrow bit the wizard, though the men on the palisade sent many his way. Some flared into brief blue flame, others flew wild, others simply vanished.

Arrogant and contemptuous, Balamung stood, dry, under a rain of death.

He opened the Book of Shabeth-Shiri and began to chant. Even fighting desperately afurlong away, Gerin felt the power the wizard gathered, saw the air around him shimmer with pent-up energies. His hair tried to prickle upright under his helm.

The Trokmoi who had been assaulting the wall of the palisade on which the spell would fall sprinted away for their lives. Balamung's chant rose to a crescendo. He shouted in the dread Kizzuwatnan tongue, paused, shouted again.

Sheets of red flame flowed from his fingertips. The fire engulfed the wall of the palisade. Gerin watched in awe and consternation. Not even ashes, he thought, could remain when that incandescent flood receded. But the palisade withstood the fiery bath unharmed, still the same sour green which had bemused the Fox before.

"I think your own wizard has won a point," Rihwin said, parrying a spearthrust. That was a notion new to Gerin. It had not occurred to him that the ugly paint might be a sorcerous defense.

Balamung shouted in frustrated wrath. His flapping black cloak gave him the aspect of a starveling vulture. He loped toward the repaired section of the palisade, crying to Siglorel, "Southron fool, you'll pay for not bending the knee to me!" Less than a bowshot from where Gerin battled his minions, the Trokmê mage opened his fell grimoire and began another spell.

Redoubling their efforts, the baron and his men tried to close with the wizard while his sorcery distracted him. But they had all they could do to stay alive; pushing forward against the barbarians was impossible.

The Fox could only watch as fire shot once more from Balamung's hands. It caught and clung to the untreated timbers of the improvised barricade—and to the back of a woodsrunner not quick enough to get away. A human torch, he shrieked and fell and burned. Gerin's men within Fox Keep braved arrows to beat at the flames with hides and pour water and sand on them, but could not douse the wizardfire.

Then Siglorel, clad in robes no less black than Balamung's, appeared at the top of the burning stretch of palisade. As Rihwin had said, when faced with the supreme challenge of his life he turned his back on the alepot and fought Balamung's spells to a standstill. Now he worked with unhurried skill, ignoring the missiles flying around him. His fingers flashed in intricate passes. As his hands fell when his spell was done, the flames fell too, leaving the bulwark smoldering but intact.

"You dare to show yourself in my despite?" Balamung hissed. Gerin shuddered at the malice in his voice. Siglorel gave his foe a tired, grave nod. "Then dare—and die!" Balamung's arm swept down. Lightning cracked from a clear sky. A flick of Siglorel's hand sent the bolt smashing harmlessly to the ground.

The backlash of energies from the wizards' duel—and simple fear, too—held Trokmoi and Elabonians frozen where they stood, unwilling witnesses to a struggle more dire than any in which they fought. Balamung was clearly the stronger. The lightnings he hurled crashed ever closer to his enemy, his whirlwinds spun up great clouds of choking dust that all but hid the palisade, his demons flew shrieking through the winds and dove on Siglorel like huge batwinged falcons.

No levinbolt, though, seared through Siglorel's heart, no wind seized him and flung him to his doom (though the warrior who had been at his side had time for but one brief scream of terror as Balamung's tornado tore him from Castle Fox), no demon drank his blood. Face gone dead white from strain, hands darting now here, now there like those of a man wracked by fever, Siglorel somehow kept an ever-tightening circle of safety round himself.

Once or twice he even managed to strike back. Balamung contemptuously swatted aside his lightnings, as if they were beneath his notice. The end, Gerin saw, was inevitable. Balamung cursed in balked outrage as his weaker opponent evaded destruction again and again, but each escape was narrower, each drained more of Siglorel's waning strength.

Then the Trokmê wizard chuckled terribly. He briefly checked the Book of Shabeth-Shiri. At his gesture, a plane of pulsing violet light sprang into being on either side of Siglorel. As Balamung brought his hands toward each other, the planes of force he had created began to close upon his antagonist. Siglorel tried to check the inexorable contraction, but all his knowledge, all his cantrips, were of no avail against the ancient, mighty sorcery Balamung commanded.

Ever nearer each other drew the planes of force, so that now Siglorel held them apart not with his magic, but by the power of his strongly muscled arms and shoulders. The desperate tableau held for half a minute, no more; then only a crimson smear lay between the glowing planes.

Gerin expected his own life to be similarly crushed away, but Balamung, a cat toying with a helpless mouse, took too much pleasure in the baron's dismay to end the game so quickly. Full of noxious confidence, his voice sounded in the baron's ear: "First you can watch your fine keep fall. Then I'll get round to dealing with yourself—if my lads have not done it for me."

That seemed likely. Gerin and Van fought back-to-back much of the time now. Many of the warriors who had accompanied them were gone. Attacked at the same time by one Trokmê with a sword and two more with spears, Priscos went down while Balamung was speaking. Rihwin and Gerin killed the spearmen, but Priscos lay where he had fallen.

Balamung began another spell. A clot of black smoke rose before him. It quickly began to take shape and solidity. Even after his invocation ceased, that which he summoned continued to grow.

The demon was roughly anthropoid, but twice the height of any man, and broad in proportion. Forced to bear its huge mass, its short thick legs were bowed, but they carried it well enough. Its huge arms, hanging almost to the ground, ended in grasping, taloned hands. Its skin was black and green, and wet like a frog's. It was grossly male.

Its chinless lower jaw hung slack, showing row on row of saw-edged teeth. A bifurcated tongue lashed in and out. The demon had no nose, only red slits to match the banked fires of its eyes. Above those eyes, its forehead sloped straight back. Its batlike ears swiveled and twitched at every sound.

Obeying Balamung's shouted command, it waddled toward Castle Fox. The Trokmoi scattered before it. As he watched it near the keep, Gerin saw a plume of smoke curl up from within the palisade. One of the outbuildings was alight, whether from Balamung's magic or a mere fire-arrow he did not know.

The wizard saw it too. He laughed. "You'll no more be putting your betters in the stables to sleep, will you now?"

At their mage's order, the Trokmoi raked the palisade with arrows, forcing its defenders to keep their heads down. A few Elabonians shot back. Two arrows pierced the demon. It wailed and gnashed its teeth, but did not slow.

Then Nordric rushed at it, a sword in either hand, curses rising even over its cries. All the barbarians around him had fled at the demon's onset, but in his blind fury he knew only the attack. The demon stopped as he charged. It was confused, no doubt, to see a human running toward it.

Then confusion gave way to a full-throated bellow of pain and rage, for Nordric's first stroke ripped into its thigh. Purplish-red ichor spurted from the wound. Gerin and the Elabonians cheered frantically, and were joined by more than a few Trokmoi not happy with the unholy ally Balamung had given them.

But the demon, faster than its bulk suggested, slipped by Nordric's next rush. An arm longer than he was tall snaked out. A huge hand seized him in a chest-crushing embrace. No last oath passed his lips as his swords fell from nerveless fingers. The demon brought the fresh-killed dainty to its mouth. The horrible jaws slammed shut. The monster flung what was left of the broken body behind it and resumed its advance on the palisade.

Reaching the repaired section of wall, it grasped a charred timber near the top. Enormous muscles bunched under its glabrous hide. The timber groaned, screamed, and came loose with a splintering crash. The demon tossed it aside, grabbed another and pulled it free, then another and another.

More arrows thudded into its flesh, but so thick were its muscles that they guarded its vitals almost as well as a corselet. The Trokmoi shouted in excitement as they saw the barrier torn apart.

When the breach was all but complete, an Elabonian with more courage than sense attacked the demon with a spear. A heavy forearm knocked aside his weapon. The demon lashed out with a broad, flat foot. The Elabonian's body, torn nearly in two by that terrible kick, flew through the air to land well within the courtyard of Fox Keep.

Balamung cried out once more in whatever fell

tongue he used to control the monster he had summoned. It turned away from the keep, moved ponderously toward Gerin and his embattled comrades. The smoke from the burning stables grew thicker as the warriors who had been fighting the flames abandoned that task to meet the Trokmoi swarming into the breach.

More afraid of their hideous partner than the men they were facing, the woodsrunners who had opposed the Fox gave way as the demon neared. Out of the corner of his eye, Gerin saw Van closely studying the oncoming monster. The tight smile on the outlander's face puzzled him until he realized his friend had at last found a foe to overawe him.

Then shouts from the keep made every head whirl. The demon, bat-ears unfurled to the fullest extent, turned to meet the new challenger bearing down on it. Duin the Bold, mounted on a horse and carrying the biggest spear he could find, had rammed his way through the Trokmoi at the breach. He thundered toward the monster, shouting to draw its attention from Gerin and his companions.

The part of the Fox's mind which, regardless of circumstances, observed and recorded fine details, now noted that Duin was not riding bareback. He sat on a rectangular cloth pad cinched tight round the horse's middle. His feet were in leather loops depending from either side of the pad.

Duin rode straight at the demon, which gathered itself to meet him. His lance, powered by the hard-charging horse, plunged deep into the monster's belly. The improvised stirrups kept him atop his mount and added even more impact to the blow. The gore-smeared bronze spearpoint jutted from the demon's back.

Its roar of agony filled the field. Though blood bubbled over its lips, it plucked Duin from his horse and slammed him to the ground. He lay unmoving. The demon's shrieks faded to gurgles. It swayed, toppled, fell. Clawed fingers opened and closed on nothing, then were still.

But Balamung did not let the Trokmoi dwell on the defeat of his creature. "Have no fear, lads," he said. "I'm after having more of the beasts, which they'll not find easy to stop. And look: the palisade's broken, and there's fire in the courtyard. One more good push and we'll need push no more." He opened the Book of Shabeth-Shiri, began again the dreadful invocation which had called the demon from its plane.

Gerin looked from the congealing smoke of the Trokmê's magic to the smoke puffing up from the stables—the stables where Balamung had slept three years before, the stables which, as his brother's ghost had reminded him, had not been well cleaned from that time to this.

Sudden wild hope burned through him. If a single one of Balamung's hairs was buried in the old dry straw of the burning outbuilding—and if his own memory still held the spell he had learned from Rihwin more out of sheer annoyance from any expectation it would ever be of use . . . "What have I to lose?" he muttered to himself, and began.

A woodsrunner leaped at him when he dropped his sword and shield. Van stretched the man lifeless in the dirt. The outlander had no idea what his friend was doing, or indeed whether he still had all his wits, but would guard him as long as breath was in his body.

Chanting in the harsh Kizzuwatnan tongue, left hand moving through passes fast as he dared, the Fox went to his knees in the first of the three required genuflections. As he rose, he remembered the words of the Sibyl of Ikos, words he had thought filled only with doom. Confidence tingled along his veins, warm like wine. He grinned savagely. Aye, he was bowing to the mage of the north, but he did not think Balamung would appreciate the compliment.

That newfound confidence almost made him careless. His tongue stumbled in a particularly intricate passage of the spell. For a moment, his body filled with frightening heat. But he recovered and raced on, driving to be done before Balamung could finish his own magic and realize himself attacked. He bowed for the last time, shouted the last Kizzuwatnan curse, and stood. If he had blundered, he would soon be dead, either from the recoil of his spell or the overwhelming power of his foe.

He had won the race. Balamung was still incanting, his demon materializing before him. Half a minute passed in anticlimax. Gerin watched his enemy in baffled despair. Then the fire in the stables reached the two or three hairs still left from the wizard's visit long before.

Balamung paused for an instant, brushing a sleeve of his robe across his forehead as if to wipe away sweat. Then little yellow flames licked at the robe, and at his flesh as well. Smoke poured from his body.

The half-formed demon vanished.

Balamung screamed, a cry of utmost anguish that stirred horror though from the throat of a foe. The wizard beat at his flaming chest with arms no less afire. He knew the author of his destruction the instant his dreadful eyes seized the Fox's. A clawlike hand speared at Gerin for a final malediction. Flame dripped down the pointing index finger before the spell was cast.

The all-consuming fire left of Balamung only gray flakes of ash. The wind tossed them high in the air and blew them away. He had read his stars aright: no man would ever know his grave, for there was nothing of him to bury.

And with him burned the Book of Shabeth-Shiri. That evil tome, which had survived so long, seemed at the end more tenacious of life than the wizard who briefly owned it. Only slowly did the flames grip its pages. Gerin would have taken oath that he saw those pages flutter and rustle in an almost sentient effort to put out the fire and escape their fate. But the spells Shabeth-Shiri had amassed in ancient days now turned to smoke one by one, and as each was destroyed the power of the Book grew less. At last the fire engulfed it altogether, and it was gone.

A strange pause followed; neither side could quite believe Balamung had truly perished. Gerin's men in Fox Keep recovered first. Shouting, "The Fox! The Fox!" they battered their way through the dismayed Trokmoi at the breach and rushed toward the baron and his few remaining comrades. The woodsrunners scattered before them.

Drago the Bear took Gerin in an embrace that hurt even through armor. Right behind him were Rollan, Simrin Widin's son, and most of the borderer crew. They were thinner and dirtier than the Fox remembered, but still men to be reckoned with, and happier than he had ever seen them.

Gerin had hoped their onslaught, coupled with the death of the wizard at his moment of triumph, would send the Trokmoi fleeing for the Niffet. But a northern chieftain stopped the rout before it began. He cut down with his own hand a barbarian running past him. "Are we men or snot-nosed weans?" he roared. "It's but southrons we're fighting, not gods. They bleed and they die—and it's not many of 'em are left to be killed!"

The Trokmoi sensed the truth in his words. So, with sinking heart, did the Fox. Though magic had failed the barbarians, edged bronze might yet suffice. "We haven't enough men to fight in the open here. Back to the castle before they cut us off," he commanded. "Keep the best order you can."

Drago began to protest. He looked from the regrouping barbarians to the white scar over Gerin's eye and thought better of it. For the first hundred yards or so, the retreat went smoothly. Then the Trokmoi gave a hoarse cheer and charged.

Direct as always, Van went straight for the northern leader, reasoning that his death might kill the spirit he'd given his men. But not even the outlander's might let him bull his way through the Trokmoi. Their noble commander declined combat. Like few barbarians Gerin knew, he was aware he had more value for his band than his sword-arm alone.

The baron and his men were within the shadow of the palisade when Rihwin swore and fell, an arrow through his calf. An axe-wielding Trokmê leaped in for the kill. Though prone, Rihwin turned the first stroke with his shield. Before the woodsrunner could make a second, Drago speared him in the side. Gerin's burly vassal slung Rihwin over his shoulder like a sack of turnips. He ran for the breach with the rest of the Elabonians.

Thus, through the gap torn in the palisade, Gerin re-entered Fox Keep, the outbuildings afire before him, the Trokmoi hard on his heels. Cursing the noble who had rallied the northerners, he shouted for pikemen to hold the gap.

The barbarians outside the keep listened to the passionate oratory of their self-appointed leader. With much argument and wasted motion, they formed a ragged line of battle. "At 'em!" the noble cried. Now he led the charge himself.

Arrows and javelins took their toll of the onrushing

barbarians, but they did not waver. They slammed into the thin line the Fox had built against them.

Spear and shield, sword and corselet kept them out. Van was everywhere at once, smiting like a man possessed, bellowing out a battle-song in the twittering tongue of the plains. He hurled his spear at the leader of the woodsrunners and cursed foully when he missed.

He took out his rage on the Trokmoi nearest him. Blood dribbled down the leather-wound handle of his mace and glued it to his hand. As always, Gerin fought a more wily fight, but he was in the front line, his left-handed style giving more than one woodsrunner a fatal half-second of confusion.

When at last the Trokmoi sullenly pulled out of weapon-range, though, Gerin realized how heavy his losses had been. Simrin Widin's son was on his knees, clutching at an arrow driven through his cuirass into his belly. Fandor the Fat lay dead behind him, along with far too many others. Almost everyone who could still wield a weapon was at the breach, and almost everyone bore at least one wound.

Shouts of alarm came from the watchtower and two sides of the palisade. "Ladders! Ladders!" The few defenders still on the wall raced to the threatened spots. One ladder, another, went over with a crash, but already red-mustached barbarians were on the walkway. They fought to hold off the Elabonians until their comrades could scale the wall for the final, surely victorious assault on Fox Keep.

Gerin knew such weariness as he had never felt before. He had endured the terrors of the werenight, slain a wizard more deadly than the world had known for a score of centuries . . . for what? An extra hour of life. Merely for the lack of a few men, his holding would fall despite all he had done. A double-bladed throwing axe hurled from the walkway flashed past him. It buried itself in the blood-soaked ground.

But instead of pressing home their attack, the Trokmoi cried out in despair and fear. The Fox's troopers shouted in sudden desperate urgency. The barbarians on the wall fled back to their scaling-ladders and scrambled down them, trying to reach ground outside the keep before its defenders sent their escape routes toppling.

Bewildered, the baron looked south and saw the most unlikely rescue force conceivable thundering toward Fox Keep. Wolfar of the Axe, in man's shape once more, still had with him a good third of the two-hundred-man army he had led before the werenight. Gerin more than half expected Wolfar's men to ignore the Trokmoi and attack him, but they stormed down on the barbarians, the bloodthirsty baron at their head.

The Trokmê noble tried to rally his men yet again. Wolfar rode him down. At his fall, the woodsrunners broke and ran, flying in all directions. They had already taken one assault from the rear, and had kept their courage after Balamung died just as his triumph seemed assured. Now courage failed them. They threw away weapons to flee the faster. Most ran for the Niffet, and most never reached it, for Wolfar's warriors fought with savagery to match their overlord's.

Gerin did not let his men join the pursuit. He kept them drawn up in battle array at the breach, unable to believe his long-time enemy would not try to deal with him next. Their numbers were near even, though Wolfar's men were fresher. But when Wolfar returned from the killing-ground, he and his vassal Schild stepped over the contorted bodies of the Trokmoi who had died before the palisade to approach Fox Keep unarmed.

"I ought to cut your liver out, Fox," Wolfar said by way of greeting, "but I find I have reason to let you live."

The notion galled Wolfar so badly, he could go no further. Schild spoke for his chief, over whom he towered—he was as tall and lean as Wolfar was short and stocky, and was one of the few men serving under Wolfar whom Gerin respected. He said, "As you can guess, once we pulled ourselves together after whatever madness struck last night"—Gerin started to explain the werenight, but decided it could wait—"we came north after you. But a little south of here, we caught a woodsrunner fleeing your keep. He told us you'd killed their wizard, the one you warned me of not long ago. Is it true?"

"Aye, it's true. Dearly bought, but true."

"Then you've earned your worthless life," Wolfar said, looking toward the corpse of the demon Duin had killed. It was already starting to stink. "You've done a great thing, damn you, and I suppose I have to let it cancel what's between us from the past." He started to offer Gerin his hand, but could not bring himself to do it. The Fox knew there was still no liking or trust between them.

That was not so of their men—soldiers from both sides broke ranks to fraternize. In their shared victory over Balamung and the Trokmoi, they forgot the enmity that had existed between them. Though he did not want to do it, Gerin felt he had no choice but to invite Wolfar and his troops to help man Castle Fox and make it defensible once more.

To the baron's secret disappointment, Wolfar accepted at once. "A holding with too few soldiers in it is almost worse than none at all," he said. "I worry about my own keep; the men I left behind rattle around in it like dried beans in a gourd—do they not, Schild?"

"Hmm?" Schild gave him an unclassifiable look. "Aye, my lord, the garrison there is very small indeed."

As Wolfar's men filed into the holding, Gerin assigned them duties: some to the palisade, others to help some of his own men plug the breach, still others to help the wounded or fight the fires still flickering in the outbuildings. Wolfar did not object to his dispositions. He seemed content to let the Fox keep overall command inside Fox Keep.

Gerin was glad to find that Rihwin's injury was not serious. "You're not hamstrung, and the arrow went clear through your leg. Otherwise we'd have to cut it out, which is nothing to be taken lightly," the baron told him. "As is, though, you should heal before long."

"If I put spikes on my wrists and ankles, do you think I'll be able to climb trees like a cat?" Rihwin asked, adjusting his bandage.

"I see no reason why not."

"Odd," Rihwin murmured. "I never could before."

"Go howl!" Gerin threw his hands in the air and went off to see to other injured men. If the southerner could joke at his wound, he would soon mend.

Had they taken place at any other time, Gerin would have reckoned the next days among the most hectic of his life. As if was, they scarcely stood comparison to what had gone before.

True, four days after Balamung's fall, the Trokmê chieftain who had turned longtooth in the werenight led an attack on Fox Keep. By then, though, the breach in the palisade was repaired, and the holding had fresh supplies drawn from the countryside. Nor did the woodsrunner have patience for a siege. He tried to storm the walls, and was bloodily repulsed. He himself jumped from a scaling ladder to the palisade walkway.

Wolfar took his head with a single stroke of the heavy axe that gave him his sobriquet.

Then the ladder went crashing over. Half a dozen Trokmoi tried to leap clear as it fell. The ladders that stayed upright long enough for the barbarians to come to grips with the Elabonians were few. After their leader was slain inside the keep, they lost their eagerness for the fight.

In a way, that second attack by the Trokmoi was a gift from the gods. It further united Wolfar's men and Gerin's against a common foe, and again reminded them how petty their old disputes were now. A good lesson, Gerin thought. He regretted that the province north of the Kirs had not learned it sooner.

Wolfar, surprisingly, seemed to take the lesson to heart. He did not much try to hide his animosity toward Gerin, but he did not let it interfere with the running of the keep. He never mentioned Elise. He was as cordial as his nature allowed toward the baron's men, and insisted on praising Fox Keep's ale, though by now it was coming from the barrel-bottom and full of yeast.

Gerin would sooner have seen him surly. He did not know how to react to this new Wolfar.

For Schild, on the other hand, his admiration grew by leaps and bounds. When the Fox learned from a prisoner of a band of Trokmoi planning to raft over the Niffet, Wolfar's lieutenant led a joint raiding party to ambush the barbarians as they disembarked. The ambush was a great success. The Trokmoi paddled back across the river after leaving a double handful of men dead on the shore.

On the raiders' return, Wolfar was so lavish in their praise and so affable that Gerin's suspicion of him redoubled. But beyond this uncharacteristic warmth, the thick-shouldered baron as yet showed no hint of what was in his mind.

"He's given me every reason to trust him," Gerin told Van one night, "and I trust him less than ever."

"Probably just as well for you," Van said. Gerin was not sorry to find his worries shared.

Word of Balamung's death spread quickly. It raised the Elabonians' spirits but disheartened their foes, who had leaned on the wizard's supposed invincibility. Two days after the defeat Schild had engineered for the band of southbound barbarians, a large troop of Trokmoi came north past Castle Fox. Except for keeping out of bowshot, they ignored the keep, intent on returning with their booty to the cool green forests north of the Niffet.

Another large band came by a day later, and another two days after that. As if the appearance of the third group of retreating Trokmoi had been some sort of signal, Wolfar stumped up to the Fox in the great hall and said abruptly, "Time we talked."

Whatever Wolfar had been hiding, it was about to come into the open. Of that Gerin felt sure. Stifling his apprehension, he said, "As you wish. The library is quiet." He led his western neighbor up the stairs.

Wolfar seemed less disconcerted by his strange surroundings than Gerin had hoped. "What a bastardly lot of books you have, Fox!" he said. "Where did you pick them all up?"

"Here and there. Some I brought back from the southlands, some I've got since, a few came from my father, and a couple I just stole."

"Mmm," Wolfar said. Then he fell silent, leaning back in his chair.

At last Gerin said, "You said you wanted to talk, Wolfar. What's on your mind?"

"You don't know, Fox?" Wolfar sounded honestly surprised.

"If it's Elise, she won't marry you, you know. She'd sooner bed a real wolf."

"As if what she wanted had anything to do with it. Still, she's only a—what word do I need?—a detail, maybe."

"Go on." Now Gerin was genuinely alarmed. This cold-blooded calculator was not the Wolfar he had expected, save in his utter disregard for anyone else. The Fox wanted to keep him talking until he had some idea of what he was dealing with.

"I'd thought better of you, Gerin. We don't get along, but I know you're no fool. You have no excuse for being stone blind."

"Go on," Gerin said again, wishing Wolfar would come to a point.

"All right. On this stretch of the border, we have the only two major holdings that didn't fall. Now tell me, what aid did we get from the Marchwarden of the North or our lord Emperor Hildor?" Wolfar tried to put mockery in his voice, but managed only a growl.

"Less than nothing, as well I know."

"How right you are. Fox, you can see as well as I—better, I suppose, if you've really read all these books—the Empire hasn't done a damned thing for us the past hundred years. Enough, by all the gods! With the confusion on the border—and deep inside, too, from some of the things you've said—the two of us could be princes so well established that, by the time Elabon moved its fat arse against us, we'd be impossible to throw out, you and I!"

No wonder Wolfar had changed, Gerin thought, whistling softly. Anyone carrying that big an idea on his shoulders *would* change, and might buckle under the strain of it. Something else bothered the Fox too, but he could not place it. "What would you have us be princes of?" he asked. "Our side of the border is so weak the Trokmoi can come down as they wish, with or without their wizard. For now, we can't hope to hold them."

"Think, though. We can channel their force into whatever shape pleases us. Save for them, we're the only powers on the border now, and we can use them against whoever stands against us."

That idea Gerin liked not at all. He wanted to drive every woodsrunner back across the Niffet, not import more as mercenaries. He said, "After a while, they'd decided they'd sooner not be used, and act for their own benefit, not ours."

"With their sorcerer gone, they could never hurt us, so long as we kept up enough properly manned and alert keeps," Wolfar argued. His elaborate calm worried Gerin more than any bluster or nervousness.

But at last he had it, the thing Wolfar was trying to hide. The blank look Schild had given his overlord, a few odd remarks from Wolfar's men ... everything fell together. "Wolfar," he asked, "what were you doing on my land, away from your properly manned and alert keep, when you ran into me just before the werenight?"

"What do you mean?" Wolfar's deep-set eyes were intent on Gerin.

"Just this: you've tried to bury me in a haystack without my noticing. It almost worked, I grant you—you're more subtle than I thought."

"You'll have to make yourself plainer, Fox. I can't follow your riddles."

"Very well, I'll be perfectly clear. You, sir, are a liar of the first water, and staking everything on your lie not being found out. Your keep must have been sacked, and almost at once, or you'd still be in it, not trotting over the landscape like a frog with itchy breeches. In fact, you're as homeless as a cur without a master."

Wolfar took a long, slow breath. "Reasoned like

a schoolmaster, Fox. But your logic fails you at the end."

"Oh? How so?"

Heavy muscles rippled under Wolfar's tunic. "I do have a home keep, you see: this one." He hurled himself at Gerin.

The Fox sprang from his seat and threw a footstool at Wolfar's head. Wolfar knocked it aside with a massive forearm. Like a crushing snake, he reached out for the Fox. In the first moment of fighting, neither man thought to draw sword. Their hatred, suppressed these past few days, blazed up out of control, too hot for anything but flesh against flesh, Gerin mad as Wolfar.

Then Wolfar kicked the Fox in the knee. He staggered back, hearing someone shriek and realizing it was himself. The bright pain cut through his bloodlust. When Wolfar roared forward to finish him, he almost spitted himself on Gerin's blade.

His own was out the next instant. Sparks flew as bronze struck bronze. Wolfar used his sword as if it were an axe, hacking and chopping, but he was so quick and strong Gerin had no time for a telling riposte. His movement hampered by his knee, he stayed on the defensive, awaiting opportunity.

It came, finally: a clever thrust, a twist of the wrist, and Wolfar's blade and one finger went flying across the room. But before the Fox could pierce him, Wolfar kicked the sword from his hand and seized him in a pythonic embrace.

Gerin felt his ribs creak. He slammed the heel of his hand against Wolfar's nose, snapping his head back. In the capital they claimed that was often a fatal blow, but Wolfar merely grunted under it. Still, his grip loosened for an instant, and Gerin jerked free.

He wondered briefly what was keeping everyone from bursting into the library and pulling the two of

them apart. They were making enough noise to scare
the Trokmoi in the woods, let alone the men in the
castle. But no one came.

Wolfar leaped for a sword. Gerin tackled him
before he could reach it. They crashed to the floor in
a rolling, cursing heap. Then, like a trap, two horn-
edged hands were at the Fox's throat. Almost of their
own accord, his reached through Wolfar's thick beard
to find a similar grip. He felt Wolfar tense under it.

Gerin tightened his neck muscles as he had learned
in the wrestling schools of the capital, tried to force
breath after precious breath into his lungs. The world
eddied toward blackness. In one of his last clear
moments, he wondered again why no one was breaking up the fight. Then there was only the struggle to
get the tiniest whisper of air and . . . keep . . . his . . .
grip . . . tight . . .

After that, all he knew was the uprushing welcom-
ing dark.

The first thing he realized when his senses returned
was that he was no longer locked in that death
embrace. His throat was on fire. Van and Schild Stoutstaff bent over him, concern on their faces. He tried
to speak. Nothing came from his mouth but a croak
and a trickle of blood.

He signed for pen and parchment. After a
moment's incomrpehension, Van fetched them. Quill
scratching, Gerin wrote, "What happened?"

As reading was not one of his many skills, Van held
the scrap of parchment in some embarrassment.
Seeing his plight, Schild took it from him. " 'What
happened?' " he read. "My lord Gerin, you are the only
man who knows that."

Gerin looked a question at Van.

"Aye, Wolfar's dead." The outlander took up the
tale. "When he and you went up to have your talk,

the rest of us sat around the great hall wondering what would come of it. Then the racket started. We all looked at each other, hoping it was something simple, say a demon from one of the hells or Balamung back from the fire.

"But no, sure as sure, it was you two going at each other. We could have had a fight down there to match the one up here. If anybody had tried going up the stairs, that's just what would have happened. So, though nobody said much, we figured whoever came out would rule here, and anyone who didn't like it or couldn't stand it would be free to go, no hard feelings. And we waited.

"And nobody came out.

"Finally we couldn't stand it any longer. Schild and I came up together. When we saw you, we thought you were both dead. But you breathed when we pried Wolfar's hands off your neck, and he'll never breathe again—you're stronger than I gave you credit for, captain."

Gerin sat up, rubbing his bruised throat. Looking at Schild, he managed a thin whisper. "You knew Wolfar was tricking me with his talk of a keep he could go home to, and you helped him do it."

Van barked a startled oath, but Schild only nodded. "Of course I did. He was my overlord; he always treated me fairly, harsh though he was. He was not altogether wrong, either—it's long past time for us to break away from the Empire's worthless rule, and I cannot blame him for wanting the power he saw here for the taking."

Schild looked Gerin in the eye. "I would not have called you 'my lord,' though, did I not think you would do a better job with it." Slowly and deliberately, he went to one knee before the Fox. Van followed, though his grin showed how little he thought of such ceremonies.

Dazed more ways than one, Gerin accepted their homage. He half-wished he could flee instead. All he'd ever wanted, he told himself, was to read and think and not be bothered. But when the responsibility for Castle Fox fell on him, he had not shirked it. No more could he evade this greater one now.

He looked at his books, wondering when he would find time to open them again. So much to be done: the Trokmoi ousted, keeps restored and manned, Elise wed (a solitary bright thought among the burdens), Duin's stirrups investigated (which reminded him how few horses he had left), peasants brought back to the land ... Dyaus above, where was there an unravaged crop within five days' journey?

He climbed to his feet and walked toward the stairs. "Well," he said hoarsely, "let's get to work."

AFTERWORD

When in the early 1970s Poul Anderson reissued *The Broken Sword* after it had been out of print for some years, he noted that, without changing the plot, he had cleaned up the writing. I didn't fully understand when I read his afterword: he'd published *The Broken Sword*, hadn't he? How could it need cleaning up?

Now the shoe is on the other foot. *Werenight* was written in bits and pieces from 1976 to 1978 (often in time stolen from my dissertation); it first appeared in 1979 broken into two parts, titled by the publisher *Wereblood* and *Werenight*. The same publisher also tagged me with the pseudonym Eric Iverson, on the assumption no one would believe Harry Turtledove, which is my real name.

And now it's time for the book to see print again. When I looked over the manuscript, I discovered, as Anderson and no doubt many others had before me, that I'm a better craftsman than I used to be. Without interfering with the story or characters I invented in my younger days, I have taken this chance to cut adjectives, adverbs, and semicolons, and generally tighten things up, and I've changed a couple of bit-players' names where I'd used others that struck me as too similar to them in later fiction. All in all, this is the book I would have written then if I'd been a better writer. I hope you enjoy it.

—Harry Turtledove
October 1992

There Are Elves Out There

An excerpt from

Mercedes Lackey
Larry Dixon

The main bay was eerily quiet. There were no screams of grinders, no buzz of technical talk or rapping of wrenches. There was no whine of test engines on dynos coming through the walls. Instead, there was a dull-bladed tension amid all the machinery, generated by the humans and the Sidhe gathered there.

Tannim laid the envelope on the rear deck of the only fully-operated GTP car that Fairgrove had built to date, the one that Donal had spent his waking hours building, and Conal had spent track-testing. He'd designed it for beauty and power in equal measure, and had given its key to Conal, its elected driver, in the same brother's-gift ceremony used to present an elvensteed. Conal now sat on its sculpted door, and absently traced a slender finger along an air intake, glowering at the envelope.

Tannim finished his magical tests, and asked for a knife. An even dozen were offered, but Dottie's Leatherman was accepted. Keighvin stood a little apart from the group, hand on his short knife. His eyes glittered with suppressed anger, and he appeared less human than usual, Tannim noticed. Something was bound to break soon.

Tannim folded out the knifeblade, slit the envelope open, and then unfolded the Leatherman's pliers. With them he withdrew six Polaroids of Tania and two others, unconscious, each bound at the wrists and neck. Their silver chains were held by some-*things* from the Realm of the Unseleighe—inside a limo. And, out of focus through the limo's windows, was a stretch of flat tarmac, and large buildings—

Tannim dropped the Leatherman, his fingers gone numb. It clattered twice before wedging into the cockpit's fresh-air vent. Keighvin took one startled step forward, then halted as the magical alarms at Fairgrove's perimeter flared around them all. Tannim's hand went into a jacket pocket, and he threw down the letter from the P.I. He saw Conal pick up the photographs, blanch, then snatch the letter up.

Tannim had already turned by then, and was sprinting for the office door, and the parking lot beyond.

Behind him, he could hear startled questions directed at him, but all he could answer before disappearing into the offices was "Airport!" His bad leg was slowing him down, and screamed at him like a sharp rock grinding into his bones. There was some kind of attack beginning, but he had no time for that.

Have to get to the airport, have to save Tania

from Vidal Dhu, the bastard, the son of a bitch, the—

Tannim rounded a corner and banged his left knee into a file cabinet. He went down hard, hands instinctively clutching at his over-damaged leg. His eyes swam with a private galaxy of red stars, and he struggled while his eyes refocused.

Son of a bitch son of a bitch son of a bitch. . . .

Behind him he heard the sounds of a war-party, and above it all, the banshee wail of a high-performance engine. He pulled himself up, holding the bleeding knee, and limp-ran towards the parking lot, to the Mustang, and Thunder Road.

Vidal Dhu stood in full armor before the gates of Fairgrove, laughing, lashing out with levin-bolts to set off its alarms. It was easy for Vidal to imagine what must be going on inside—easy to picture that smug, orphaned witling Keighvin Silverhair barking orders to weak mortals, marshaling them to fight. Let him rally them, Vidal thought—it will do him no good. None at all. He may have won before, but ultimately, the mortals will have damned him.

It has been so many centuries, Silverhair. I swore I'd kill your entire lineage, and I shall. I shall!

Vidal prepared to open the gate to Underhill. Through that gate all the Court would watch as Keighvin was destroyed—Aurilia's plan be hanged! Vidal's blood sang with triumph—he had driven Silverhair into a winless position at last! And when he accepted the Challenge, before the whole Court, none of his human-world tricks would benefit him—theirs would be a purely magical combat, one Sidhe to another.

To the death.

* * *

Keighvin Silverhair recognized the scent of the magic at Fairgrove's gates—he had smelled it for centuries. It reeked of obsession and fear, hatred and lust. It was born of pain inflicted without consideration of repercussions. It was the magic of one who had stalked innocents and stolen their last breaths.

He recognized, too, the rhythm that was being beaten against the walls of Fairgrove.

So be it, murderer. I will suffer your stench no more.

"They will expect us to dither and delay; the sooner we act, the more likely it is that we will catch them unprepared. They do not know how well we work together."

Around him, the humans and Sidhe of his home sprang into action, taking up arms with such speed he'd have thought them possessed. Conal had thrown down the letter after reading it, and barked, "Hangar 2A at Savannah Regional; they've got children as hostages!" The doors of the bay began rolling open, and outside, elvensteeds stamped and reared, eyes glowing, anxious for battle. Conal looked to him, then, for orders.

Keighvin met his eyes for one long moment, and said, "Go, Conal. I shall deal with our attacker for the last time. If naught else, the barrier at the gates can act as a trap to hold him until we can deal with him as he deserves." He did not add what he was thinking—that he only hoped it would hold Vidal. The Unseleighe was a strong mage; he might escape even a trap laid with death metal, if he were clever enough. Then, with the swiftness of a falcon, he was astride his elvensteed Rosaleen Dhu, headed for the perimeter of Fairgrove.

He was out there, all right, and had begun laying a spell outside the fences, like a snare. Perhaps in his sickening arrogance he'd forgotten that Keighvin could see such things. Perhaps in his insanity, he no longer cared.

Rosaleen tore across the grounds as fast as a stroke of lightning, and cleared the fence in a soaring leap. She landed a few yards from the laughing, mad Vidal Dhu, on the roadside, with him between Keighvin and the gates. He stopped lashing his mocking bolts at the gates of Fairgrove and turned to face Keighvin.

"So, you've come to face me alone, at last? No walls or mortals to hide behind, as usual, coward? So sad that you've chosen *now* to change, within minutes of your death, traitor."

"Vidal Dhu," Keighvin said, trying to sound unimpressed despite the heat of his blood, "if you wish to duel me, I shall accept. But before I accept, you must release the children you hold."

The Unseleighe laughed bitterly. "It's your concern for these mortals that raised you that have *made* you a traitor, boy. Those children do not matter." Vidal lifted his lip in a sneer as Keighvin struggled to maintain his composure. "Oh, I will do more than duel you, Silverhair. I wish to Challenge you before the Court, and kill you as they watch."

That was what Keighvin had noted—it was the initial layout of a Gate to the High Court Underhill. Vidal was serious about this Challenge—already the Court would be assembling to judge the battle. Keighvin sat atop Rosaleen, who snorted and stamped, enraged by the other's tauntings. Vidal's pitted face twisted in a maniacal smirk.

"How long must I wait for you to show courage, witling?"

Keighvin's mind swam for a moment, before he remembered the full protocols of a formal Challenge. It had been so long since he'd even seen one. . . .

Once accepted, the Gate activates, and all the Court watches as the two battle with blade and magic. Only one leaves the field; the Court is bound to slay anyone who runs. So it had always been. Vidal would not Challenge unless he were confident of winning, and Keighvin was still tired from the last battle—which Vidal had not even been at. . . .

But Vidal must die. That much Keighvin knew.

From Born to Run *by Mercedes Lackey & Larry Dixon.*

*   *   *

Watch for more from the SERRAted Edge:
Wheels of Fire by Mercedes Lackey & Mark Shepherd

When the Bough Breaks by Mercedes Lackey & Holly Lisle